l. a. cotton

Published by Delesty Books

First Paperback Edition
Copyright © 2017 L A cotton
All rights reserved.
ISBN: 9781976759833

Edited by Andrea M Long
Cover Designed by Lianne Cotton
Images licensed from Adobe Stock and Shutterstock

Dedication

For Andrea.

Also By L A Cotton

Chapter One

Maverick

I balled my fist against my thigh, clenching until it hurt. Pain was good. Pain distracted me from the present. The awkward-as-fuck present that was Christmas Day in the Stone-Prince house. The whole thing was a joke. Playing happy families. Ignoring the herd of elephants in the room.

Kyle caught my eye from across the table and flashed me a knowing grin.

Fucker.

He loved seeing me squirm during *family* time. Usually, I bailed, but it was Christmas. Even my heart wasn't that black. I glanced around, checking no one was watching, and pulled my hand from under the table flipping him off. Laughter rumbled deep in Kyle's chest and all heads snapped in his direction.

"I, hmm…" he spluttered. "Eggnog… I drank too

much."

Take that jackass. I smirked at him.

"Everything smells delicious, Rebecca," Stella, the woman Uncle Rob was banging, smiled, inhaling for effect. I'd only met her a couple of times, but it was like she tried too hard. I preferred people who talked less. Like her six-year-old daughter, Beth, who sat fidgeting with the table cover, eyes darting all over the place, unsure what to make of us all.

Mom beamed as she fussed over the table, straightening pans and making room for everything. "I can't take all the credit. Loretta came in yesterday to help me prepare. But I glazed the ham myself."

Halle-fucking-lujah. Our family needed more than a glazed ham to mend the deep cracks.

"So, Cous," Kyle piped up and my eyes slid to her. Lo was sat opposite me and one seat over, but she kept her focus on my stepbrother, refusing to look in my direction. My fist clenched tighter. The urge to bail was strong—rushing through my veins, heating my blood. I couldn't leave her though. I wouldn't. Even if she thought she didn't want me here, even if she planned on ignoring me all day, I wasn't going anywhere.

"Yes, *Kyle?*"

"What did the big red man bring you?" His brows quirked up with amusement. *Motherfu*—I tamped down the urge to throw Mom's green bean casserole at him. He knew exactly what he was doing. After he'd asked me if I planned on buying Lo a present and I'd told him no, Kyle had given me nothing but shit. *"It's too soon for that,"* I'd grumbled at him. He didn't know I'd already gotten her something, but I didn't want him running his mouth. The two of them had developed a tight bond. Between last-minute meetings with Coach, and the school's guidance counsellor, Miss Tamson; and then Lo shutting me out, I hadn't had chance to give it to her yet.

"Nothing special." Her frosty glare moved right over me, and I groaned under my breath. If being suffocated by Mom's fake smiles and Kyle's passive aggressive bullshit wasn't bad enough, Lo's mood was a fuse to my temper, and I was one match away from losing it.

"Now, come on, sweetheart," Uncle Rob said, "You had a nice pile of presents under the tree."

She rolled her eyes. "I know, Dad, I just—"

"It's ready," Mom appeared in the doorway—her timing not completely sucking for once—lost behind the huge ham in her gloved hands, "and it tastes divine."

"Darling," Gentry went to her. "You're not supposed to eat it before bringing it to the table."

"Hush now and make room. Everyone be careful, the pan is hot."

Ham safely situated on the table, Gentry pulled out her chair and Mom sat down, beaming at him. Even after all this time, it was hard to watch the two of them—a testament to how screwed up I was.

"This looks great, Rebecca," Uncle Rob echoed Stella's words, patting his girlfriend's hand affectionately, and I risked peeking over at Lo. Her face was impassive. A stone mask. But I saw the hurt glittering in her eyes, and I knew exactly what it was doing to her watching her father with a new woman. A woman who wasn't her mom. Because I knew first hand that no matter how high you built the walls around you, they would never be impenetrable. And part of me wanted to leave the table; to grab her hand and take her far away from this mess… but I couldn't. Right now, I couldn't be who she needed me to be.

And it killed me.

Something vibrated beside me and Macey peeked under the table, fumbling with her cell phone. I elbowed her, whispering, "If I have to endure this, so do you," while everyone else started helping themselves to the food. In typical Kyle fashion, he already had his plate piled high. I was built, but he could out eat me any day of the week thanks to all the conditioning and drills Coach Munford made the football team run.

"As soon as dinner's over, I'm out of here," my sister hissed through gritted teeth, refusing to look at me.

Lo wasn't the only girl around the table pissed at me.

"Macey, pass the greens, please," Mom said to her.

"Sure," she mumbled, passing her the dish.

"Robert tells me you want to pursue a career in dancing?" Stella angled herself to Macey, who tensed up at the mention of her future.

"Maybe." It came out clipped. "I haven't decided. Senior year is a long way off yet."

"Not really, sweetheart," Mom said. "Maverick will be graduating before you know it and then you'll be thinking about college applications."

I sucked in a sharp breath, my fingers tightening around the silverware. *Not here. Not now.*

"And you're hoping to play basketball, Maverick?"

Shit.

Silence descended over the table and Mom shot me an apologetic smile. *Too late for that, Mom.*

"I..." the words lodged in my throat.

"Maverick knows putting all of his hopes on basketball is a risk. The likelihood of being drafted to the NBA is what?" She looked to me. "Five out of every ten thousand high school players?"

"Three." My voice was flat.

"Yeah, but Rick's got what it takes to go all the way," Kyle chimed in. "He holds the three-point record for the State."

I shot him a look that said, *'not helping'*. I didn't want to discuss this. Not in front of strangers. Or Lo—definitely not Lo. Not when she still didn't know everything.

"It's sensible to have other options," Gentry weighed in, surprising me, but then Stella had to go and ask the question I dreaded.

"What would you do instead of play basketball, Maverick?"

Mom's face blanched this time. It was one thing to pretend I was keeping my options open, another to have to tell a barefaced lie to the people she considered family.

"Maverick's always had a natural instinct for business."

Could have fooled me. I swallowed the sarcastic reply souring on my tongue. Mom was only trying to help—it's all she ever did. Mediated between me and my father, Alec Prince. Ruthless businessman and the devil in an Armani suit.

Anger speared through me. It came hand-in-hand with him. The very mention of his name. The sound of his voice. The weight of his demands and loaded threats.

"I have a boyfriend."

Mom's fork clattered to the table as she stared at Summer with wide eyes. "Excuse me?"

"I, hmm, sorry." Summer tucked her hair behind her ear, unable to meet Mom's heavy gaze. "I've been trying to tell you since school got out for the holidays."

"That's lovely, sweetheart. And this, boyfriend…" Gentry swallowed hard, loosening his collar. "Will we get to meet him soon?"

Summer's eyes darted around the table, landing on me, and understanding passed between us. She was taking the heat from me to her, and it was more than I deserved after how I treated her and Nick. But I wouldn't forget.

"He's a good guy," I said, forking potatoes into my mouth, trying to act normal. It was the least I could do.

"You knew about this?" Mom tilted her head and I shrugged.

"We all know," Kyle added. "And for what it's worth, Nick has my seal of approval."

"Kyle," Summer and Lo said at the same time and he threw his hands up.

"What? It's a good thing."

"Okay, okay everyone. Let's calm down and finish eating," Gentry said. "Summer, I'm sure he's a good guy. Me and your mother very much look forward to meeting him."

My little sister's face turned crimson as she said, "Good, because he'll be here in about an hour."

~

When dinner was finally done, Lo was the first up to help Mom clear away the dishes. Macey made her excuses and left. If it was possible, I think she hated family time more than I did. Usually, we were a team. A united front. But ever since I'd played things down with her when she confronted me about Lo, that had changed. My sister wasn't blind… or stupid, but I wasn't ready to have *that* conversation, and she'd pretty much given me the silent treatment ever since.

"Laurie?" I asked Kyle as he texted someone.

"Yeah," he grinned. "I'm trying to convince her to come over, but her mom is pretty into the whole family thing."

I heard his words, but my eyes were too busy tracking Lo as she moved around. When she came out of the kitchen and disappeared down the hallway toward the back of the house, I pushed out of my chair. Kyle cocked his eyebrow. "You think that's a good idea?" He flicked his head in the direction Lo had gone.

"If anyone asks, I'm upstairs." I could take the other door out of the dining room and double back around past the stairs. It was risky, but I couldn't go another second without seeing her.

"It's not just your head on the block, you know."

I narrowed my eyes at him, casting Uncle Rob and Stella a sideways glance, but they were busy entertaining Beth. Kyle was right. This wasn't the way anyone needed to find out about us, but I needed to know we were okay.

Excusing myself, I left the room, breaking out into a gentle jog as I neared the downstairs bathroom. The vibrations of the faucet filtered through the door confirming she was inside. I waited, ready to bolt up the stairs if anyone came this way.

When the door swung open and Lo saw me standing there, her walls slammed down. Arms folded across her chest, chin high, she said, "Let me past." Her attempt at a scowl was too fucking cute, and I stepped closer, forcing her to back up.

"Not until you talk to me."

"What's to talk about? It's been two weeks since the dance and nothing has changed. Not one thing."

Not true. A lot had changed for me, but I didn't want to anger her further. Not when I was unable to do anything about it right at this precise moment.

"It's complicated; you know that." I stepped into the room and closed the door behind me, locking it. Her eyes widened with disbelief and I dragged a hand down my face. I didn't want to fight. Lo was my constant. My calm. She had no idea how much I needed her.

And I had a feeling she needed me too, not that she'd ever admit it.

She went to move around me, but I caught her wrist tugging her into my arms. "Don't be like this. It's you and me, okay?" I ran my nose along her cheek pressing a kiss to the corner of her mouth. "When we tell them—and we will—things will change. I just want it to be us, for a little while."

It wasn't the whole truth. But she didn't need to know that yet. I'd crossed a line going to the dance for her—the kids at school were already talking—but when I found out what Caitlin had planned I couldn't just stand by. Besides, it was killing me seeing her around school, watching Lions follow her around like a lost fucking puppy, and not being able to touch her. To show everyone she was mine.

So, I had made a choice.

Her.

I knew things would blow up once everyone found out though. I just needed her to give me some time to figure stuff out. To protect her from the fallout.

"London, come on," I buried my face in her shoulder, inhaling deeply.

"Maverick," she sighed, and I felt some of her irritation ebb away. "I don't want to play games."

I lifted my head and touched it to hers, forcing her to look at me. "This is not a game. It's real, Lo. I just need time."

Indecision flickered in her eyes, and I couldn't blame her. I'd been a bastard. The worst kind. But I was only protecting her.

It was all only ever about her.

Lo's fingers curled into my t-shirt and she pulled me closer, igniting a fire in my stomach. "What was that all about at dinner? The college stuff?"

My spine went rigid. Of course, she'd witnessed the whole conversation, but I didn't want to do this here. I'd have to tell her eventually, but not now. Not when I needed her so much. My lips crashed down on hers, hungry and possessive, as my hands buried themselves deep in her hair. I thought Lo would fight me. Push me away and demand answers. But she didn't. She let me in, swirling her tongue with mine, and I groaned, feeling myself grow hard.

"I want you," I murmured against her mouth, rolling my hips into hers, showing her just how much.

"We can't—"

"Lo, sweetie. Everything okay in there?"

She scrambled out of my arms, breathless and flushed. "Coming, I'm just coming."

I hooked my hand around her waist and pulled her back to me, my mouth brushing the shell of her ear. "Not yet, you're not, but it can be arranged."

Shuddering in my arms, her eyes darkened with lust as she bit down on her lip, staring up at me. I wanted nothing more than to—

"Lo, honey." A soft knock at the door echoed around the tiled room. "Are you sure you're okay?"

She slipped out from between me and the wall and I stumbled forward, my breath ragged. "We should get back out there before she sends a search party," Lo whispered.

I cussed quietly. My mother, the cockblock. "Fine. But this isn't over," I said in a low voice.

As soon as the adults were tipsy on Loretta's infamous eggnog, we would finish this. By then, there was every chance I wouldn't care who saw us.

"Stay here and I'll distract her." Lo sighed deeply, her eyes still blazing with lust.

She slipped out of the door, closing it behind her. I heard Mom hovering, asking questions, but soon their voices disappeared. Coast clear, I gave myself a couple of seconds for my racing heart to calm down then left the bathroom and returned to my version of hell.

Chapter Two

Lo

"My god, I thought I'd never escape." Laurie flounced into the pool house looking every bit the sun-kissed beauty. I still hadn't adjusted to seeing people dressed in t-shirts and sunglasses despite it being December. Winter in England was usually cold, wet and dreary. But not here. Every day was summer.

She stopped dead in her tracks when her eyes landed on the small group of people playing Monopoly. Laurie grabbed my arm tugging me to one side. "Is that Maverick Prince?" There was a lilt to her voice that had me smiling. "Maverick Prince playing Monopoly?"

I shrugged. "Stranger things have happened."

"No," she glanced back over at them, her brows furrowed. "No, they haven't. So, you and him, it's the real deal?"

"Ssh," I whisper-hissed. "You promised not to make a scene. He just wanted to lie low. Dinner was... intense."

"I can only imagine." Laurie blew out an exasperated breath. "Jesus, Lo, you sure don't do things by halves. I hope you know what you're getting yourself into."

It wasn't the first time she'd offered her advice, but

like I'd told her then, there wasn't a choice to be made.

"Will you two quit gossiping and get over here, already?" Kyle called. "You need to witness me kick Prince's butt."

"Sore loser, Stone?"

Laurie rolled her eyes, "Here we go," she sighed just as Kyle grumbled, "Low blow, Prince. It wasn't like we didn't give it our all."

"I know. I'm just yanking your chain. Chill," Maverick conceded, hearing the disappointment in his stepbrother's voice. Kyle had sulked for two weeks straight when the football team didn't make it past the semi-finals of the regionals.

We joined the boys, Summer, and a wary looking Nick. I didn't blame him. Maverick almost strangled him when he'd found out he slept with Summer, but things were calmer now. Although dinner had been awkward for other reasons. The conversation about college had taken a strange turn and I couldn't help but feel I was missing a piece of the Prince puzzle. I'd tried numerous times to ask about his father, but every time his impenetrable walls slammed down, and Maverick forced me out.

He wasn't shutting me out now though as his eyes dropped to the spot beside him. I arched my brow, flicking my gaze to Nick and Summer. Kyle and Laurie knew about us. Talk of the dance had spread like wildfire through the school hallways, but we hadn't officially gone public yet. Not even to Summer or Macey. Although from the cold-shoulder she'd been giving Maverick, I suspected Macey believed the hallway gossip, despite Kyle being as good at starting rumours as he was killing them. I'd heard more than one story which painted Maverick as the doting step-cousin. A real knight-in-shining-armour, swooping in to save me—the poor defenceless British relative—from the big bad bitch Caitlin.

Most didn't buy it. Especially Caitlin. And for the last few days of classes, her eyes followed me, burning holes into my back. She knew the truth. But you didn't argue with a Stone-Prince. Strangely, Maverick neither confirmed nor denied anything, only stoking the fire. In public, he went back to ignoring me and I ignored everyone else. The stares. The whispers, pointed fingers and smirks. They could believe what they wanted for all I cared. The people who mattered knew the truth. Well, most of them.

I didn't mind the kids at school not knowing, but I hadn't expected him to want to keep it from our families. Or maybe I had. I mean, this was Maverick Prince. The world's most closed book. But I didn't want to sneak around. Not when I'd fallen out with Dad over the very same thing.

"Lo, you're up." Summer smiled over at me from the shelter of Nick's side. I reached for my playing piece, purposefully brushing Maverick's arm. He stilled, his breath hitching, and I couldn't help the smirk tugging at my mouth. He wanted to play games, fine?

But it didn't mean I had to play fair.

We played until the main house became pitched in darkness. Rebecca stopped by more than once to check on us and try to persuade us to hang out with them. Each time she slunk off with disappointment gleaming in her glassy eyes.

It was Kyle's turn to roll, but I was too busy watching Summer and Nick. They were so cute, pressed close to one another. The way he touched her tenderly as if she was the most important thing in the world to him. They were young, Summer not yet sixteen, but their love was obvious. It was nice, being here with them and her brothers. Even with the odd growl from Maverick, and Kyle's inappropriate comments about Nick's hands and what would happen to them if he didn't stop groping his *baby* sister, and I made a mental note to thank them both later for giving her this.

"Babe, I'm getting tired." Laurie yawned, stretching her arms out in front of her. She stood up wiping her hands down her jeans. "I should probably head home."

"No way." Kyle leapt up and slung his arm around her shoulder, pulling her close. "You're staying. They'll all be sleeping off one of Loretta's infamous nog hangovers, you can sneak out first thing."

A shudder rolled through me. I didn't want to imagine Dad in one of their spare rooms cuddled up with Stella, her daughter sleeping soundly next to them on a blow-up mattress. Why we couldn't have just gone home was beyond me, but Rebecca and Gentry insisted we stay over for the night. I suppose it had its advantages. My eyes roved to Maverick beside me, heat flooding my stomach. When I looked back at my friend, she was chewing her lip nervously.

"I'm not sure," Laurie said, "I don't want to cause any problems."

Kyle leaned in and whispered something in her ear and her cheeks flushed a deep red. "Okay." She had that dreamy look about her and it didn't take much to work out what he'd promised if she stayed over.

"I guess I should head home too," Nick declared. "Thanks for letting me hang out."

"Jesus, Nick," Maverick groaned raking his hand through his hair. "We're not that bad."

Nick's jaw fell open, but Kyle chimed in, "Speak for yourself, Prince." He flashed his stepbrother a cocky grin, but it soon slipped away when Laurie elbowed him in the ribs.

"Ignore them, Nick. It's been fun hanging out. We should do it again sometime." Laurie smiled. "Lo, are you coming?" She gave me a pointed look, and I narrowed my eyes back at her.

"I, hmm…" Heat flared in my cheeks and I was unable to meet Summer's gaze as Nick helped her up.

I hated lying to her, the one person who had been nothing but nice to me since I arrived in Wicked Bay four months ago, but Maverick had asked for time. And I couldn't deny that the thought of keeping this—*us*—to ourselves for a little longer was tempting.

"Come on, babe." Kyle saved me. "She's a big girl. I'm sure she can find her way back to the house." Laurie mumbled something under her breath, but Kyle was already pulling her out of the pool house. Nick said goodnight and followed them, but Summer lingered behind.

Maverick had disappeared somewhere, leaving just the two of us and when Summer's eyes fixed on mine, I knew she knew.

"You could've told me, you know?"

"I'm sorry."

"It's okay. I understand, but I'm here for you, Lo. Always."

I nodded over the lump in my throat.

"Everything okay?" Maverick said from behind me and I twisted around to him.

"Yeah. Summer was just saying goodnight."

"I'll see you tomorrow." She hesitated, as if she wanted to say more, but with a faint smile she disappeared into the darkness.

"What was that about?" Maverick dropped down beside me.

"She knows."

"And?"

"And what?" I raised an eyebrow.

"Did she try to warn you off me?" He leaned closer, taking the air with him, and my reply died on my tongue as his hungry gaze dropped to my mouth. "I thought they were never going to leave."

I blinked, trying to focus. "Oh, I thought you wanted to hang out?"

It had been his suggestion, much to everyone's surprise.

"No." He inched closer until we were eye-to-eye. "I wanted an excuse to get you in here."

"Someone might see us."

"Right now…" His breath fanned my cheek, fluttering over my earlobe and a shiver danced up my spine making my hairs stand on end. "I'm not sure I care." Deft fingers glided up my shoulder and curved around my neck, and then his lips slanted over mine, gentle and unhurried. A complete contrast to the hot-headed ruthless boy I knew Maverick to be.

He pulled me closer, pressing the lines of his chest against the soft curves of mine. His other hand slipped around my hip and down my thigh, dragging me onto his lap until I was straddling him, my knees either side of his thighs.

"Maverick, wait." I pushed my hands against his chest, steadying myself. Catching my breath, I pulled back to meet his heated gaze. "It's too risky."

"I need you, Lo. I need to know we're okay." Uncertainty flashed over his face, rendering me speechless. "I need you." His lips connected with my neck and he sucked the skin, teeth scraping the sensitive spot, eliciting a breathy moan from me.

"Not here," I pulled away again.

"You'll stay?" Victory danced in his eyes and I shook my head with gentle laughter.

"On one condition." The words flew out before I could stop them. It was the perfect time and although using sex wasn't entirely fair, I didn't know how else to reach him.

"You have terms? I'm not sure that's how this works, *London*." His voice was low, a flicker of irritation in the way my nickname sounded rolling off his tongue. But I wasn't about to back down now.

"I do." An amused smirk tugged at my lips. "I'll stay if you tell me what that was all about at dinner?"

His expression was unreadable. "Lo," he warned, but I held firm. "Maverick. If we're doing this, you're going to have to let me in eventually."

He'd said that this was real, that *we* were real, but I needed more. It had to be more than just a physical connection.

Maverick scooped me off his lap and moved me beside him, dragging a hand down his face. "My dad wants me to attend Cal State East Bay in the fall. It's where he went to college and I guess he wants me to carry on his legacy or some bullshit."

"That's not so bad, is it? You can still play basketball there, can't you?" Didn't all colleges have sports teams? But when Maverick tensed, his jaw clenched in frustration, I had my answer.

"He doesn't want you to play basketball?"

"He'd prefer I pursued business studies." His fist clenched against his knee, the anger in his voice startling me. I'd seen Maverick bruised and bloodied; I'd witnessed his temper first hand, but I'd never seen him like this. The corded muscles in his neck pulsated, and I knew if I reached out and touched him, I'd feel the tremble of fury underneath his sweater.

"But you're good, right? You can get a scholarship and go to another college? Kyle said—"

"It's complicated."

"But it's your dream."

"Dreams don't always come true, Lo." All the fight, the need to hurt, melted away in those six words and he hunched over, staring at the floor.

"Maverick." I slid my hand over his bicep and squeezed. "There has to be another way."

His head turned slowly, and a sad smile tugged at the corner of his mouth. "Maybe."

I didn't know the first thing about basketball, college scholarships, or going pro, but I couldn't imagine a world where a parent didn't support their child's dream. And despite my lack of knowledge, I'd seen Maverick play. I'd witnessed the boy he became on the court. He was at home. Free.

He belonged on the court.

"But—"

"Come on." Maverick cut me off as he stood and pulled me up with him. "I'm beat and it's late."

He guided us to the bedroom, to the room that used to be mine, his palm pressed against the small of my back. Once inside, he let me go, and I turned to face him. Soft light filtered in through the blinds casting shadows across his face. His profile was so strong, so confident. But I knew it was the armour he wore to keep people out. To protect himself and the secrets he carried. And I wanted nothing more than to strip it away, piece by piece.

Maverick wasted no time stripping out of his clothes until he stood before me in just black boxer shorts that hugged his thighs. My gaze swept down his body, the years of physical training and conditioning evident in his lean sculpted muscles. My insides coiled tight as warmth spread through me. He was breathtaking. But when my eyes landed on his, he didn't return the sentiment. He looked lost... defeated. And I hated it. In that moment, I hated Alec Prince, a man I barely knew, for causing Maverick such pain. Because that's what I saw in his expression. Raw pain.

"Maverick," I whispered closing the distance between us.

"No more questions, Lo. Not tonight. Please?"

My heart cracked. This wasn't my Maverick, and I realised that he was still keeping things from me. That although I'd peeled away one layer of him tonight, there were so many more I had yet to uncover.

I went to him, sliding my hands over his broad shoulders and pressed a kiss to the underside of his jaw. Maverick responded by hooking his hands underneath my jumper and sliding it up off my body. His fingers traced a path down my chest between the swell of my breasts, and I sucked in a shaky breath as they continued down, pushing my leggings down my hips.

"I don't deserve you," he said in a broken whisper. "The way I treated you when you arrived." His cool gaze dropped away.

"Maverick, look at me." I grabbed his jaw forcing his face to mine. "We all make mistakes. This, us, it isn't a mistake."

He wanted to protect me from something—most likely his father. I understood that now. But I wanted to do the same for him. I wanted to help.

I crushed my lips to his, trying to pour everything I felt into the kiss. It ignited something in him and he scooped me up. My legs went around his waist as he carried us to the bed, and we didn't speak another word as he lay me down, hovering above me. Dark eyes, almost black with need, stared down at me as he ground his hips against me before capturing my lips and kissing me hard.

We became a blur of limbs and breathless moans. My hands explored his chest, shoulders, slid into the hair at the base of his neck. Maverick's mouth owned my skin. Nipping and biting, soothing the sting with his tongue. He walked a fine line of control. It poured from him, crackling in the air around us. But then he rolled us, settling me on top of him, handing me the power, and I felt the shift between us. His walls had come down tonight. He'd let me in. I wasn't foolish enough to believe that tomorrow, when the sun rose and the light streamed in through the blinds, everything would be the same. But as I wiggled into position and sank down on him and his head tipped back, eyes shuttering in ecstasy, it didn't matter. Tonight, I'd helped him forget. I'd grounded him.

In some small way, I'd helped.

Chapter Three

Maverick

"Shit, Lo, we overslept."

"What? Huh?" Her voice was thick with sleep as she roused in my arms. "What time is it?" She smiled at me through half-opened eyes.

"Seven-thirty." I brushed my lips overs hers in a lingering kiss. "You need to go before someone realizes you're not in your room." Pulling my arm free, I threw back the covers and started yanking on my jeans.

Lo stretched her body with a soft sigh and my dick jumped to attention. Fuck. What I wouldn't do to climb back into bed and lose myself in her again. But I'd be losing a lot more if anyone found her in here. Naked. In my bed.

Grabbing her sweater off the floor, I balled it up and threw it at her. "Put this on. You have ten minutes before I drag you out of here and throw you in the pool for a morning dip."

Her eyes snapped to mine, and she tried her best to glower at me, but she looked too damn cute. I chuckled, running a brisk hand over my head, and left her to it. I needed coffee or a cold shower. Anything to calm my racing pulse and the urges rushing through me.

When I'd woken with Lo wrapped around me, her face buried in my chest, her silky hair plastered everywhere, it took a few seconds for my brain to register. It was the first time she'd stayed over after two weeks of stolen kisses and dry humping in the back of my Audi. I'd stayed at her place once when Uncle Rob was out of town for business but other than that, time alone was a luxury we didn't have.

For a second, I wondered if it was real; if she was truly here, in my arms. Lo had that effect on me. Shifted some of the unrest in my chest. Made me believe things could be okay, that the darkness living inside of me could be erased. But then the memories came quick and fast, a surge of waves crashing against the shore. Christmas Dinner. All the talk of college. Mom's pale face as she tried to cover for *him*. Lo asking me questions—too many fucking questions. I'd surprised myself when I'd answered her. But she was right, if we were really doing this, I needed to let her in. Even if it went against my default setting of shutting everyone out.

But Lo wasn't everyone.

Not even close.

Since that very first night, last summer, she'd reached me in a way no other had. Maybe it was because she didn't know who I was. She wasn't driven by some ulterior motive to get close to me. She didn't want to use me to get to my dad or to win some popularity contest. I was no one to her and yet, she cared enough to ask me if I was okay. To stay with me, despite being a rabbit caught in the headlights.

To give herself to me.

Shit.

I'd really fucked up that night. And almost every other day since she arrived in Wicked Bay. The things I'd said, how I'd treated her... she deserved better. But it was all for her. To protect her from becoming collateral damage in the shitstorm of my life.

The second I felt her enter the room, I turned slowly, drinking in the sight of her, bed hair and all. "Morning," I said, trying to disguise the emotion in my voice. Lo had barreled into my life and turned my world upside down, but I didn't want to play all my cards, not yet. Not with so much on the line. Because once she found out the truth, there was every chance Lo would fold, and I'd lose her.

I couldn't lose her. Not now I knew the curves of her body. The taste of her lips. How perfect she fit against me.

I just couldn't.

"Hey." A deep blush spread up her neck and into her cheeks as she tugged her sweater down, and I wanted nothing more than to kiss her there, right in that very spot. "Do we have time for coffee?"

My eyes flickered to the window. There was no sign of life from the main house yet, and I figured if anyone was stirring, Kyle would send a signal. He might have enjoyed seeing me get chewed out by Gentry or my mom, but he wouldn't do that to Lo. She had him wrapped around her finger almost as much as me.

"Sure, if we're quick."

She sat at one of the stools while I turned on the coffee maker. "You have done this before, right?" Amusement laced her voice, and I glanced over my shoulder with a scowl, but Lo shrugged. "I just figured that with Loretta around you never had to fend for yourself." She smirked around her words. Taunting me.

"You think I'm spoiled?" I acted insulted.

Lo tilted her head to one side and chewed her bottom lip before replying, "Aren't you?"

I was on her before she could escape. My fingers dug into her sides, tickling and squeezing. Lo shrieked, trying to fight me off, but I was bigger. Stronger. And she'd known exactly what she was doing when she baited me.

"Maverick, stop. Stop," she panted, pressing her face into my shoulder to drown out her pained laughter.

"I never had you down as ticklish." I'd have to remember that.

My touches became slower, surer, and she gasped for breath. "Maverick... Rick. Stop. Stop, I'm sorry." It came out muffled.

"Sorry," I said. "What was that?"

Lo pulled back and met my eyes. "I'm sorry, okay. I take it back."

My fingers brushed back and forth in gentle movements and she pressed her lips together to contain her cries... or were they moans?

"Does that feel good?" I cocked my head, and she stared at me, squirming on the chair as my hand moved lower, skating across her bare thighs. Over the scars she still refused to talk about. I knew they from the accident but Lo wouldn't go there. And I'd tried. More than once, I'd tried to get her to open up. I guess we were both strangers to letting other people in.

"You really should have put on pants," I leaned in close, whispering in her ear, and Lo shivered as I ran my hand up the inside of her thigh. It rippled through her body like a shockwave and it was my turn to smirk. As I pulled away, my lips grazed her ear... her cheek... the corner of her mouth.

Fuck, I would never get enough of her.

"Too bad we have to get back to the house," I said against her lips before I pulled away fully.

Her palms slammed into my chest and I staggered back with a whoosh of breath. Lo slid off the stool and made her escape, mumbling something about my unfair games, and continued with the coffee.

"I'm proud of you," the words tumbled out and her head snapped up to mine as she added sugar to the mugs.

"You are?"

"For yesterday, for keeping it together in front of Stella."

"I didn't do it for her."

"I know."

I'd seen how painful it was for her. Watched as she tamped down the urge to bolt every time Stella spoke or laughed or so much as looked in Lo's direction. She was a better person than me because if it had been me in her shoes I doubted things would have played out so smoothly.

Lo pushed my mug across the counter with a heavy sigh. "She's not going anywhere. I guess I have to get used to it."

"Your dad, he seems happy."

"Yeah." Lo's gaze moved to the window that looked out on the house. "I still don't understand it, though. I've tried to process it but it's like my mind can't unravel it all. It's too much."

I caught her hand and tugged her around to me, trapping her between my legs. "Give it time."

She didn't answer, too lost in her thoughts.

"Wait here a minute." I dropped a kiss on her head and switched us, helping Lo onto the stool. "Wha—" she started, but I was already moving. When I'd spotted it in a store downtown, I knew I had to get it for her.

After retrieving the package from its safe place in my nightstand drawer, I returned to Lo. She eyed my hands and said, "Maverick?"

"I don't think I got to say it yesterday, but Merry Christmas, Lo." I kissed her again. Just a quick peck but it was still like a bolt of thunder in my chest, then I handed her the gift.

"Merry Christmas," she swallowed as her fingers

traced the edge of the parcel in her hands. "What is it?"

"Open it and see." I ran a brisk hand over my head, a sudden burst of nerves flooding my chest. What if she didn't understand? What if she didn't like it? What if it was too soon?

"You got this, for me?" She stared at the journal in her hands and then slowly slid her tear-filled eyes to mine. "It's beautiful."

"I saw it and it reminded me of your tattoo." The black floral design was handstitched into the silk material binding the journal.

"It does, it's..." her voice wobbled. "Maverick, this is... I don't have words. I love it." She clutched it to her chest and leaned forward, pressing her lips to mine. My fingers slid into her hair, anchoring us together as I ran my tongue along the seam of her mouth. Lo let me in, let me take what I needed. When I was one second away from hauling her back to the bedroom, I pulled away.

"I thought it might help," I breathed out. "Writing stuff down." Miss Tamson had suggested it to me more than once over the last year. But my answer was always the same.

"I- I used to keep a diary, when I was younger." She swallowed, and I saw tears in her eyes. "Thank you, this is... it's perfect, Maverick. I feel bad now, though. I didn't get you anything. I didn't think—"

"Stop." I cupped her jaw, staring at her. "I don't need anything from you, Lo. Just you."

"You mean that?" I gave her a pointed look and she blushed again. And then she said, "You really think they'll be upset?"

"Gentry won't be happy. He thinks I'm a bad influence."

Lo placed her gift on the counter and looped her arms around my neck. "I like your bad influence." A suggestive smile tugged at her lips and I gave her a smirk of my own.

"Is that right?"

She nodded up at me through thick lashes and I leaned in again to kiss her, but she leaned back out of reach. "But I don't like the idea of you getting hurt, Maverick."

"Lo," I warned. She'd asked me once about the fighting, the day after the dance. And I'd told her then, she didn't need to worry.

"I just want to understand," the uncertainty in her whisper crushed me, but I couldn't tell her. Not that. Anything but *that*.

"It's just something I need right now."

"But—"

"I'm not doing this, Lo, not today. Not now." I moved away from her.

"You were hurt, Maverick. You got hurt."

My body went rigid as I clenched my jaw.

"Maverick." The inflection in her voice cooled the molten lava running through my veins, just enough for me to look at her. "I didn't mean to push. I just," she swallowed. "I care about you, a lot."

Closing the distance between us, I looked at Lo. Really looked at her. We were both broken. Products of our fucked-up pasts. But where I wanted to hurt and feel pain, she wanted to fix and make everything better.

"This is who I am, Lo. I'm not the good guy. I fight. I lose my shit and see red. It lives inside of me and when it gets too much, I have to let it out."

"What happened to you?" Her voice was a gentle caress and it would have been so easy to tell her. To bare the demons that haunted me. But I couldn't do it. Not now. Maybe not ever.

I gathered her against me, tucking her head into the space between my jaw and chest. Lo's fingers curled into my t-shirt and we stood there in silence. I knew what I was asking of her was a lot. But I also knew she had her own demons. Things she still hadn't laid to rest. And when—*if*—the time was right, she'd tell me.

"I want you, Lo," I said. "I want this. But there are some things I need to handle myself."

I wish it could be different. I wish I could be the kind of guy who deserves you. But I didn't say the words. Because I was a selfish prick.

"Okay."

It was so quiet I almost missed it but Lo wiggled free, craning her neck up at me. "I trust you. When you're ready to tell me, I'll be here."

As I stared down at her—the girl who held my heart in the palm of her hand—I knew I was going to hell. One way or another, my secrets would ruin us. But it was too late to walk away.

Because in the end, maybe I was more like my father than I wanted to admit.

Chapter Four

Lo

"Slipping into the kitchen, I clicked the door shut behind me. It was quiet with only the rhythmic tick tock of the wall clock and the soft hum of the refrigerator making a sound. I glanced back at Maverick as he lingered by the pool house. The familiar sensations in my stomach tugged sharply but it wasn't only desire I felt. After our intense conversation, waves of dread rippled through me too, swirling with my lust. Tainting the amazing night we'd spent together.

I'd pushed him too far, demanded answers he couldn't give me. But I wanted to know all of him. Even the parts I might not like.

Tiptoeing across the kitchen, I reached the stairs, taking two steps at a time until I was safely inside the guest room. The door clicked shut behind me, and my eyes landed on the bed with its crisp fresh sheets and fluffy pillows. It looked so inviting, but the house would come alive within the hour and I'd have to play my part. Again. Have to pretend that Maverick was nothing to me... again. I peeled off my clothes and slipped into the white, silky-soft robe hanging on the back of the door, smiling to myself at Rebecca's preparedness, and headed for the bathroom.

"Sleep well?" Kyle grinned cockily as he came out of the bathroom and I rolled my eyes choosing silence as my only reply. His laughter followed me all the way down the hallway.

When I was showered and changed, I made my way downstairs. Everyone was gathered in the kitchen. Dad, Stella and Beth sat huddled at one end of the island, talking and laughing over their breakfast plates.

"Good morning, sweetheart," he said as I helped myself to a glass of juice.

"Morning," I replied, unable to meet his gaze, worried that if he saw my flushed skin and undisguisable smile, he might see the truth on my face.

"There's toast, pancakes, bacon, and cereal," Uncle Gentry added. "Help yourself, Lo.

"Thanks." I picked a stool away from Dad and Stella, and loaded my plate with pancakes despite my hunger disappearing the second I laid eyes on them.

It was weird being back and yet, in some ways, I felt more at home here, in amongst the secrets and lies than I did in my own house.

"It really was a lovely day, yesterday." The sound of Stella's voice sent my spine rigid. "Thank you for inviting us."

I risked a sideways glance at her, the woman my father loved. All day yesterday, she'd been polite. Laughing and chatting with Gentry and Rebecca as if they were old friends. Mum never wanted this life—had fought Dad on it—but Stella fit in so easily. As if she was supposed to be here.

As if she belonged here all along.

I swallowed over the lump of pancake stuck in my

throat as my eyes burned with unshed tears. But then I felt Maverick behind me. His fingers grazed the small of my back so lightly I might have missed it. But I didn't. I felt that single touch all the way down to my crushed soul. Maverick got it. He understood.

"Something smells good," Kyle bounded into the room, freshly showered, and the spell was broken. Maverick went to him and some unspoken message passed between them. And then my cousin's gaze settled on me, "Laurie wants to know if you're coming to hang with us later?"

"Kyle," Rebecca sighed. "I wanted us to spend the day together."

"No can do, Momma P. We have plans." He waggled his eyebrows and stuffed a piece of bacon in his mouth.

"It's fine, darling. We can take Robert and Stella out on Dad's boat? Someone might as well get some use out of it since Mom and Dad are off on their travels again."

"Oh, that would be wonderful," Stella crooned, the sound vibrating in my skull. "Wouldn't that be wonderful, Bethany?"

The little girl smiled showing the rest of us a mouthful of half-chewed cereal.

"Beth," her mother blushed, covering her daughter's mouth and whispering something about table manners.

"Be ready by ten," Kyle said to me and I nodded. I was ready to get out of here.

So ready.

~

"Laurie snuck out unnoticed then?" I said to Kyle as he backed his Jeep out and did a U-turn before setting off down the winding drive.

"It seems the two of you are pretty stealthy that way." He flashed me a sideways grin. "He's taking care of you, right?"

"Seriously, Kyle?"

"What? I'm just looking out for you. Rick is..." He blew out a long breath. "Look, I'm pleased the two of you finally got your shit together, maybe you can rein him in, but it doesn't mean I don't worry." His voice trailed off and I curled my fingers into the soft leather. "Alec Prince is... well, he's a ruthless bastard. I don't know what's going on between him and Maverick but it's nothing good, Cous. Things could get very messy when he finds out."

"I know," I whispered.

I wasn't stupid. And I hadn't missed the pure rage that flowed out of Maverick whenever talk of his future or father came up.

"He won't talk to me about it." I admitted.

"Give him time. This, you, it's new for him. Rick doesn't let people get close, Cous."

Another thing he didn't need to tell me, but then he added, "You're the exception. I don't know what happened that night last summer, but it stayed with him. When I realized it was you, I couldn't tell him. You were back in England. Unlikely to ever show up here again."

He held my gaze, keeping his hands tight on the wheel as we sped toward wherever we were going. "But then Dad told us you were moving here. I didn't know what to do. After everything you'd been through... the stuff I heard my dad tell Rebecca," he gulped. "You sounded as broken as him."

Silence filled the space between us. Thick and heavy with the ghosts of my past and I struggled to breathe.

"I'm sorry," was all he said, and I wasn't sure which part he was apologising for. But it didn't matter. The emotion in Kyle's voice, the way he'd taken me under his wing and protected me from the start, it was all I needed to know.

"Thank you," slipped from my lips and Kyle chuckled

low in his throat.

"You're family, Cous."

We rode the rest of the way in comfortable silence. Until I realised we were going in the opposite direction to Laurie's house. "Hmm, Kyle where are we going?" I said, and then I saw it. "Luke Taffia's house?" It was the last place I expected.

"Change of plans," he said as he turned into the sloping driveway. When he cut the engine, he added, "Come on, the Prince awaits."

Maverick was here?

Of course he was. It was his best friend's house, but he hadn't said a single word about this when I managed to covertly ask him what his plans were for today. I climbed out and smoothed down my hair suddenly feeling unsure.

"Hey, its fine. It's nothing crazy. Rick and the team hang out here over the holidays. Luke's parents vacation for the New Year in Cabo."

I gave him a tight nod and followed him up the path. Maverick's car was tucked between two cars I didn't recognise. When I didn't follow him inside, Kyle glanced back over his shoulder, "What's wrong?"

"Last time we were here…" I dropped my eyes. We'd been drunk, and Maverick had given us a ride home—with the girl he'd come downstairs with.

"They didn't sleep together."

"What?" My head shot up, eyes wide, and I hated how insecure I sounded.

Kyle turned to face me, dragging a hand down his face. "You didn't ask him about it, did you?"

Lips mashed together, I shook my head. I hadn't asked. We weren't together then. Maverick was a free agent. Despite how much it hurt to see them, so intimate and close, I hadn't asked.

He rolled his eyes. "You're as bad as each other."

"Kyle." I gritted my teeth, aware that we were standing on the threshold of Maverick's best friend's house and that he was probably in there.

"Maverick didn't sleep with Selina. I asked him," he hesitated. "He wouldn't tell me the whole story, but I believed him. You should ask him about it."

More secrets.

I had a feeling if I was going to be with Maverick, I needed to get used to them.

Reluctantly, I followed Kyle inside, closing the door behind me. Laughter floated down the hallway. The house reminded me of the Stone-Prince's place. Posh. Big. It was beautiful. But unlike my family's house back in England, it lacked the personal touches I was used to. No photographs or family portraits hung on the wall. It was all very perfect. And all very cold.

We entered a room toward the back of the house. A typical boy cave with huge sofas; bean bags; the biggest TV I'd ever seen, mounted on the wall; and a crowd of boys cheering at the screen.

"Stone, get in here." Trey, the guy from that night at the party, said with a grin. But when his eyes roved to me they narrowed, and he tipped his chin. "Hey."

I opened my mouth, a sarcastic reply on the tip of my tongue, but Maverick's voice cut through the room. "Trey, back off."

"Hey, man," the boy's hands shot up. "I'm just messing. Sorry, Lo."

"Learn some manners, dude. She's family." Kyle threw me look I didn't quite understand as he wedged himself between Trey and another guy I vaguely recognised from school and the basketball team.

My eyes moved from person to person, trying to place them. But I quickly realised, these were Maverick's inner circle. The boys he hung out with at school, his teammates.

So why the hell was I here?

"Can I get you something to drink, Lo?" Luke said from his leather gaming chair.

"I'd take a water," I said. But it wasn't him who got up.

Maverick stalked toward me, his eyes holding mine. "Come on." He took my hand and led me out of the room and across the hallway to the kitchen. All I could do was follow, my mind swimming at the strangeness of the situation.

Maverick had Kyle bring me here. To his friend's house... to hang out with them?

"I can hear your thoughts from here." He released my hand and went to a cabinet, retrieving a glass.

"No, you can't," I shot back.

Maverick slid the drink across the counter and then stalked around the island to me. "Yes, I can." His eyes narrowed. "You're thinking what the hell am I doing?"

He was close. His breath fanning my cheek as he leaned in and pressed a kiss to my shoulder. "You're not my dirty little secret, Lo. I want you here, with me."

"Maverick." My hands slid to his chest as I pulled away to look up at him. "It's okay. This thing with your dad. College. It's okay. You'll let me in when you're ready."

Understanding danced in his eyes, but I saw the flecks of surprise. Confusion. Had he done this, brought me here, to reassure me?

Or himself?

"Prince, bring supplies," someone yelled, breaking our connection. Maverick mumbled under his breath before capturing my lips in a quick peck.

"You okay with this?"

Was I?

I nodded.

When we returned to the game room, no one batted an eyelid as Maverick moved to one of the empty chairs and pulled me down on his lap. They noticed. I felt their intrigue. Their discreet glances in our direction. But no one said a word. Maverick was the Prince and them his Court. Luke was the only one who dared meet my gaze. He smiled broadly and gave me a nod of approval. And I don't know why, but it meant something.

It meant a lot.

~

If I'd been confused by the whole situation, Laurie's face blew my expression out of the water. Her eyes had widened to saucers when Kyle led her into the room and introduced her to everyone. Of course, she already knew everyone, but this was different. We were in their world now. It was a sight to behold—Laurie Davison speechless. Kyle laughed, tucking her into his side, as the rest of the boys continued with their game. Maverick chatted and took his turn, leaning around me to control his character, and day soon turned into late afternoon. Luke ordered in pizza and someone disappeared, returning with beer and more snacks. It was nothing like the parties I'd attended before with Laurie and Kyle.

The doorbell chimed and one of the guys, Aaron, leapt up.

"About fucking time, I'm starving." As if on cue Kyle's stomach grumbled and me and Laurie stifled a laugh.

"I'll get plates." Luke rose from his chair and looked to us. "You guys eating?"

We shared a look and Laurie grinned. "Hmm, hells yeah. But I need to pee first."

"Babe, too much information," Kyle scolded but she wasn't fazed as she followed Luke out of the room.

"Scoot over, I'll go and help Luke." Maverick lifted

me to the side, so he could slide out from under me and I nestled back in the soft chair.

"So, Lo, you and Rick, huh?" Trey's eyes were guarded. Not hostile but not particularly welcome either, but there was something in his voice and I couldn't get a read on him.

"Trey, come on, man." Kyle went straight to my defense, but I shook my head slightly at him.

"That's between me and Maverick." I lifted my chin a little and looked him dead in the eyes. He was concerned for his friend. I got it. I did. I'd swept onto the scene and Maverick, for all they knew, had hated me. Had wanted nothing to do with me. And now... well, I could see how it might be confusing.

"Yeah, but how did it even happen? I mean, one minute he's gunning for your blood and then the next he's all up in your—"

"Everything okay here?"

Our heads whipped around to the door. Maverick stood there, jaw clenched and his hard gaze set firmly on his teammate.

Chapter *Five*

Maverick

Luke stacked plastic forks on top of the pile of paper plates balanced in my hands. His parents were happy for us to come by and hang out, as long as we didn't touch Mrs. Taffia's chinaware.

"I take it from the look on her face when she stepped into the room, she had no idea Kyle was bringing her here?"

I shrugged. "I didn't think she'd come if I asked."

"Why?" He rubbed his jaw and I could see his mind working overtime.

I shrugged again. Luke knew how I felt about Lo—he'd known the second she flipped me off her first morning at school. Even though I'd refused to fess up to him in the beginning, it all ended the second she walked into the warehouse with me. Looking back, that was the day I claimed her as mine. Instead of forcing her out of my car and chewing her out, I saw the pain in her eyes—the fierce determination to run—and made a split decision.

One that changed everything.

Because there was no going back now, not for me.

"Does she know?" he added when I didn't answer.

"Not everything, no."

"Shit. You're playing a dangerous game, man. What do you think he'll do when he finds out?"

My eyes hardened, my spine ramrod straight, and the anger deep inside of me flared. Luke saw it. I didn't let many people in, but Luke wasn't just anyone. He was my best friend. Family. But there were some things even he didn't know. Things that were just too difficult to say.

"I'll deal with it when it happens." Because it would. My father would find out about Lo eventually. I just needed time to figure shit out. To figure out how I felt about all of this. I didn't let people in. I didn't trust easily. But Lo was different.

"You're really into her, aren't you?"

"I…" How did I even begin to put into words the way her presence calmed me? Soothed the roaring beast living inside me. Even with that smart mouth of hers she reached a place few could.

"Just be careful. Don't give him a reason to go after her." My mouth dried at Luke's warning. "Take those and I'll get the rest of it," he added.

I smirked, relieved his *Dr. Phil* routine was over. "Yes, *Mom*," I smiled around the word and he flipped me off.

Out in the hallway I could hear the others chatting. Kyle, Lo… Trey.

"So, Lo, you and Rick, huh?"

I froze, my senses on high alert. I should have known that cocky bastard wouldn't be able to follow orders. *Don't push her*, I'd warned them all before she arrived with Kyle. They didn't understand it—what I'd done for her at the dance. Since Caitlin, I hadn't so much as looked at another girl. It was rule number one. No distractions. And I'd stayed true to form, spending weeks ignoring Lo around school or barking orders at her as if she was nothing more than an unwanted burden. An annoying thorn in my side.

"Trey, come on, man." Kyle warned but Lo cut in, her voice steady. "That's between me and Maverick."

I edged closer to the room as pride swelled in my chest. But it was quickly tamped down by something that resembled thunder in a storm, building at the fact the fucker had even asked the question. I knew he was only feeling her out, protecting me. But I didn't need it, not from Lo.

Never from Lo.

Her motivations were pure, and if anything, she was the one who needed protecting from me. From the piranhas circling me.

"Yeah, but how did it even happen? I mean, one minute he's gunning for your blood and then the next he's all up in your—"

"Everything okay?" I stepped into the room, ignoring Trey and fixing my eyes on Lo, silently letting her know I heard their exchange. The corners of her mouth curved up and she gave me a small nod letting me know she was okay.

"Fine. Trey was just telling me the Wreckers have a real shot at the Championship.

"He was, was he?" My eyes swept over him, cold and calculated, and he gulped, shifting on the bean bag uncomfortably.

"Yeah, I—" he spluttered dragging a hand down his pale face. "You need to get your girl up to speed, Prince."

I held his unsteady gaze. *One... two... three.* Satisfied he'd gotten the message, I went to the table and dumped the plates. Lo lifted off the chair to let me slide beneath her. My arms wound around her waist and I entwined my fingers in hers. Trey didn't look at us, but Kyle flashed me a knowing smirk and I tipped my chin at him. He had my back. *Our* back. And I appreciated him far more than he realized.

"Pizza is served." Aaron's face was barely visible over the stack of boxes in his hands and the smell of tomato and peperoni filled the room. My stomach grumbled in response and Lo twisted around to me. "Someone's hungry." She laughed, and my arms tightened around her as I leaned into her, brushing my lips over hers.

"Yeah, but it's not the pizza I want to eat," I whispered, and her body hummed at my words. When I eased away, her pupils were dilated, and her lips were parted with surprise. I smirked. "Come on."

We joined the others, helping ourselves to the food. When I'd asked Kyle to bring her here, he'd been wary. These people were my friends, my inner circle. But they were good guys, mostly, if you overlooked Trey's earlier fuck up.

"Thank God, the food's here." Laurie poked her head around the door. "I'm starving."

"You'd better hurry before your guy eats it all," Trey joked, and everyone laughed. Except Kyle, who was too busy piling his plate high.

"Seriously, man, I don't know where you put it. You must have hollow fucking legs."

"It's called exercise, Trey," Kyle said. "Maybe you should try it some time."

Trey grabbed a dough ball and launched it at his head. Kyle ducked, and it hit the wall.

"Chill, fuckers," Luke snapped. "Mom will know if so much as anything is damaged, out of place, or missing."

That shut them up.

When we were all seated again, Luke flicked through the channels. Some Christmas chick flick filled the screen and Laurie shrieked, "I love this one."

We all looked at her. Even Lo laughed.

"And this," Trey grumbled, "is why we don't invite

chicks over more often."

"But it's Jude Law. He's so delicious, right, Lo? And British," she added with a dreamy sigh. "His voice, hmm."

"Okay, okay, boyfriend, sitting right here. Turn it off before she starts dry humping the screen."

"He's okay, I guess. I've never really thought about it," Lo said before taking a bite of pizza. When she swallowed, she added, "But Charlie Hunnam, now there's a guy I could totally get on board with."

Laurie's eyes lit up and she grinned like the cat who got the cream. "Oh yeah, his body is like—"

Kyle shoved his slice of pizza in her mouth, declaring, "And that is how you shut her up."

My stepbrother liked to think he was in control of *that* situation but we all knew Laurie would make him suffer later, behind closed doors. It'd taken months for her to finally let him back in and there was no way he would screw it up again. He loved her too much. And despite never knowing what was going to come out of her mouth, Laurie was kind of cool.

"That was so good, I'm stuffed," Lo said, standing. "Want anything?" She turned to me and I raked my gaze over her body, lingering on the curve of her chest, letting her know exactly what I wanted. Color bloomed in her cheeks and she stuck out her tongue at me before leaving the room.

When she'd gone, Aaron looked right at me and said, "You are so whipped, man."

"Jacks," I warned but he grinned broadly, unfazed by my tone.

"Hey, it looks good on you," he went on. "About time you got some. Maybe it'll remove that giant stick from your—" My plate skimmed his head and his eyes grew to saucers. "Shit man, I'm only messing."

Luke threw me one of his looks and I picked it up before I went in search of Lo. She was in the kitchen, cleaning up the empty glasses. "You don't have to do that," I said.

She shrugged, throwing me a quick look over her shoulder. "I know but I don't mind." Her movements slowed as I stalked toward her, and her body turned as if she felt it. The pull. The tether between us.

I placed my hands either side of her, caging her against the counter. "Charlie Hunnam, really?"

Lo dipped her head but kept her eyes on me, desire swirling in them. "What? He's hot."

I didn't reply but I didn't break eye contact either.

"Jealous?" she whispered, leaning closer, looking up at me through hooded lids.

My resolve cracked. I curved a hand around her neck and kissed her. Slow and deep, it took everything I had not to unleash all the tension that had been building over the last few hours, with her sitting in my lap, wiggling against me. Teasing me. Our tongues tangled together and my whole body went off like a rocket.

"I want you," I breathed rocking into her. Showing her just how much.

"Shit, fuck," someone choked out from the doorway. "Are you trying to scar me for life?"

I broke away, dropping my head to Lo's, dragging air into my lungs. "Nice timing, Stone," I said with a hint of agitation.

The fucker had the balls to laugh as he came over to us. "I need to bleach my eyes."

"Kyle," Lo sighed. "Your timing sucks."

That's my girl. I smirked at him and his face screwed up. "Me and Laurie are going to bail. Do you want a ride?"

"No," I said as Lo answered, "Yes."

I looked to her and cocked my eyebrow. "You want to

leave?"

"No, but I need to get back somehow, and we can't exactly turn up together."

Kyle glanced between us, but I only saw Lo. I didn't want her to leave, not yet. But she was right. Fuck. She was right. I flicked my head at my stepbrother for him to give us a minute and he stalked off.

"Is your dad home tonight?"

"I don't know."

"Tell him you're staying at Laurie's and sneak into the pool house. No one has to know."

"Maverick…"

It was on the tip of my tongue to persuade her. To push until she gave in. But I knew what I was asking of her was unfair. To lie to her dad, to deceive him. Especially after what he'd done with Stella behind her back.

"Can I see you tomorrow? I want to hang out, just the two of us." And I knew the perfect place to take her.

"Will it be safe?"

"Safe? I'm not going to hurt you, Lo." Anger rippled under my skin but then her hands were there, pressed against my chest. The simple touch soothing my rage.

"I didn't mean that." She leaned up and brushed her lips over mine. "I would love to spend the day with you. I'd better go before Kyle comes back in here and really does have to bleach his eyes. Text me later."

Nodding over the lump in my throat, I stood paralyzed as she moved around me. But at the last second, I snagged her hand. "Thank you," I said, "For today."

"You don't need to thank me, Maverick. I'll talk to you later."

I lingered in the kitchen, listening as Lo, Kyle, and Laurie, thanked Luke for his hospitality. The front door slammed shut and I was about to go back into the game room when Kyle's head appeared around the doorjamb.

I wasn't surprised.

"I, hmm, forgot something." He waggled his eyebrows pretending to look for whatever he'd *forgotten*. "Everything good here?"

I knew what he was asking me, and I folded my arms over my chest and gave him a tight nod.

"Good. You have Lo to think about now. Don't do anything stupid."

"Get out of here before Laurie comes looking."

He barked a laugh and saluted me before disappearing into the hallway. When the door slammed again, I leaned back against the counter and let out a heavy sigh. I didn't even have to say anything, and he knew—that fucker knew where my head was at.

"Prince, you're up," Luke yelled, and I ran a hand down my face, the familiar restlessness building in my chest. Lo hadn't even been gone two minutes and I already felt it. The simmering energy. The darkness creeping in.

And there was only one thing that would stop it.

~

"Are you sure about this?" Luke's eyes narrowed, searching my face, but I only nodded, pushing my way into the circle, his mumbled words rolling off my back, *"She's going to kill me."*

I stepped up to the two men in the ring. Bobby, the referee, tipped his head at me and I returned it, banging my fists together. The other guy, a guy I'd seen around here before, did the same.

"No body shots. No biting. No…" Bobby's voice was lost in the chants and yells from the crowd. Blood-thirsty and wild. The bitter smell of sweat hung in the air, suffocating and overpowering. But I breathed it all in, letting it center me. Letting it fuel the beast.

Bobby lifted his megaphone and started prattling off his usual intro speech. I found Luke across the ring and understanding passed between us. He knew I needed this, that without it I couldn't think, I couldn't breathe. Restless energy zipped through me as I bounced on my feet, eyeing my opponent, assessing his weaknesses. The bell sounded and the beast inside me exploded.

Chapter Six

Lo

"Lo, I'm just leaving."

"Okay, Dad," I replied, trying to tame my hair into a ponytail. His head appeared around the door and I stifled a laugh. "Hmm, nice hat."

"Don't. Bethany picked it out for me yesterday."

"Oh. Well, she has great fashion sense." I forced a smile but knew it probably resembled a grimace.

"You'll be okay?" If he noticed my pained expression, he ignored it.

"Yeah, I'm hanging out with Laurie and the others. Don't worry. Go, have fun."

Guilt tightened around my heart but then I remembered he was leaving me to go to Stella's, so I felt a little better. It was sad, really, that this was what our lives had become—lies wrapped up in fake smiles and forced words.

"I'll see you later, bye, sweetheart." He left, and I finished up getting ready. Maverick had texted me earlier to say he'd pick me up at nine-thirty, and that I needed to wear comfortable shoes, as if I ever wore anything else.

Although my tummy hummed with nervous energy, I

was excited to be spending the day with him. Just the two of us. Our time alone had been limited since the dance, and we'd spent most of that kissing or touching. Losing ourselves in one another. I wanted to get to know him, to learn his hopes and fears, his dreams and aspirations. I wanted to know everything there was to know about Maverick Prince.

My phone vibrated, and I picked it up, smiling when I saw Maverick's name.

Maverick: The coast is clear

With one last check in the mirror, I grabbed my Oxford University hoodie off the back of my door and left my room. Dad was gone. Although he was around more than he'd ever been at the Stone-Prince's, he still spent a lot of time with Stella and Beth, and I'd grown used to the quiet.

I slid my feet into my favourite Converse and went to meet Maverick. He stood against the Audi, eyes glittering with some indecipherable emotion. But my gaze went straight to the purplish bruise along his cheek, the faint split in his lip.

"What the hell did you do?" I hissed as I reached him, tracing his injuries with my fingertips. He recoiled from my touch, causing my stomach to drop away.

"Come on, we need to get going." He went to move but I grabbed his arm. "Maverick," I softened my voice, trying to reach him. "What happened?"

He dragged a hand down his face and blew out a frustrated breath. "Lo, come on. I want to spend the day together. Just you and me. No bullshit. No drama."

I blinked my eyes in disbelief. "You were fighting again." I couldn't disguise the pain in my whisper and his stone mask slammed down.

Just when I thought we were getting somewhere. Yesterday had been a first. We'd hung out with his friends. He'd let me into that part of his life. He must have left Luke's after me and gone to that godforsaken place.

"Why?" I snapped, feeling the bubble of irritation and disappointment.

"You left and I—" His eyes darted around, refusing to meet my narrowed gaze.

"Don't you dare blame this on me. I left because it made sense, because *you* want to keep this,"—I motioned between us—"a secret."

"Lo," his voice was low, heavy with regret. But it was too late for that. Jesus, how often did he do this to himself? I slid my hand down to his wrist and inspected his hands. Angry red marks marred his knuckles and I winced imagining them slamming into bone. A faceless man's cheek. His ribs.

"Why, Maverick? Just tell me why."

Eyes clamped shut, he let out a long breath. "Because I need it."

"But why?" I dropped his hand and curled my fists into his black sweater. "Try to help me understand?"

He dropped his head, his eyes open now and fixed on me. "It's the only way I know how to make it stop." His admission hung between us and I waited for him to continue, but instead he said, "I'm fine. It's barely a scratch."

"Not the point," I let out a deep sigh. We were getting nowhere. Maverick wasn't going to tell me what I wanted to know. Sensing my worsening mood, he looped his arms around my waist and gathered me close.

"I'm sorry, okay. I didn't think." His warm breath danced over my skin. "You never have to worry about me Lo. I've got it under control. I promise."

But that was just it, I did worry. Maverick stepped into

that ring because he needed it. Not for victory or sick satisfaction at crushing his opponent, but to battle his own personal demons. And I knew first-hand it wasn't a battle easily won.

"Can we start over? I have the whole day planned." Hope sparkled in his brown eyes bringing out the flecks of gold.

"The whole day?"

"And tonight, if you're lucky." The corner of his mouth lifted in a smirk and he was back—the Maverick I knew. Cocky and self-assured. But for a second, I'd seen another glimpse of the boy from the beach that night last summer. Uncertain. Vulnerable... Damaged.

"So where are we going?" I asked, shelving the argument for now.

"It's a surprise." He dropped a kiss to my head and went around to the driver's side.

I climbed inside grumbling, *"I hate surprises."* Maverick chuckled and the tension from seconds earlier evaporated. As he backed out of our small driveway, I couldn't help but trace the bruise. Irritated and sore, I could imagine the crunch of knuckle against his cheekbone, and my stomach roiled.

Back in Surrey, after the accident, there had been days when I wanted it to be over. The crippling grief. The gaping jagged hole left in my heart by my mum and Elliot. I'd drank or smoked, swallowed or inhaled anything I could, just to forget. To numb everything. So I knew all about wanting to replace one feeling with another. To transport myself to another place. I'd woken up in pools of my own vomit, in stranger's houses. I'd even woken up in the hospital once after having my stomach pumped... but it was self-inflicted. Self-destruction at its finest. I couldn't imagine wanting someone, another human being, to hurt me. It made me wonder what could have possibly happened to Maverick to make him step into that ring... to *want* to hurt in order to forget.

As if he felt me watching, he turned to me and smiled. A rare sight for the boy who carried a darkness within him. A darkness I knew I'd barely uncovered.

~

"Disney? We're going to Disney?" I'd spotted a couple of signs but hadn't wanted to get my hopes up.

"Is that okay?" Uncertainty lingered in Maverick's voice, but my squeal of approval had him relaxing in his seat.

"Is it okay? For real? Do you know how disappointed I was when we didn't get to visit last year?" A pang of sadness washed over me. Maverick noticed, his hand slipping over my knee and squeezing gently.

"You okay?"

"Yeah, I'm fine." If I didn't let the memories in, didn't give them notice, I could almost pretend I was just a girl on a date with a boy.

A date at Disney.

I let out a squeak of excitement again.

"You really like Disney, huh?" Maverick mocked, and I frowned over at him as he turned off the highway.

"You're telling me you don't like Disney?"

He shrugged but I saw how his mouth was curved slightly. "It's okay, I guess."

"Okay, he says," I mumbled watching as we drove down Disney Drive. But I caught the flicker of amusement in his eyes, and a frisson of anticipation ran through me at the thought of seeing another side of Maverick.

We rode in silence while Maverick concentrated on the signs directing us to the huge parking lots. "It's busy," I said noticing the queue of cars waiting for entry, my anxiety trying to push its way to the surface. But I tamped it down, not wanting to ruin the day before it even got started.

"Yeah, I guess you're not the only one who loves Disney." He smirked at me and I poked my tongue out at him. "I got us tickets for both parks."

"I want to ride Guardians of the Galaxy first, and the parades, we have to see the parades."

"You really do love Disney," Maverick grumbled as he followed the line of cars until we were directed to an empty bay. I was first out, excitement buzzing in my veins. I couldn't remember the last time I was this excited. It was a feeling I wanted to cling to.

To hold on and never let go.

"You look so cute right now." Maverick came around to me and offered me his hand. I slid my palm into his, sparks of electricity dancing over my skin.

"Thank you." I grinned at him. "In case I forget to say it later, thank you for this."

He let out a smooth chuckle tugging me toward the streams of people.

So. Many. People.

Ugh.

But I ignored the masses, following Maverick to the line. Keeping my mind busy on all of the amazing things we would get to do today. "It's so pretty," I said as we made it through security, my eyes taking it all in. The Christmas trees, the twinkling lights, fake snow, and music.

"Come on." Maverick wrapped his arm around me and guided me down an off-shoot pathway. The queues had dispersed now, and I inhaled a deep breath. I could breathe. I was fine.

It was going to be fine.

Better than fine, it was going to be great.

"For someone who doesn't get the whole Disney

thing, you seem awfully sure of where to go," I mocked.

"It used to be my favorite place to come."

Used to be. I swallowed over the giant lump in my throat.

"I can't imagine your mom traipsing around this place in her Louboutin's."

"Mom didn't bring us."

Oh. If Rebecca hadn't brought them then it must have meant... Shit. Me and my big mouth.

"It was our yearly vacation with Dad," Maverick continued, surprising me. "He'd bring me, Macey, Alex, and Elle, out here for the weekend over the holidays. There isn't a ride in this place we haven't conquered." He flashed me a smug grin, but I saw the pain behind his eyes.

"Alex and Elle?"

"Yeah, my half-brother and sister. Alex is sixteen like Summer, and Elle is thirteen."

"Oh, I didn't know..." my voice trailed off. Laurie had told me Alec Prince had children with his wife, but no one ever talked about them. "They don't go to our school?"

Maverick shook his head. "They go to the private school."

"Oh."

I wanted to ask more, to find out about his half-brother and sister. But talking about his father hurt, I could see that. So, I wouldn't push. Not when he was finally opening up. The Guardians of the Galaxy ride loomed up ahead and Maverick weaved through the streams of people, until we were entering the queue. He nudged me first and I waited for the people in front of me to move along, suddenly aware of how packed it was. I'd begged Dad to bring me here last summer. I loved the fairground, theme parks, thrill rides. But that was *before.* My whole body tensed up and Maverick noticed, sliding his arms through mine and pulling me back to his chest. "Scared?" he whispered.

It wasn't the first time he'd asked me that, and each time I couldn't help but wonder if there was some hidden meaning in his question. I sucked in a sharp breath, glanced back at him and pressed my lips together with a small shake of my head. My anxieties only had power over me if I let them. I could do this. It was just a ride. It was safe.

I was safe.

He laughed, dropping a kiss to my nose, and then nudged me forward again. But he didn't let go. Maverick stayed wrapped around me, moving us as one. A couple of people in the winding queue watched us and I wondered what they saw. A slow blush crept into my cheeks. We hadn't talked about what we were to one another. And we definitely hadn't labelled our relationship. But this, being here with him like this, and yesterday at Luke's, felt significant. It felt like Maverick was trying to tell me something without having to say the actual words.

And the thought comforted me more than I expected.

~

We spent the day moving from ride to ride. After the Guardians of the Galaxy, I avoided any of the rides in enclosed spaces. Maverick noticed my ashen face after that first ride, the slight tremble to my hands, but he didn't push, and I gave him no answer. I couldn't go there. Not yet. Not when he'd gone to all this effort for me. I just wanted to enjoy our day together. So, when the music filled the air and the crowds lined Main Street, I yanked Maverick with me to watch the parades. Then we ate cotton candy, and foot long hot dogs, and stood in front of the iconic blue-tipped castle to take selfies.

It was perfect.

Well, almost perfect. But our demons could wait. Disney was the place of dreams, not nightmares.

"My feet hurt so bad," I said as we walked hand in hand toward Downtown Disney.

"I told you to wear sensible shoes."

"These are sensible shoes." I elbowed Maverick's ribs. "We must have walked miles today."

"What's a little pain in the name of Disney?" he mocked drawing me into his side. "Did you want to get food, or head back?"

I checked my watch. "It's almost six."

"Is your dad expecting you back?"

"He texted earlier to say he's staying at Stella's."

Anger flashed in Maverick's eyes, but he didn't say anything. "There's this thing we could go to, if you wanted to?"

"Thing?" I said.

His eyes shifted, and I sensed his uncertainty.

"Maverick, what thing?"

"A party." He released me to rub his jaw. "Hmm, Selina invited us."

"Selina?" My eyes widened with realisation. "You mean the girl from Luke's party?"

"It's not like that, Lo. She's a friend."

"Friend, right."

"Come on." Maverick crowded me against the wall. "I know Kyle told you nothing happened. I thought you'd ask me... I was waiting for you to ask." His eyes softened, searching mine. "Why didn't you ask?"

"I... I don't know."

I did know. I just couldn't tell him the truth.

"She came to Luke's that night, looking for me. Her brother, Dex, he fights in the same circuit as I do. She's worried about him. She didn't know where else to go. Nothing happened."

"I believe you."

Relief washed over his features. "She's been pushing me to bring you around to meet her. Since I knew we were going to be in the area, I said I'd ask you. But we don't have to go."

I didn't know how to feel about Maverick having a girl in his life that knew that side of him—the side he refused to let me see—but I knew he was telling me the truth about them. And if I wanted to learn more about him, maybe she could help.

"Okay, I'll go."

A wide smile split his face but then he was kissing me. Drawing tiny whimpers from me as he pressed his hard body against my soft curves. Silently reassuring me I had nothing to worry about.

And I believed him.

Chapter Seven

Maverick

Lo stayed glued to my side as I guided us through the house in search of Selina. The same way she had on the Guardians of the Galaxy ride. I'd been joking when I asked her if she was scared, but when we came out Lo was as white as a ghost, the excited sparkle gone from her eyes, and I knew something was wrong. I didn't push. Didn't ask when she disappeared into the restrooms for ten minutes. I knew it had to be something to do with the accident. But when she was ready, she would tell me. I knew better than most that sometimes we had to deal with things the best way we knew how. It didn't make it any easier to see her uncomfortable though.

"Hey, everything okay?" I said as we moved further down the hallway. When Selina invited us to the party, my gut instinct was to say no. I knew Lo thought something had happened between us, Kyle told me as much. But Selina insisted. Said it would be good for Lo to get to know her. To have a friend, an ally.

I hated that she was right.

"Maverick, over here." Selina wound through the chaos beaming at me. "I didn't think you were coming."

"Change of plans." I eyed Lo beside me and Selina smiled broadly.

"Lo, I'm so glad you came."

"Hi."

Selina knocked me out of the way, wrapping my girl into a hug.

My girl.

Fuck. I ran a brisk hand over my head. She was buried deep. Deeper than I ever expected, but after the last couple of days of just being together, something had shifted. I felt it every time she looked at me.

Taking her to Disney was a risk. I hadn't been lying when I told her it was once my favorite thing to do. I'd lived for those vacations with my father. But that was before I learned what a piece of shit he really was, and the truth tainted every good memory I had.

Before today, I hadn't stepped foot in the place in almost five years. The excitement in Lo's eyes though, made it all worth it. I stuffed down the bad memories, the anger flowing through me, for her. And somewhere during the day, I realized I was having fun too. Whether she meant to or not, Lo filled some of the black holes in my soul, replacing them with light. Blinding white light. And, unknowingly, she'd given me back a piece of my childhood.

"Come on," Selina's voice yanked me back into the present. "Let's get some drinks. I think my jerk of a brother is around here somewhere."

Dex was here?

I scanned the room, but it was dark; difficult to see through the tendrils of smoke swirling in the air. Lo gripped my hand, her pulse fluttering wildly underneath her skin.

"Hey, are you okay?" I asked again, leaning into her. She nodded but I felt the tension radiating off her. Just as I had on the ride earlier.

As we neared the kitchen, the air became cleaner, people coming and going from the open door. It was quieter in here, easier to breathe, and Lo visibly relaxed, the tension painted on her face melting away.

"What can I get you, Lo?" Selina began sifting through the collection of bottles of liquor, but she said, "Just a beer, please."

"I'll have the same."

"Here you go." Selina handed us each a beer. "Dex is out back, I know he'd like to see you," she said to me.

"The two of you'll be okay?" It was a question for Lo, but Selina answered.

"We'll be fine, right Lo?"

Lo nodded, taking a long pull on her beer. "Go, I'll be fine."

"Sure?"

"Go, it's fine." She flicked her head to the door and with one last silent look, I made my way outside spotting Dex immediately. It was hard to miss him with his blue-tinged mohawk.

"Maverick, my man." He got up and came to me, pulling me in for a one-armed guy hug. "Selina know you're here?"

"Who do you think invited me?" I eyed his friends, gathered around a table, recognizing a couple from the fight circuit.

"She got you checking up on me?"

"Nah, man. She wanted to meet Lo."

"Your new girl?"

I nodded and followed him to two empty chairs away from the others.

"Prince has finally settled down, never thought I'd see the day." A crooked smile split his face as he retrieved a packet from his jean pocket, sliding a smoke between his lips. "She know what you like to do to let off steam?"

"She knows."

Surprise flashed in his eyes. "And she didn't have anything to say about it? Kellie never let me hear the end of it."

I answered him with silence. I wasn't here to talk about Lo. As far as I was concerned she was off limits, separate to the ties that bound me to Dex.

"I get it, my man. You want to protect her from the bullshit. Keep her out of that world." He dragged a lungful of smoke into his chest. "But you know one day they'll cross paths and then what?"

My fingers scraped along my jaw, over and over, as his words sunk into my bones. He was right. Of course, he was fucking right. I'd seen to that when I took her to the warehouse. *I'd* already brought her into that world. Only then, I hadn't known what she was to me. Not really. Sure, I'd felt the pull, but I didn't ever plan on making her mine. Or maybe I had. Shit. I didn't know which way was up lately. Between things with Lo and my father, and Caitlin and JB, and with graduation right around the corner, my life was freefalling.

"How is the old man?" Dex asked as if he could hear my thoughts.

My eyes snapped to his, narrowing with contempt. Dex didn't know the whole story but he knew enough.

"Easy, Prince. It's just a question but from the death stare you're throwing my way I'll go out on a limb and say things are still pretty fucked up."

"Something like that," I mumbled forcing down the dark urges swarming my chest.

"Some of the guys said you annihilated Suffolk."

I flexed my fingers. In and out. The marks were barely visible now, but I knew I was sporting a pretty gruesome bruise around my eye. "He knew what he was getting when he stepped into the ring."

"Yeah, but the last man standing match? You've got to be more careful, man."

Silence stretched out before us. Dex knew the score. We didn't fight for fame or fortune. We fought because we had to. Because we needed a release—a way to tame the beast.

"Selina's worried," I said, cutting the quiet and he shifted uncomfortably.

"I know but she doesn't get it." He blew out smoke rings. "No one does."

"Have you tried talking to her?"

"Talking's not my style, you know that."

Another thing we had in common.

"You're keeping up with classes though?"

"Yes, *Mom*," he mocked stubbing out his smoke. "I can't switch it off. I've tried. It's in me, man. In me deep. I'm different. I have been ever since…" Dex stared off at nothing, lost to his memories.

I only knew this Dex. The guy he became after losing his girlfriend, Kellie, to a drunk driver. But I knew pain and hurt and anger. I saw it reflected back at me every time I looked at him.

"Just watch your back. Lacroix is gunning for blood after what you did last month."

"Dex," one of his friends called, and he met my hardened glare.

"Look, Prince, I appreciate the concern, but I can take care of my own shit. You should do the same."

"Dex, man, get over here."

"Chill, fuckers, I'm coming." He stood up and clapped me on the back. "Don't be a stranger, Prince. And take good care of your girl." Pain flashed in his eyes and then he was gone.

I finished my beer and went back inside. Selina and Lo

were talking like old friends and some of the tension in my shoulders evaporated. I wanted them to like each other. Even though I wasn't close to Selina the way I was Kyle or Macey, she knew parts of me they didn't. I didn't have to hide or pretend with her.

"Speak of the devil," she grinned, tipping her bottle in my direction.

"I hope you're behaving, Lina?"

"Me? As if I wouldn't."

"I'm trying to get her drunk, so she'll reveal all your secrets." Lo smirked, and I hooked my arm around her waist tucking her into my side.

"There's nothing worth knowing," I said, the words calm and measured. Nothing like the storm raging inside me. Because I did have secrets. I had a boat load.

"You two are so cute." Selina watched us with nothing but happiness shining in her eyes. "I'm glad you found each other." Her gaze settled on me and I saw the understanding there, the silent message, and I flicked her a small nod.

Me too.

~

Lo was quiet on the ride back to her house. I wanted to know what she was thinking—if today had been too much too soon. But the coward in me kept quiet.

The house was pitched in darkness as I pulled into the driveway and cut the engine. "You're quiet." I turned to her.

"Just thinking." She gave me a small smile, but it did little to ease my racing pulse.

"Lo, I—" I said at the same time as she said, "Maverick."

"You go," I insisted, and she twisted around to me. My heart jackhammered in my chest as I gripped the wheel. Why did she look so worried? What had changed in the last hour? I racked my brain for a clue. Any hint she hadn't enjoyed today. But all I could picture was the happiness in her eyes. The sound of her laughter. The feel of her hand in mine as she stood squashed between overexcited kids as we watched the parades.

"Thank for you today. It was..." Her gaze darted around me and I held my breath waiting.

Fuck, if she wanted space, after everything, what would I do?

"I had a really nice time, Maverick."

Relief seeped into my veins. Slowly, at first, and then like a tidal wave. She wasn't letting me down, she was thanking me.

"You don't need to thank me, Lo. I wanted to share a piece of me with you."

And Disney had seemed like the lesser evil.

I reached for her, gliding my fingers along her jaw, and tilted her face to mine. "Thank you for coming to the party with me."

"Selina is nice. I can see why you like her."

"Lo," I warned.

"I don't mean it like that, Maverick. I just meant I can see why you trust her." I saw the hesitation flicker in her eyes. "But Kyle, he doesn't know?"

Mouth pulled tight, I shook my head.

"Because she's part of that? The fighting?"

"Dex is a part of that, not Selina." Who was I trying to kid? I met Lo's soft gaze with my own. "But yeah, she worries. Dex has been through stuff. He's still healing."

Selina had given Lo the cliff notes on what went down with her brother, but she'd stayed true to her promise to me and not revealed anything about me and my story. Even though she didn't know everything, Selina knew enough. After watching me and Dex beat each other to a bloody pulp during my first fight at the warehouse, she'd drawn her own conclusions about me. By the time she was done with us that night, we left the place with more than just our pride in tatters. I'd sought her out after that and apologized. She told me Dex's story and I gave up snippets of mine, and I promised to look out for her brother where I could.

We'd been friends ever since.

Silence hung heavy in the space between us. She wanted more. I saw it in her eyes. But I'd already given her as much as I could today. So I deflected. "What happened today, Lo?" I said.

"What do you mean?" Her voice quivered and she tried to pull free, but I cupped her jaw, holding her face firm.

"On the ride. You were so excited, but something changed. You were barely there and when we came out you looked... I don't know, shell-shocked."

"I..." Unshed tears lingered in her eyes but then her expression changed. Hardened. "I'm fine," Lo said. "I guess it was scarier than I thought it would be after all."

She was lying.

But then so was I. Neither of us ready to bare our truths. To face our demons.

"You want company?" I flicked my gaze to the house. She'd already told me her dad was staying at Stella's for the night and I wanted nothing more than to hold her. To feel the soft curves of her body pressed against me.

"I'm kind of exhausted. Raincheck?" Her smile was strained, and I saw it now, the dark circles around her eyes. Whatever had happened today had weighed more heavily on her than I anticipated.

I leaned in, brushing my lips against hers. Featherlight. And not nearly enough. But I wouldn't push tonight. "I'll text you tomorrow," I said pressing one more kiss to her mouth.

"Okay. Goodnight, Maverick." She climbed out of the

car and made her way up to the house. When she reached the door, she glanced back and gave me a small wave.

Once she was inside, I waited for a couple of seconds before backing out of the drive. Maybe time apart would be a good thing. Give us chance to get our heads straight and process everything.

Or maybe it would make the darkness bite back with a vengeance.

Chapter *Eight*

Lo

New Year's Day came and went. With Luke's parents still out of town, he threw a party for the team, and I let Kyle and Laurie drag me along. But with more kids from school going I knew Maverick would keep me at arm's length. And sure enough, he did.

It hurt. More than I expected. It was like he'd opened up to me—about his dad, his past—only to slam his walls back down and push me out. Even though, deep down, I knew he was only trying to prepare me for when school started back, and I tried to brush off the dejection, I was only human.

At least he wasn't sporting any fresh cuts or bruises. And while I wasn't deluded enough to think he'd stopped fighting altogether, I couldn't help but hope I'd reached him on some basic level.

"All set?" Dad called, and I grabbed my bag and made my way into the kitchen.

"I think so. Kyle said he'd be here soon."

"Where did the last four months go?" His eyes creased as he sipped his coffee. "A new year," he sighed. "I feel like good things could happen this year, kiddo."

"Sure, Dad." I helped myself to juice from the fridge.

"Before you know it, it'll be summer, and you'll be thinking about college."

My stomach sank, and the glass wobbled in my hand. In eight months, I'd be a senior and Maverick would be off at college. Away from Wicked Bay.

Away from me.

Alec Prince wanted him to follow in his footsteps and attend California State East Bay as a business major. Almost four-hundred miles away, it might as well have been another planet. And I still didn't truly understand why Maverick would just give up his dream for his father—a man, for reasons I'd yet to uncover, he hated.

A horn blared outside, and Dad chuckled. "He sure likes to make an entrance. Have a good day, sweetheart. It could be a late one. You'll be okay?"

"Sure, Dad. See you."

I made my way out to Kyle. His hair had grown out over the holidays, falling over his eyes and he looked even more roguish than usual.

"Mornin', Cous."

"Hi," I said slipping into the seat. "No Laurie?"

"She's riding in with Autumn. Besides, I thought you and I should have a little chat."

My eyes rolled on a groan. Kyle had taken it upon himself to become my relationship counsellor. It was sweet at first but now… well, it was bloody annoying.

"I'm fine. No pep talk required."

The Jeep joined the steady traffic and Kyle tapped the steering wheel with his finger. "After the party, I just thought…" he trailed off.

"You thought I'd what? Have some kind of breakdown because Maverick hardly looked in my direction? Yeah, not likely."

"You don't sound bitter at all."

"Seriously, Kyle, what do you want me to say? Maverick wants time. I'm trying to give him time. And maybe he's right. Maybe it is better if no one knows about us yet. I mean you heard some of the things they were saying about me before school finished for the holidays. I'm not sure I'm ready for that."

"If you think people don't know, then you're wrong, Cous." My eyes flashed at him, but he continued, "Hey, I'm on your side, remember?" His lips curved in a warm smile and I sank back in the seat, feeling the fight leave me.

"I know, I'm sorry. I just…"

"I know, Cous, I know. Maverick thinks he's protecting you. But sometimes he makes the wrong call. Sometimes he needs someone else to make the decisions."

"You think I should…" I couldn't even say the words. If I walked into school this morning and did something crazy like kiss him in front of everyone he would go nuclear. "He'd kill me."

"Are you sure about that?" He threw me a sideways glance.

Maverick had already said he wanted to protect me— told me he didn't think he was good enough for me. But was he really so vulnerable? So uncertain about how I felt about him?

He was Maverick Prince for God's sake. He could have any girl he wanted.

We bailed out of Kyle's Jeep and met Laurie and Autumn. Much to my relief there was no sign of Liam… or Devon. After the dance, he'd tried to talk to me once, but I walked away and never looked back. As far as I was concerned he'd made his bed.

"Hey, Lo." Autumn made a beeline for me, and we left Kyle and Laurie all up in each other's business as we headed for the main building. "Did you have a nice Christmas?"

"Yes, thanks. You?"

She shrugged. "It was okay. It's always hard when Derrick is away. My mom and dad struggle. But we visited my papa down in Tijuana which was nice."

So that was where she got her tan skin and big brown eyes from. Hesitation lingered in her voice and I knew she probably wanted to ask about Maverick but thankfully, Laurie barged in between us, looping her arms through ours. "I've missed you both."

"I saw you like three days ago," I chuckled.

"Yeah, but now I get to see you every day again." She clutched my arm. "Don't look now but there's Caitlin."

Of course I looked. My eyes found her immediately walking into school with her friends.

"What a bitch. We so have to make her pay for what she did to you at Winter Formal."

"Laurie," Autumn and I said in sync. "I don't want to start anything with her," I added. She had enough ammunition to go after me without me handing her anymore.

"I know, I know," Laurie sighed. "It's just so unfair. She pulls this kind of shit all the time on people and I'm sick of it. Someone needs to bring her down a peg or two."

I didn't disagree, but I also wanted to try to not draw any more attention to myself. But as I joined the stream of kids entering the building, I felt their stares, heard the low rumble of their whispers.

Kyle was right.

They knew.

They all knew.

~

Maverick: I like your sweater

Lo: Stop perving on me and eat your lunch. You have practice tonight, right? You'll need the energy

I risked a peek over at Maverick's table. Wedged between Luke and Trey as they laughed about something, his fingers flew over his phone screen.

"Someone important?" Laurie's eye dropped to my phone and I shoved it onto my lap.

"Just my dad."

"And how is daddy dearest?" I heard the playful lilt in her voice, but I gave her a disapproving glare and she went back to her lunch while I discreetly read Maverick's text.

Maverick: I can think of better things to be doing right now

Lo: Behave!!!

Maverick: With you? Never.

His intense stare burned through me even from the distance between us, and I knew if I looked at him, I'd see desire swimming in his eyes. His jaw tight with frustration.

Need.

So, I didn't look.

I kept my head bowed, half-listening to Laurie and Autumn as they discussed their boyfriend's successes and failures at gift-buying. Before I knew what I was doing, I'd retrieved my journal from my bag, running my fingers over the intricate stitching.

"That's beautiful," Laurie said craning over me to see. "Where did you get it?" There was no ulterior motive in her voice this time just genuine interest.

"It was a gift."

This time I did allow myself to glance over at Maverick. He chatted to Luke, their heads close. But, as if he felt me, our eyes met, and for a split second, there was just the two of us. No school. No busy cafeteria. No kids discussing their holidays over stale sandwiches and wilted salad.

Maverick broke away first, jolting me back into reality. Laurie watched me knowingly and gave me a sad smile. But I didn't want or need her pity. I wasn't some victim. A weak girl letting her boyf... the boy she cared about treat her like she was no one. I was a survivor and I understood pain and desperation and anger. I probably understood Maverick better than anyone else here. And if he said he needed time, I would respect that. Because when he looked at me I knew the truth.

Our truth.

And that's all that mattered.

~

I survived the first day of classes. By the time the afternoon rolled around, I'd barely noticed the way heads followed me into a room. They could think what they wanted. Kyle insisted on driving me home, despite my protests I could walk. So it was no surprise to find him leaning against his Jeep when I filed out of the building along with my classmates. But his eyes narrowed to something over to my left, and I followed his line of sight, releasing a heavy sigh when I spotted Devon. He was hovering, waiting for something... or someone. When he spotted me, and started in my direction, I had my answer. Hitching my bag up my shoulder, I quickened my pace, wanting to avoid a scene.

"Lo, wait up," he called, but I'd reached the edge of the parking lot. "Lo, come on, please let me explain."

Something in his voice had me whirling around to face him. "Explain? Are you fucking kidding me? Is this another joke?"

"Lo." His eyes darted around me. Anywhere but at me. "I... I fucked up. I just..." he spluttered.

"I don't have time for this, Devon. Stay away from me." I didn't look back as I hurried for the Jeep. Satisfied he didn't need to intervene, Kyle climbed inside and I joined him a couple seconds later.

"What did he want?" He flicked his head over to Devon who stood rooted to the spot, watching us.

"To apologise, I guess."

"Motherfu—"

"I told him to stay away."

"You think he will?" Kyle sneered.

Devon had sounded desperate. Broken. But if he knew what was good for him, he would walk away.

And stay away.

"Maverick will lose his shit."

"Don't tell him."

"Lo." Kyle blew out a long breath, raking a hand over his face. And it didn't escape me that he called me Lo instead of 'Cous'. "Do you think that's a good idea?"

"He doesn't need to know. Besides, nothing happened. I didn't even hear him out."

"You're playing a dangerous game, Cous."

"It's not a game, Kyle. Devon screwed me over. I won't forget that in a hurry, but I don't need you or Maverick fighting my battles."

"Try telling Prince that."

Once we were out of the school parking lot Kyle said, "So how was it, today? You know with the pretending and all?"

I shrugged. "Okay, I guess."

"You're a terrible liar, Cous. If it's any consolation, I happen to know it almost killed Rick."

It had?

Kyle's smooth chuckle filled the Jeep, but I didn't reply, too busy mulling over the day's events. Caitlin ignored me in the one class we shared. Macey too. It was more than I could have hoped for.

"What did he tell Macey?" I said.

"Who? Rick?"

"Who else, Kyle?"

"Does it matter?" I shrugged again watching the town roll by and he added, "Why, did she say something?"

"She barely even acknowledged me in class."

"Let him worry about Macey."

My phone vibrated, and I dug it out of my bag, my heart swelling when I saw Maverick's name on the screen.

Maverick: I miss you

My fingers typed out a reply.

Lo: I miss you too. Now go to practise

Maverick: You know, keep talking like that and I might start to think you're trying to get rid of me

Lo: Like I have a choice

Kyle eyed me, a smirk playing on his lips, but I ignored him. Waiting for Maverick's reply. It came seconds later.

Maverick: You're right. You don't. I'll text you after I'm done

I slid my phone away and continued staring out of the window. Kyle was desperate to ask, it radiated from him. But when he did finally speak, his words spun my head.

"Prince has it so bad."

Chapter Nine

Maverick

"Take the shot, Prince." Coach's voice boomed across the court, and I swiped my brow with my arm, lining up the ball. I loved this part. The anticipation crackling in the air. The rush of adrenaline. Just me, the ball, and the absolute self-belief in making the shot. The sweet, sweet sense of relief when it sailed through the hoop wasn't so bad either.

"Now!" he yelled, and I pushed up in one fluid movement, extending from my knees and through my hips until I hovered above the ground. My wrist snapped at the perfect moment and the ball flew through the air, finding its way home.

"Nice," Aaron clapped me on the back as we moved into position to run the play again. I glanced to the wall clock as I gathered the hem of my jersey and tugged it up, rubbing the sweat off my face. We'd been at it an hour already. Coach would want at least another thirty minutes before he'd let us go. Which meant at least another hour, more like two, before I got to speak to Lo, or even better, see her.

Today had been torture. Knowing she was close but not being able to touch her. When she'd passed me in the hallway between second and third period, I'd almost caved and dragged her to my car. But I'd laid down these stupid rules, and I needed to stick to them.

Tonight.

I'd find a way to see her tonight.

"Prince, get your head in the game," Coach seethed as I fumbled the ball and Trey scooped it up and shot an easy two-pointer.

"My bad, sorry, Coach," I said just as Luke caught my eye. Amusement danced in his expression as if he knew exactly what I'd been daydreaming about. I flipped him off and moved back into position.

By the time Coach called time and let us head to the locker room, I was restless. My blood simmering with unbound energy.

"Someone needs to get laid," Aaron smirked in my direction and I mouthed, *"Fucker"* at him as I toweled off my hair.

"You mean that sweet piece of British *arse* isn't putting out?"

"Watch it, Bryson," I said yanking on a clean jersey.

"Ignore him, man." Luke came to my defense. "He's just jealous you're getting some, and he's not."

Bryson mumbled something but was interrupted by Coach's voice. "Prince, my office please."

The guys hollered and cheered as I grabbed my bag and made the short walk to the office. I knocked and waited for a second before slipping inside.

"Take a seat, son," he yanked off his ball cap and dropped it on his desk, raking a hand through his graying hair.

"What's up, Coach?"

"I got a call this morning from my contact at Bruins."

My ears perked up, and I straightened off the chair.

But when I saw his grim expression, I knew I wasn't going to like what he had to say.

Mouth down-turned at the corners, rubbing his jaw, he met my eyes. "It's not looking good, son."

The room zeroed in around me. He was wrong. He had to be wrong. But as my stomach plummeted down into my fucking toes, I knew he was serious. "What? I don't understand... I thought it was looking good?"

"I'm not sure what's going on over there. My contact didn't have all the details but there's been a discrepancy..."

His words became white noise in my eardrums. Bruins was my out. My shot at breaking free from my father's chains. This was not happening.

"Maverick, son, are you hanging in there?"

"Hmm, what?" I blinked at him, scratching my head. I'd barely heard anything he'd just said, my pulse crashing against my skull like a sledgehammer.

"Look, let's not assume the worst, yet. I'll do some more digging. See if we can find out what's going on. I just wanted to give you a heads up, son. I know how much this means to you."

"Thanks, Coach." I stood and gave him a tight nod, but I was numb.

"Don't give up yet, Maverick. You deserve this; no one deserves it more." His words bounced off my back, and by the time I reached my car, I couldn't remember the walk from Coach's office to the parking lot. Watching your dream evaporate in front of your eyes had that effect. It was so close—so fucking close—I could almost smell it.

Bruins...

Basketball...

Freedom.

It had been snatched away from me in the blink of an

eye and now I was stuck in this nightmare with no escape.

My pocket vibrated, and I pulled out my cell phone. Lo's incoming text flashed over the screen but I didn't open it. Instead, I scrolled to Kyle's number and fired him a text asking him to distract her tonight. I needed time to process, to work out my next move, and my mood was worsening by the second.

He texted straight back.

Kyle: Anything I should know about?

Maverick: Just some shit I need to take care of. Watch my girl for me.

Kyle: Your girl?

Maverick: Stone!

Kyle: Don't push her away, Rick. Whatever's going on, she can handle it.

I threw my cell phone inside the car and climbed inside, irritated that he saw through my bullshit so easily. Kyle's intentions were good, but he only knew half the story. He didn't know that this changed everything. Without Bruins, I was royally screwed. Stripped of who I was, and with no chance of escape.

Fuck.

~

For the next two days, I avoided Lo. It was easier than seeing her and trying to explain. Most girls would have grown clingy, demanding answers. But not Lo. She knew what I needed.

Somehow, she always knew.

"You're being a dick." Kyle dropped down beside me as I ate my sub in a quiet corner of the cafeteria. I'd waited until the rush cleared so I could eat in peace—and avoid the dark-eyed angel who saw into my black soul.

"Nice to see you too, Stone."

"She's not stupid, you know? She knows something is wrong. Maybe if you just told us, we could help?"

"I'm dealing with it," I snapped.

He glanced around at my pity party for one and arched his brow. "Well, if this is what you call dealing with it, looks like you've got it covered."

"Stone."

"*Prince*," he mocked. "Just talk to her. She's put up with enough of your bullshit so far. I'm sure she can handle whatever it is that has you eating on your own like a sad, lost puppy."

He held my stare. Daring me to disagree. To reel off any one of the numerous excuses I used when I needed to shut someone out.

"It's complicated," I said, earning me an over-dramatic eye roll.

"Of course, it's complicated, this is you we're talking about."

My cell phone vibrated. It was Lo. I knew without even looking. "Getting that?" Kyle said, and I scowled at him.

Lo: I missed you last night

Maverick: Coach pushed us pretty hard, I crashed when I got back to the house

Lo: It's fine, Kyle and Laurie dragged me to The Shack to play pool... again

Maverick: I hope you kicked his ass

Lo: Of course

Maverick: I have a thing with the guys tonight, but tomorrow?

Guilt swarmed my chest.

Lo: Maverick, is everything okay? You've been, I don't know... distant

Maverick: Everything is good, it's just a crazy time with classes and practice

Lo: Okay

The word stared back at me. Taunting me. I was a bastard. I hadn't so much as looked at Lo all day—well, not in plain sight. But I felt her everywhere. In the hallways, at lunch, in the parking lot. She haunted me, and all because I was too cowardly to do the right thing. But things were already spiraling out of control.

One day.

We'd managed one fucking day before my shit caught up with us. So, I did what I did best, pushed people away. It was for her own protection while I figured shit out.

When she didn't text again, I sent her another one.

Maverick: I miss you

It wasn't a lie. I missed her like I needed air to breathe. But it wasn't the answer she wanted or deserved either. Another text came through, but it wasn't the name I'd hoped to see.

"What's wrong now?" Kyle said noticing how rigid I'd gone.

"I'm not sure, but I intend on finding out." I rose from the table and shoved my tray at him. "Lunch is on me."

"Rick, come on," he pleaded, but I was already gone.

Five minutes later, I was back inside Coach Callahan's office.

"Take a seat, son."

"I think I'll stand."

"Suit yourself." He leaned back in his chair and let out a heavy breath. For someone who coached basketball for the last fifteen years, he was surprisingly out of shape. "I spoke to my contact again. It would seem the board received some additional information regarding your application."

"I don't understand... what are you saying?"

He looked me dead in the eye as he said, "They know, son. Bruins know."

~

"We need to talk." I barged into my father's study and stormed straight over to him. He looked up from his desk and went back to his stack of papers.

"Nice to see you too, Son."

I bristled, my teeth grinding. I hated it when he called me that. As far as I was concerned, he lost that right a long fucking time ago.

"Tell me this wasn't you. Tell me you didn't screw me over, your son. Your own fucking son." Anger burned through me and I clenched my fists. If he was affected, he didn't show it as he placed his papers down and regarded me.

"Why don't you calm down, take a seat, and tell me what it is that has you so worked up?"

So he wanted to play it that way?

Fine.

I took a seat on the leather sectional opposite his desk and leaned forward on my fists, propped up by my elbows. "I heard from college today."

"East Bay, I presume?" His mouth curved into a smug grin and he leaned back in his chair. "I didn't think acceptance letters were issued until March. But then, we know you're a sure thing. I spoke to the Dean myself, only last week."

How convenient.

"He's very much looking forward to welcoming you in August."

My mouth soured as I absorbed his saccharine words. The lying piece of shit was baiting me, trying to trick me into confessing.

"You think you're so fucking slick, don't you?" I stood up, eyes narrowed on his face, fists clenched at my side. "Well you can go to hell for all I care."

His unforgiving gaze flickered there, and he cocked his head to the side, rubbing his jaw. Did he remember?

Because I sure as hell hadn't forgotten.

We were at an impasse. He refused to bend, and I refused to concede. It was a mistake coming here, I realized that now. Alec Prince didn't apologize or own his mistakes. And he certainly didn't compromise. He was infallible, and I was screwed.

As I stormed toward the door, his voice halted me. "I suggest you re-evaluate your attitude, Maverick. I'm handing you your future on a silver platter. Don't screw it up. There's a lot at stake here, you'd do well remembering that."

I slammed the door behind me, the wood ricocheting off its frame. My blood boiled and before I could stop myself, my hand collided with dry wall. Every step away from his office, was like another fuse to my anger and a wildfire swept through me. My fingers trembled as I dug out my cell phone and found the number I needed.

Maverick: Call Bobby, see if I can get on tonight.

Luke: Tonight? You're sure?

Maverick: Just do it.

I waited, my breath coming in short, sharp bursts. And then the answer I needed was there.

Luke: It's on.

Chapter Ten

Lo

"As soon as Kyle's Jeep stopped, I was out of there, running toward the warehouse, fear propelling me forward.

"Lo, wait up," he yelled after me, but I didn't stop.

I couldn't.

Maverick was in there and something was wrong. I'd known the second Kyle turned up at the house. After a week of pushing me away, keeping me at a distance, I didn't even need to hear the words from my cousin's mouth. It was a gut feeling. Intuition.

And I should have seen it coming.

The deafening noise as I slipped inside the building, made me falter. Just for a second while my senses adjusted. But then I was moving, pushing through rabid men ignoring their grunts of agitation. Someone grabbed my hand, and I swung around, ready to fight. But Kyle stared back at me, concern shining in his blue eyes. "It's me," he said over the noise. "It's just me."

"Come on." I pulled him with me, moving deeper into the room. A different sound filled the air now. Bone on bone. Fist crushing soft tissue. It was sickening, and I clutched my stomach barely able to stand it. But when I burst through the thick of bodies and my eyes landed on Maverick, everything disappeared. Sucked out of my world until I could see nothing but him and a faceless man beating the shit out of one another. Deep red rivulets ran down their faces. A busted eye. A thick split lip. A patchwork of cuts and bruises. If it wasn't for the sharp tug in my stomach reassuring me it was Maverick, I would have looked twice. His broken face was barely recognisable.

"Holy shit," Kyle breathed beside me, his grip on my hand tightening.

"Do something, Kyle," I managed to croak out. "You have to do something."

"I... I'm not sure, fuck." We both gasped when the other man got Maverick with a strong right hook. His head snapped back, blood splattering the spectators to his side. They roared, fuelled by blood and bone.

But Maverick came back swinging. His hands jabbed in perfect synchronicity and despite the sheer brutal nature of the scene, despite my conscience screaming at me to look away, I couldn't take my eyes off him. He moved like a cat. Lithe and quick. Crowding his opponent. Forcing him back against the frenzied crowd. Maverick was hurt, but he was in control. Cold... calculated... deadly. And my heart ached for him.

"He's got this, Prince has—" The roar of the crowd drowned out Kyle's words. It was like every crunch, every snap, they responded. A pack of hyenas circling, waiting for their next bloody meal.

The man got in a couple of rib blows and pain flashed across Maverick's face. He eased off, trying to catch his breath, but it was the wrong move. The man closed in. Pushing forward with everything he had. The noise reached a crescendo as if the hungry crowd felt the nearing victory. Maverick pushed back, jabbing quick and precise. Each hit like a bullet to my chest. But his opponent swung wide and hard, clipping Maverick's jaw, and he staggered back, shaking his head.

"Kyle, oh my god..." I couldn't watch. I couldn't breathe.

"He's got this, Prince has got this," Kyle kept repeating to himself as if the alternative was not an option.

It happened so quick. One minute, Maverick was ready to pounce, the next he was met with an onslaught of fists raining down on him. *Snap. Crack. Snap. Crack.* The sound reverberated around my skull as my stomach churned and I clapped a hand over my mouth in a desperate attempt to stop myself vomiting.

Forfeit my mind urged. But I knew he wouldn't. Maverick wouldn't go down without a fight.

"NOOO!" My plea was lost in the final roar as the faceless man landed one more fist to Maverick's face. His head twisted at an angle that seemed to defy logic and I screamed again and then I was running toward Maverick as his body began to fall.

~

"We should take him to the ER," I insisted for the third time, keeping one eye on Maverick's bloody and lifeless body slumped in the back of the Jeep.

"I don't know, Cous."

"Kyle," I ground out. "Look at him. He's a mess. He needs—"

"No hospitals."

Relief flooded me at the sound of Maverick's groggy voice, followed by anger. Red hot fury exploded in my chest and I lost it. "You could've died," I snapped, unable to stop the tears as they rolled from my eyes.

Maverick groaned, his eyes half-closed. "I'm fine."

"You look like something off the Walking Dead."

Kyle's attempt at humour was lost on me. We'd watched, unable to do anything, while Maverick let a man pummel him into shreds.

"It's nothing a hot shower and some Advil won't take care of. Maybe a beer or two."

I glared at him through the mirror, but Maverick's eyes were closed again, or swollen shut. It was hard to tell; there was so much blood and bruising. But as if he sensed me watching, he added, "The on-site medical guy checked me over. Mild concussion from the fall. Possible broken rib. Nothing else to worry about.

"Pull over," I demanded, and Kyle cast me a sideways glance.

"Hmm, Lo, we're in the middle of nowhere, I can't just sto—"

"Pull. Over."

With a heavy sigh and a string of cuss words under his breath, Kyle pulled the Jeep over to the side of the road and climbed out. "I'll give the two of you some space."

I shot him a look of gratitude. When he was out of earshot I twisted my body around and traced every cut and bruise marring Maverick's face. There were a lot. A couple looked worse than the rest. Blood seeping from deep gashes. He needed proper medical attention but part of me—the part swarming with rage—thought maybe he deserved to suffer. To feel even an ounce of the pain and hurt churning through my stomach.

"Why, Maverick? Why would you do this?"

He shifted up the seat, one arm wrapped around his waist as if he was holding himself together. Pain twisted into his marred face. His brows knitted tight. Breathing shallow. "You wouldn't understand."

That's it.

That's all he had?

"Wouldn't understand?" my voice wavered. "You

haven't even given me a chance. You shut me out, Maverick. All week, you've been avoiding me. Keeping me at a distance. I thought it was me. I thought you'd changed your mind about us. But it's him, isn't it? Your father did something."

It was the only thing that made sense.

"London…"

My heart crashed against my chest. I was so conflicted. Part of me wanted to nurse him better. Soothe his cuts and bruises. Tend to his wounds. But another part wanted to finish the job.

How could he go there… for *that*?

"You need help Maverick. This—whatever you think you are doing by stepping into that ring—it's not working. I want to help you. I want to understand but I can't… I won't stand around and watch you self-destruct."

His eyes finally snapped open to mine. Daring me to say the words. To end us before we ever got started. But I swallowed them down leaving the threat hanging between us.

Kyle chose that moment to open the door and poke his head inside. "Are you two done? I'm freezing my balls off out here."

"We're done," I said holding Maverick's hard glare for another second before throwing myself back against the seat.

We weren't done.

Not by a long shot.

But I meant what I said. I couldn't keep watching him do this to himself. Not when he refused to let me help him.

We rode the rest of the way in silence. Kyle threw me a few concerned looks, keeping one eye on Maverick in his rearview mirror. He was sleeping. Or too exhausted to make a sound. God. Seeing that, watching a man bigger and stronger pound his fists into Maverick's face over and over. It was something I never wanted to see again.

When I'd reached him, unconscious on the ground, everything started to blur. My heart beat so fast I felt queasy, and I went into shock. Kyle later told me it had taken two men to hoist Maverick up and carry him to the 'medical room' which turned out to be some abandoned office where they had a gurney and a sparse first aid kit.

Some good that did.

"Okay, how are going to do this?" Kyle said as he turned off for their house, and I glanced back at Maverick.

"I have no idea. Are your dad and Rebecca home?"

"They were going to some gala. They should be gone for a while."

"And Summer and Macey?"

There was no way Summer needed to see Maverick in this state. Macey neither.

"Who knows? But if I park by the garage, we can carry him through the back entrance and straight to the pool house.

"And then what, Kyle?" I hissed. "He needs—"

"I know, I know. Let's just get him inside and reassess the situation. Once he's cleaned up, he'll probably look and feel better."

Kyle pulled up as close to the back gate as possible. The place was pitched in darkness, no sign of Gentry's car in its usual spot. He climbed out and came around to my side. I got out and watched as he opened the back door and scrubbed a hand down his face.

"This is fucked up," he breathed out. "Rick, do you think you can stand?"

Nothing.

"Rick, man, you have to help us out here. C'mon."

A garbled reply came from inside the car and then

Maverick appeared, dragging himself to the door. "Shit," he groaned. "That hurts."

Kyle caught him and between us we managed to wrestle him onto his feet. Limp and exhausted, Maverick's upper body hung forward, pain lingering in every breath. By the time we reached the pool house, beads of sweat were rolling down my back.

"Get the door, Cous." Kyle shifted his weight to take most of Maverick's and I slid out from his side to let us in.

Maverick's pained groans filled the silence as we helped him into his bedroom and guided him down onto his bed. He landed with another groan. Kyle caught my eye and mouthed, *"What now?"* and I released a weary breath.

"I'll get the first aid kit. You help him strip out of his clothes."

"I'm not getting him naked." Kyle's eyes bunched together.

"His vest, Kyle. Take off his vest."

"His vest? You mean his tank, right? I can do that."

"Keep your fucking hands off me," Maverick choked out, groaning some more.

"He speaks. He's alive."

"Kyle, not helping," I scolded. "Just watch him, I'll be back."

I gathered the first aid kit, paper towels and a bowl of warm water. In less than five months, this was the second time I was cleaning blood from Maverick's face.

But I never anticipated *this*.

When I returned to the bedroom, I paused. Kyle had pulled up the desk chair beside the bed and was talking in a hushed voice to his stepbrother, concern written all over his face and I wondered how many times he'd witnessed this over the last year.

But that conversation would have to take place

another time before Maverick bled out all over his clean sheets.

"Okay, scoot over," I said to Kyle, and he moved out of the way.

"This is going to hurt."

"You could never hurt me, London," Maverick whispered. He sounded out of it—lost to the pain radiating through his body. But even in his current state, I could have sworn I saw the faintest of smirks on his busted lip.

"Kyle, tear off some towels and fold them into squares."

He did as I asked, stacking them into little piles on the nightstand. I took the top one, dipping it in the water and squeezing it out and then started wiping. Maverick hissed and swore and, at one point, I thought he had passed out. Blood tinged the water red, but I didn't stop. *Dip. Rinse. Squeeze. Wipe.* The cloying metallic tang overwhelmed my senses and a couple of times I had to turn away just to drag a little fresh air into my lungs. But slowly, Maverick—*my* Maverick—came into view. Kyle had been right, the amount of blood smeared over his face made his injuries appear worse than they actually were. Aside from a deep gash over his right eyebrow and the jagged split in his bottom lip, it was mostly bruising and surface grazes. There was swelling around his eye, but Kyle dug out ice from the freezer and wrapped it in a towel, and applied it to the area.

"See, almost as good as new," he joked, but not even his attempt at humour could disguise his concern.

"Okay, I think we're done," I said after twenty-minutes of cleaning wounds and applying plasters. I dried my hands on a clean sheet of paper towel and stood up to take everything away, but Maverick's hand shot out and snagged my wrist.

"Thank you," he croaked, his eyes flickering in and out of consciousness.

"I'll get you some painkillers and then you can sleep it off. You might need to get your ribs x-rayed." There was a lot of bruising.

"Stay," he said.

"I can't." I shrugged out of his grip and started gathering up the bowl of water and bloody towels, forcing down the tears and bile burning the back of my throat. "I'll check in on you tomorrow. If you need anything Kyle will be here." My eyes shot to my cousin's, and he nodded.

"Sure thing. I'll be right here on Prince duty." He gave me a two-fingered salute.

"Try to get some rest." My fingers itched to touch him, to reach out and trace the lines of his broken face but I was barely holding on and I didn't want to break. Not here.

I rushed out of there with Kyle hot on my heels. "Cous," he called.

"I have to go. I'll call a taxi from the house. Stay here, in case he needs you."

"He needs you, Cous." Kyle narrowed his eyes.

"I can't…" I couldn't explain it, but I had to get out of here. "I'm fine. I just need some air. I'll text you when I'm home. He should be fine but if anything changes, don't risk it and take him straight to the emergency room."

"I think we both know the only way I'd get him there is if he's de—" His face went pale as he realised what he'd been about to say. "Shit, Cous, I'm sorry."

"It's fine. I'm fine. Goodnight, Kyle. I'll text to see how he is later." I turned, and all but ran out of there.

Chapter Eleven

Maverick

Pain radiated through me, jolting me awake. "What the fu—"

"Welcome back, Prince." There was an edge to Kyle's voice that had me searching my foggy mind for some memory of why he sounded so pissed at me.

"Wh- what happened?" I tried to sit up, but my ribs exploded with blistering heat forcing me to stay down.

"You don't remember?"

Remember?

Memories flooded my mind like a bad home movie. The warehouse. Bobby's grimace as I told him to put me on the roster. Some hulk of a guy more than willing to step up to the plate.

Lo...

Lo?

Fuck, Lo was there.

"Oh, shit," I whispered, bringing a hand to my face to inspect the damage, because from the agony splintering around various parts of my body I knew there had to be a lot.

"What the fuck were you thinking?" Kyle spat, pushing from the chair and jamming his fingers into his hair.

"Lo was there? You let her—" Fuck, it hurt to talk. Everything hurt. But the ache in my chest at the idea of her seeing me like this was worse. She wasn't supposed to be there... to see me like that.

"You think I wanted her to go there?" he seethed. "To see that? But I didn't know what else to do. Luke called me..."

Fucking Taffia. Traitorous motherfucker.

I slowly swung my legs off the edge of the bed. My fingers curled into the mattress as I breathed through the pain. My face was sore, the skin across my cheekbones and around my eyes tight and tender. And from the stinging across my ribs, I knew if I looked down there would be bruises.

"I get it. You need to exorcise whatever demons haunt you, man. And I've tried to be understanding, but last night was fucked up. Lo didn't deserve that. Hell, I didn't deserve that."

More memories came. Hazier this time. Her gentle touch as she cleaned my wounds. The brokenness in her voice as she said goodbye.

"I need to see her," I rushed out and tried to stand but my body crumpled back down.

"This is what you're going to do. You're going to take a shower." He gave me a pointed look adding, "You're on your own there, bro. Then I will drag your sorry ass to get your ribs looked at. Coach will shit a brick when he sees the state of his star player. You will not call Lo, or text, or try to see her. Handle your shit first. Give her time. And then you and I are going to have a little chat."

"Fine," I groaned as I tried to test the waters again, standing slowly. Finally upright, I loosened my hold on my midriff. The pain was immense. Burning and deep.

And when I breathed in it stung like a bitch, but I was upright. And for as much as I hated to admit it, Kyle was right.

"I'll go do damage control. There's no way you'll be able to hide this one but maybe I can lay a few breadcrumbs." He gave me one last look and turned to leave but I called out, "Stone."

"Yeah?" He glanced over his shoulder.

"Thanks, I owe you."

"Yeah. Yeah, you do."

I shuffled unsteadily around my room. When I found what I was looking for, I located Lo's number and started typing.

Maverick: I'm sorry. For everything. Kyle said I need to give you space, so that's what I'm going to do. But don't take too long, Lo. I need you. I will always need you.

When I caught sight of my reflection in the bathroom mirror, I realized now why Kyle was so pissed. It looked like I'd survived the end of the world. Dried blood clung to a deep cut in my lip. My right eye was almost swollen shut. And my ribs were an ugly patchwork of black and blue. Shit.

It was a feat, but I managed to shuck out of my sweat pants and turn on the shower. Steam misted up the glass screen as I stepped inside, wincing when the hot water slid over my tender spots. It hurt so damn much, I had to press a hand to the tiles to keep myself from buckling. Last night was a blur. I couldn't even remember the guy's face. But I remembered his fists. The feel of them hammering into my ribs, into my face. It had hurt, but the pain was good. It switched off everything else—gave me something to focus on. It made me forget.

My failures.

My fuck ups.

Him.

It made everything pale into insignificance.

But she wasn't supposed to be there. I'd told Lo once, when she'd asked me when she would get to see me in the ring, she should be careful what she wished for. And I'd meant it as a warning. To her and myself. Because I knew if she ever saw me fighting it would change everything. She'd already seen too much. If she saw that part of me as well, I'd have nothing left to protect myself with.

Too fucking late now.

She'd been there. Watched as I got my ass handed to me. It wasn't about the losing or winning for me. It was about power. About fighting back.

About reminding myself that although I was a pawn in my father's games, I still had some control over my life.

Unable to withstand the pain anymore, I turned off the shower, grabbed a towel and patted myself down. My cell phone vibrated, but it wasn't the name I wanted to see, so I ignored it. Getting dressed was a different story. Every time I tried to lift my t-shirt over my head the pain was so intense, I had to stop.

In the end, I gave up. Swiping two Advil from the nightstand, I washed them down with the glass of water from the night before and lay down on the bed. The day after a fight I usually felt renewed. Calmer. Today was different. I felt on edge. Guilt tight around my heart like a vise.

And I didn't know what the hell to do with that.

~

"Oh my god, Maverick," Mom breathed out, pushing off the stool. She came to me; her eyes dull with despair. "Why? Why would you do this to yourself?"

"Maverick," Gentry said but Kyle shot him a look and

he backed off.

"I'm fine, Mom."

Tears welled in her eyes as she took in my injuries. "This has to stop. Tell him, Gentry, tell him this has to stop."

Gentry's mouth opened but Kyle stepped between us. I couldn't see what he was mouthing to his dad but whatever it was, it worked. Gentry came and put a hand on Mom's shoulder and squeezed. "Come on, Rebecca. Let's give Maverick some space. I'm sure he's had an exhausting day."

"But..." she started to protest, but he was already guiding her back to the stool.

"I'm fine, Mom. The pills they gave me are the good kind. And nothing's broken." Thank fuck. I don't know how I would have explained that one to Coach. "I just need to rest for a couple of weeks."

"Go on." Gentry met my heavy stare. In the past, he'd been the first one to lose his cool with me. but something was different. "I'll have Loretta make you something to eat before she leaves. We'll talk about this when you're feeling more up to it."

Okay then.

I had nothing, so I gave him a tight nod and followed Kyle out to the pool house. After letting me sleep off the pain for a couple of hours, he'd woken me up, insisting I get checked out at the medical center.

"Have you spoken to her?" I asked once we were inside. Lo hadn't texted me back, but I'd noticed Kyle texting someone while we waited.

"I let her know you were okay, yeah."

"Is she... is she okay?"

He dropped into the chair and I sat down on the couch. "What do you think?" The protective edge in his voice reached some deep part of me and I bristled. He wasn't supposed to be the one protecting her, I was.

"Stone, I'm—"

"If the words 'I'm sorry' leave your mouth so help me God, I will finish what that loser started. We had to drag you out of that place barely breathing. Can you even imagine what that did to her? It hit me hard, Rick. But Lo," he hesitated. "She's still hurting. You know what she went through…"

I knew. Shit, I knew that Lo had lost her mom and brother. I knew it was still raw for her. Even though she rarely let her walls down, I knew she still carried the pain of her losses.

"And then to watch her clean you up like that. Like it wasn't killing her on the inside. If you were anyone else, I'd be telling you to keep the hell away from her. She deserves better, so much fucking better than this. But I know you, Rick. And I know something happened to make you agree to fight that animal. So, you'd better start talking, and you'd better have a good fucking reason. Or you are going to lose the best thing that's ever happened to you."

His eyes widened as if he couldn't believe he'd just said all that, then a small smirk tugged at the corner of his mouth. "And no, I'm not talking about me, I'm talking about Lo. Just so we're clear."

Fucker.

"I'll tell you," I said. "But then I need you to do something for me."

He cocked his eyebrow, leaning back in the chair. "I'm listening."

This was it. The turning point. There would be no going back after this, but he was right. If I didn't open up—reveal my deepest darkest secrets with someone— the darkness would consume me, and I'd lose Lo before I ever got a chance to really make her mine.

And I couldn't let that happen.

~

"Hello? Maverick?"

Just the sound of her voice relaxed me, seeped into my bones and made breathing easier.

"In here," I called, shifting up the bed. After coming clean to Kyle, he'd left me to go and do damage control with Lo. The fact she was here... well, my debts owed to him were stacking up.

"Hi." She appeared in the doorway, her eyes running over my face. "You look better than you did last night."

"I—" My throat closed up, and I swallowed hard trying to find the words. "Please." I flicked my head to the chair, and she nodded.

"Kyle needs to work on his persuasion tactics."

My eyebrows shot up, and she smiled. It was small, uncertain. But fuck if it didn't settle something in my soul.

"He didn't kidnap you, did he?"

"Not quite but let's just say he wasn't entirely honest."

Okay, so maybe I needed to retract my statement about owing him. But whatever he said or did to get Lo here, I was grateful.

"We need to talk," I said, not wanting to give myself time to think about it. If I paused, even for a second, I knew the words would escape me and I'd close down.

"Okay," Lo said shifting uncomfortably. "But usually when people start a conversation with 'we need to talk' it's only going one way."

"I guess that's up to you."

Confusion furrowed her brows. "I... I don't understand."

"I want to tell you the truth. About why I fight. Why I went there last night. I guess I should have told you this from the beginning, but I didn't want you to look at me with pity in your eyes."

"Maverick," she whispered. "You're scaring me."

I shuffled to the edge of the bed and sat in front of her. "Just hear me out, okay?"

She dragged her bottom lip between her teeth and nodded. I wanted nothing more than to lean in and kiss her; to capture her mouth with mine and lose myself in her. But this needed to be out in the open. Before we went any further, Lo needed to know the truth.

Chapter Twelve

Lo

My stomach lurched as Maverick inhaled deeply, the intensity in his eyes pinning me to the spot. Whatever he was about to tell me would change things. I realised that now. Maybe it's why he'd held back, pushed me away. Because he was scared of how I would react.

"When I was younger, my dad was my idol. I thought he hung the fucking moon. He was rich, successful. My friends' dads all wanted to hang out with him. Play golf. Go for drinks. People respected him. Or so I thought. In ninth grade, I heard some kids talking about how they'd overheard some of their dads talking about Alec Prince. How cold and merciless he was. It made me sit up and notice things. Because I realized they didn't respect him, they were scared of him. I knew you didn't get to where he was without being ruthless. But he was a good guy. He worked hard. Provided for his family. For me and Macey and his other kids.

"A few weeks later, I heard Mom arguing with someone. I thought it was Gentry but when I snuck downstairs, I realized it was Dad. It wasn't the same man I knew. He was aggressive. Up in Mom's face, yelling and shouting. I froze. I didn't know what the hell to do but then Gentry arrived home and I was so relieved. Things between us have never been easy—he replaced my dad. A man I worshipped." He stared off at nothing, lost to the memories.

"What happened, Maverick?" I pulled him back to me.

"I expected Gentry to put my father in his place, to defend Mom. But he didn't. Instead, he told my mom—his wife—to calm down. That's when I realized he was also scared of Alec Prince. I could barely look at him after that. What if Dad had gotten violent? Would he have stepped in? Protected her? At the detriment of pissing of the mighty Alec Prince?

"Things went from bad to worse. Dad noticed my behavior change toward him. Gentry too. But I couldn't process it. And then Macey said she overheard Beatrice and August talking about Dad and his temper... about what Mom had to put up with when they were together. It just felt like they were all keeping things from us. Lying not only to protect us, but to protect him."

His voice was raw, and it gutted me. "Do you..." God, how did I ask this? But I had to. "Do you think he used to hit your mom?"

Pain flashed in Maverick's eyes, worse than anything I'd seen last night during and after the fight. "I know he did."

"That night you found me at the party, I'd finally confronted him. We were at his house for the summer. Maxine and their kids were visiting their grandparents upstate. So it was just me, Macey and him. He took us to some business function. Left us to make our own fun while he schmoozed with business associates. He got drunk, and we had to wrestle him out of the bar with everyone watching. He was spouting all this shit about Mom, about how she'd turned me against him. Macey was so confused and upset she locked herself in her room. But I saw red. I wanted the truth. It was long overdue.

"I confronted him, came right out and asked him why they really got a divorce. He didn't answer, but I saw the truth in his eyes and I realized the Alec Prince I knew was a lie. A fake. He didn't exist. Things got nasty, he said some things, I said some things..." Maverick's voice trailed off and a feeling of dread slithered around my heart.

"Maverick, did he hit you?"

The anger.

The fighting.

Although I prayed it wasn't true, it made sense.

His head dropped, breaking our connection, and I had my answer. Tears burned my throat as I slid off the chair and kneeled in front of him, taking his face in my hands, careful not to touch the worst of his injuries. "Maverick, look at me," I whispered.

Slowly, his head lifted, so many emotions shining in his eyes, it shattered my heart.

Eyes half-closed he breathed out, "I'm not done yet."

The pain in those four words cut through my heart like a knife and I braced myself.

"He'd already made it clear he wanted me to follow in his footsteps and attend Cal State East Bay. He said it was my 'destiny'. But it was never what I wanted. I wanted to play basketball. It's all I've ever wanted to do. So, I told him to stick his *offer*. I wanted nothing to do with his legacy or his alma mater. He lost it. Before I knew what was happening, he had me pinned against the wall. I managed to wrestle him off, and I was this,"—he pinched his fingers together until they were almost touching— "close to hitting him. I just exploded. It was only his smug smirk that made me pause. As if he knew, knew we were the same. I shoved him away and punched the wall.

And then he hit me. His fists rained into me until something in me snapped. I shoved his drunk ass off me and got the hell out of there. I drove and drove not knowing where I was going until I ended up at the party."

"Maverick, I'm—" I was speechless. I remembered how I found him that night—broken and bruised, clutching the bottle of beer as if it was his lifeline.

"Don't," he said with a defensive lilt. "Don't look at me like that. I couldn't bear it. I don't want pity or sympathy. Lo, I just want you."

I closed the space between us and gently pressed my lips to his. Maverick winced as I traced the seam of his mouth with my tongue with featherlight touches. He didn't want my pity, but I could be strong for him. But he didn't let me in. Pulling back, he stared at me in awe. "There's more, Lo. I have to get all this out."

"Okay." I swallowed, my mind working overtime at what else he could possibly have to say.

"Mom called me that night. He'd rang her after I left. She was hysterical begging me to go back, to smooth things over. I couldn't believe it. She wanted me to go back to that piece of shit, the man who used to abuse her. It took me a couple of hours to calm down, but I finally went. I'd left Macey there, and she was scared. When I got back to the house, he was a different man. Sober. Calm. My head was reeling. He asked me to sit down and talk. And stupidly, I thought he wanted to apologize."

"He didn't?" I asked.

"Not even close. He said he needed me to do something for him. A favor. If I agreed, he would forget my outburst—*my* fucking outburst. I told him I wasn't interested. That I never wanted to see him again. But then he said if I didn't do as he asked, if I didn't do as he wanted, he'd see to it that I'd never get to play college-level basketball and if I ever needed a reminder of exactly how much power he had, he'd destroy Gentry's company quicker than I could blink.

"It all fell into place after that. The way Gentry cowered that night years before. Why me and Macey knew a completely different man to everyone else. He'd threatened them, bought their silence."

I'd known Alec Prince was a real piece of work, but this seemed inconceivable.

"He wanted you to date Caitlin, didn't he?" I whispered.

"Her dad is an important player in town. Owns a lot of land. Land my dad's company wants to acquire. Caitlin had always had a thing for me and Dad saw an opportunity to align our families."

Maverick looked so tired. The emotional exhaustion etched into his face. I traced my fingers over his jaw and pressed a chaste kiss on his lips. "You look tired. You should rest," I insisted.

"We should talk about this, Lo. There are still things—"

"Ssh." I shut him up, stealing another kiss. "We can talk later. Sleep. I'll be right here. And when you wake up, you can tell me the rest."

"You'll stay?"

I nodded.

"But what about my mom? Your uncle?"

"They know I'm here, Maverick."

"They do?" His brows drew together.

"There are things I need to tell you too," I said, pushing to my feet. "Come on, get comfy and make room."

A smile tugged at his mouth as he shuffled back on the bed, the first one since I arrived. It lifted my heart. There was still a lot to talk about. To confess. But he needed time. And I would wait.

I would always wait for him.

~

"Hi," I said as Maverick's eyes fluttered open. He'd slept for over an hour before he started to murmur in pain. "I think it's time for more medication." I went to move but his arm shot out and trapped me to the bed.

"Wait, let me enjoy this. Just for a second."

"Maverick, come on, you need your pills."

"No, I need *this*." He shuffled closer, grunting under his breath. "Fuck that hurts."

"Which is why you need your painkillers."

"Spoilsport."

I poked my tongue out at him as I got off the bed to fetch his medication. I'd laid beside him, watching as he slept, my stomach churning with the reality of his confession. Hatred burned through my veins at what he'd been through. All at the hands of Alec Prince—his *father*.

God, there had been times over the last few months when I'd hated my own father, but it made our issues seem so insignificant. Because for as much as I'd tested Dad's patience and pushed his boundaries over the last few months, he would never lay a hand on me. Ever.

"Here you go." I returned to Maverick's side and handed him the pills and a glass of water. He chucked them back and swallowed.

"Thanks." He handed me back the glass, and I placed it down on the desk. "You're still here," he said.

"I told you I would be. I'm not going anywhere, Maverick."

"I don't deserve you."

"Stop." I reached for his hand, entwining it with my own. "We owe ourselves this. A shot at something real and good."

"I love you, Lo." He said the words as if they were easier than breathing. "I know I'm fucked up and should let you walk away but I'm not sure I can."

He loved me?

Maverick Prince loved me.

He noticed my hesitation and a slow smirk broke over his face. "You caught that, huh?" His eyes glittered with emotion as he pushed up on his elbows. "I think I fell in love with you that very first night. An angel in the darkness."

"Maverick," I gulped over the lump in my throat.

"It's okay." He reached out to tuck my hair behind my ear. "I don't need to hear the words, yet. Just knowing you're here, that you didn't run, it's enough."

I nodded, too speechless to reply.

"I guess you want to know the rest?"

I nodded again, getting comfortable in the chair.

"I dated Caitlin for nine months. It wasn't so bad, at first. But as the weeks went by, I started to resent her. JB noticed. Kept asking me what my game was. Obviously, I could never tell him. She started making all these plans for our future. I was only a junior for fuck's sake. I panicked. We had a big argument, and I knew I had to end it. So I went to my father and sold my soul. I told him I'd go to East Bay without a fight; that I'd give up the dream of basketball if he promised not to go after Gentry's business.

"I ended it with Caitlin the next day. She played the heartbroken girl, but she didn't love me. She loved what I represented. Popularity. Money. Things had been tense with JB the entire time we dated, but that threw him over the edge. We got into it and he accused me of using his sister and since I couldn't tell him the truth, I didn't deny it."

"So that's it? You have to forfeit your dreams to protect my uncle? To be the bad guy in all of this? That isn't right, Maverick."

"I don't think he'd really do it. Alec Prince is a lot of things but ruin a man who raised his kids? Even I can't believe he's that fucked up. He rules with fear, Lo. Control. As long as I thought he would do it, he had me where he wanted me. But when Coach found out I wasn't applying to any of the colleges interested in recruiting me, he hauled me into his office and demanded answers. I gave him the short version: my place at East Bay was already a given. He refused to accept it, said he had a contact at UCLA Bruins, the only college I've ever wanted to attend."

"But what will you do if you get accepted? What if your dad makes good on his promise to ruin Gentry's business?"

"It doesn't matter now, anyway." His voice was flat as he stared off into space.

"Maverick?"

"Coach called me into his office after practice on Tuesday. He got a call from the head coach at Bruins. Acceptance letters aren't supposed to go out for another five weeks, but he wanted to give me a heads up that someone had been digging around into my transcripts."

"What... I don't understand."

"I'm dyslexic, Lo. It's pretty well managed in class but I struggle with tests. My SAT score was not where I needed it to be for UCLA but with my athletic record and Coach's connections, they were prepared to grant me special admission. It shouldn't have mattered."

"But they have to make allowances for that kind of thing, right?"

"They don't know."

"What do you mean, they don't know?"

"I didn't tell them."

"But... why?"

"Because I'm Maverick Prince."

I stared at him in disbelief. "But if it's the difference between getting accepted and not, surely it doesn't matter who knows?"

He hung his head in defeat. "It doesn't matter now. The admissions board know, and they're not prepared to support me since my score was already lower than it needed to be."

"But I thought you said you didn't tell them?" Confusion swarmed my brain.

"I didn't. My father did."

Chapter Thirteen

Maverick

"Maverick, what is it?" Lo glanced back at me.

"Maybe this isn't such a good idea." I flicked my head to the kitchen door, and she let out a heavy sigh as she spun around and came toward me.

"What's the worst that can happen?"

Gentry could skin me alive, for starters.

My eyes dropped away but Lo was there, gliding her fingers underneath my jaw, tilting my face to hers. "Come on."

"I need a minute."

"Okay." She pressed her lips to mine in a lingering kiss. "But don't disappear on me."

As if I could.

I owed her. I owed her so fucking much. But I needed a second to catch my breath. Lo disappeared inside and my eyes shuttered. There wasn't a single part of me that didn't hurt. But since coming clean to Lo about everything, I felt lighter somehow. She'd hung on my every word as I revealed my deepest secrets. And she was still here.

There had been no pity in her eyes or tears of

sympathy. Her strength knew no bounds. And then she blew my mind, explaining that before she came to the pool house she stopped by to talk to her uncle and Rebecca. Just like that, she'd told them about us.

No one had ever stood up for me before. That was my role. I protected Macey and Kyle and Summer from the bloodsuckers. The people out to use us to climb their way up the social ladder or even worse, get in with my father.

As soon as I stepped into the kitchen, silence descended. Gentry's eyes were hard on me, and I heard his silent message loud and clear. I'd broken my promise to stay away from Lo.

"Maverick." Mom rose from her stool and came to me, carefully sweeping me into her arms. "Do you have any idea how much you scared us?"

One second. I allowed myself one second to absorb her comfort. To let myself be an eighteen-year-old guy in need of a hug from his mom. Then I untangled her arms from my shoulders, wincing with pain, and put some space between us.

I didn't expect to feel a hand graze against mine, and my head snapped down to where Lo was entwining our fingers. She smiled at me and that single look fueled me. Reminded me that she was here, choosing us—choosing *me*.

"How long has this been going on?" Gentry's voice cut through the tension like a knife.

My lips parted to reply, to tell him how his niece had saved me that night last summer, but Lo cleared her throat. "Does it matter, Uncle Gentry? We care about each other. We tried to fight it. Maverick tried to push me away. But we need each other."

"I see." His jaw clenched, and I didn't miss his fists pressed into his thighs as he leaned against the counter.

"Can we assume you were sneaking around in this house? In my home?"

"Gentry," Mom soothed. "I won't pretend this hasn't come as a surprise, but there are bigger things to discuss here." She gave me a pointed look. "What on earth made you do this to yourself, Maverick? If it wasn't for Kyle and Lo," her voice cracked, and Gentry stepped up behind her, squeezing her shoulder. She covered his hand with her own and let out a long breath. "Well, Maverick, explain yourself."

It wasn't the first time we'd fought over this: the fighting, the cuts and bruises, the bloodstained clothes and bed sheets, but this was different. I'd never been beaten to a pulp before. Lo squeezed my hand, pouring her strength into me and I dragged in a long breath. "He sabotaged my shot at UCLA Bruins."

Mom's face creased with confusion and then her eyes widened with realization. "Wh-what? I don't understand."

Because she thought I was going to East Bay. She'd even agreed when my father sold the idea to her. The two of them had been ganging up on me for months, priming me for business school. But that was my father, the master in lies and manipulation. The fact Mom had been lying all of these years too, only made it worse.

I dragged a hand down my face. "You knew I wanted to go to UCLA to play basketball. It's all I've *ever* wanted. Well, Coach pushed me to apply. Helped me fill out the forms. They wanted me, Mom. Bruins wanted me. But that piece of shit sabotaged my application."

"I- I don't know what to say. This is…" she spluttered looking to Gentry for back up.

I barked out a bitter laugh. "Really, Mom? You knew how much he wanted me to go to East Bay. And you know how he'd do *anything* to get what he wants."

Her expression slipped. She knew something was up—the flicker of awareness danced in her eyes—she just didn't know what.

Not yet.

"Maverick," Lo said. "Tell them."

"Tell us what?" Mom looked from me to Lo and back again. "What's going on, Maverick?"

"I know." The words punctuated the air, and she gasped, clapping her hand over her mouth. It was ironic, really, that she'd kept the truth from me for all these years and yet, the simplest of actions gave her away.

"What do you think you know, Maverick?" Gentry finally joined the conversation.

"That he threatened you, Stone and Associates, if you told us the truth."

"Sweetheart, that isn't for you to worr—" Mom started, her mask back in place, but Gentry squeezed her shoulder again.

"Rebecca, maybe it's time?"

"No," her voice quaked. "This is not your concern, Gentry. This is between me and my ch—"

"Mom, stop," I said meeting her glassy eyes. "Were you ever going to tell us?"

"I—" Silent tears slid down her face, twisting my insides. "He was your father, sweetheart, I didn't want to..."

"When did you find out?" Gentry asked, his hard expression softening a fraction.

"About four years ago."

Mom sucked in a sharp breath, but I continued. "I heard some things in ninth grade and then I saw you arguing with him. He was angry. It was like watching a different man. But I guess part of me didn't want to believe it. It wasn't until last summer when he got drunk and started spouting a bunch of shit... I finally confronted him."

Lo's fingers tightened around mine.

"You've known, for all this time you've known... that night, I just thought you'd had another argument about school." The blood had completely drained from her face. "And... and Macey, does she know?"

I nodded.

"The fighting?"

Another nod.

"Oh, Maverick, why didn't you say anything, why didn't come to me?" Mom broke down and Gentry slipped his arm around her.

How did I tell them the truth?

How did I tell them the day I discovered who my father really was, the world as I knew it imploded? We'd been pawns in a game we didn't understand, and it unleashed something in me. A darkness I struggled to contain every second of every day.

But even now, I couldn't tell them everything.

I couldn't tell them that when he'd pinned me against the wall and I'd seen the monster underneath his well-polished façade, my own walls shattered. The darkness finally consuming me whole.

"Is it true?" I addressed Gentry. "Does he have the power to bring down Stone and Associates?"

His face paled, and I had my answer. "When I met your mother, the company was going through a rough patch. Your father offered to come on board as a gesture of goodwill, but he screwed us over."

Fuck.

"Did you know?"

"Know?" His brows knitted in confusion.

"What he'd done to Mom? When the two of you got together, did you know?"

He looked at my mom with such reverence, but I saw the flash of regret. "Not the whole story, no." His eyes met mine again. "If I had, things would be very different, Maverick."

It didn't change anything, but I believed the conviction in his voice. If Gentry had known exactly the kind of man my father was he would never have brought him into the business.

Mom sniffled, drying her eyes with a towel. "I'm so sorry. I never wanted this, Maverick. I just wanted to protect you from the truth. All of you."

God this was so fucked up. She'd lied to Gentry. Let him enter a business deal with my father knowing what kind of man he was. And they'd spent years beholden to him.

Gentry cleared his throat. "I've been looking for a way out of the contract with your father. My guy thinks there may be a way, but we have to play it right."

My ears perked up.

"I know it's a lot to ask, Maverick, but…"

"You need me to smooth things over with him." My mouth soured, anger simmering in my veins. As if Lo sensed it, she rubbed her thumb over the crease of my hand.

"If there's a way to work this so I don't lose the business," he let out a heavy sigh. "I just need more time."

At the expense of my future?

At the expense of our family's stability?

But if there was so much as a small chance we could all be free of Alec Prince once and for all, I'd take it.

I had to.

"Fine. I'll do it." The words almost choked me.

Understanding shone in Gentry's eyes and for the first time in our strained history, I saw a man with the weight of the world on his shoulders. We'd never seen eye-to-eye. I'd resented him for stepping into my father's shoes and I didn't doubt he resented me—the son of the man who threatened to destroy his business if the truth ever came out. But this, we could agree on.

"Now," he said settling his gaze on the girl beside me. "Are you going to break this to your father, or am I?"

~

"You didn't tell them?" Lo's fingers danced over my arm as we lay on my bed, her pressed into my side.

"I couldn't do it." I swallowed hard, letting my gaze slide to hers.

"I understand." Her lips curved up in a faint smile. "But, what if he does it again, Maverick? What if—"

"Ssh." I pressed my finger to her lips. "He wouldn't dare."

Because I wouldn't walk away again, and I think part of him knew that. Like Mom and Gentry, he knew about the fighting. About my raging temper. He'd been on the receiving end more than once, although it usually ended up with me smashing the nearest glass or lamp or punching the wall, only wishing it was his face.

As if she could hear my thoughts, Lo sat up with a heavy sigh. "You have to learn to control your anger around him. You can't lose control, you can't give him any more ammunition against you, Maverick."

"I know."

"But you can't fight again, I can't see you like that—"

"Ssh, come here." I pulled her down to me, tucking her back into my side. It hurt—my whole body lit up with pain—but it was worth it just to feel her close. "They took it better than I thought they would."

Especially after Gentry had been so clear that I was to stay away from Lo before she arrived. But something had changed in the kitchen. The truth hadn't fixed us—we were too broken for that—but maybe we understood one another more now.

"We still have to tell my dad."

"Are you worried about what he'll think?"

Lo lifted her head and looked at me with fire in her

eyes. "I don't care. I'm eighteen and besides, he has Stella and Bethany now."

"You know, you could have them too, Lo. It's okay to move on."

"I… I'm not ready."

"That's okay." I pushed stray wisps of hair from Lo's face. "I'm just saying, one day, you might be."

Silence enveloped us, the weight of the last couple of days heavy in the air.

"What would you have done, do you think, if UCLA had accepted you?"

"Honestly?" I breathed out. "I don't know. It's always been my dream, and I guess when Coach handed me the application, I clung on to the hope of it becoming reality."

"There has to be another way, Maverick. It's your future, your life. You can't let him win." Steel determination rang in her voice, but I was tired.

So fucking tired.

Maybe if Gentry could get out of my father's fucked up contract, I would have a shot at college, at a future I wanted for myself. But right now, all I saw was an immediate future of more secrets and games.

"Now you know why I was so hellbent on keeping you at arm's length." Turning in to her, I ran my nose along Lo's hair, breathing her in.

"You wanted to protect me… from him. From this mess."

"He'll use anything to his advantage, Lo. Including you."

"He won't come between us, Maverick, I won't let him."

"And if he starts making demands again?"

That had her attention, and Lo went rigid in my arms. "Like what?"

I shrugged. "He'll think of something." But I already suspected what he'd want. And it was the one thing that would come between us. No matter how much Lo wanted to stand beside me, there was one thing that would drive a wedge so deep I knew I could lose her.

"We'll cross that bridge when it comes."

My arm tightened around her. "Promise me, Lo? Promise me that when it does, you won't run."

I couldn't lose her. She was the only thing tethering me right now.

Silence filled the space between us and for a second, I wondered if she'd fallen asleep but then she whispered, "I promise, but you have to promise me too. No more fighting, if something happens, let me help. You have to let me help, Maverick." Panic laced her voice as she clung to me. I dipped my head, brushing my lips over hers.

"I promise."

I just hoped it was one I could keep.

Chapter *Fourteen*

Lo

"That bad?"

Kyle blew out a strained breath as I climbed into his Jeep and buckled myself in. "He's getting crankier by the second," he said, scrubbing a hand down his face.

"It's been nine days. The doctor said he can start training again after two weeks, right?"

Kyle's brow shot up and I sighed. "The doctor didn't say that, did he?"

"He advised three weeks before resuming light exercise. I think we both know Rick better than that."

"I'll talk to him."

"Do you think it'll make a difference?" Kyle backed out of the driveway.

"Probably not but it won't hurt." Things were different between the two of us since Maverick came clean about everything. Kyle wasn't wrong though; his mood was deteriorating with every day that passed. Rebecca had gone into mother hen mode, insisting he stay off school—and the basketball team—until he was healed. And for once, she'd put her foot down insisting that if he didn't, she'd go directly to Coach Callahan.

"I don't think talking is the answer, Cous." Innuendo dripped from his voice and I punched his shoulder earning me a rumble of laughter.

"If you ask me, Rick just needs a good—"

"Kyle, don't you dare…"

"What? It's all good. We're friends. I tell you about Laurie."

"No, you torture me with all the sordid little details of your relationship with my *best friend*. There's a difference."

"Whatever you say, prude."

"I am not a prude." I just didn't want to discuss my sex life with my cousin. Not when the sex involved his stepbrother.

"Are you blushing?" His laughter filled the Jeep and I gave him the finger and turned to the window, feeling the heat in my cheeks. My phone vibrated, and I retrieved it from my bag. "Hi, Dad."

"I'm sorry I didn't make it home," he rushed out in one breath.

"It's fine, I hung out with Kyle and Laurie."

"And Maverick?"

"Yes, Dad, and Maverick."

He grunted, and I could imagine him scratching his jaw the way he did whenever he was uncomfortable. "Lo, sweetheart, I'm really not sure I—"

"I thought we agreed, Dad? I'm eighteen. It's my choice."

"I know, I know, but…" he hesitated. "Just be careful, that's all I'm asking."

Maverick had wanted to come with me when I broke the news to Dad, but it was something I needed to do alone. Besides, when he realised how terrible he looked, I think he was relieved I didn't want him there. And I knew from the deep lines creased across Dad's forehead as I told him, it was the right decision. He didn't scold me the way he had so many times before, since the accident, but disappointment poured from him. And I wondered just how much Gentry had confided in him about everything. But Maverick wasn't the bad guy here. He was just a boy trying to protect those around him—his family.

"Can I expect you home later?" I changed the subject.

"I'll probably head straight to Stella's and meet you at the restaurant."

"Okay, see you later."

"Bye, kiddo."

"Uncle Rob?" Kyle asked as I stuffed my phone back in my bag.

"Yeah."

"You know, you haven't said much about *that* in a while."

"That?" I said.

"Yeah, you know, your dad, Stella, the living arrangements."

"What's to say? He's at hers more than he is at ours. But if the alternative is her at ours all the time, then I'd rather it be this way."

"You should just move back in with us. You're practically always at the pool house, anyway."

"Because Maverick's housebound. Once he's back on his feet…"

We'd been wrapped in our own little bubble for the last week. I didn't even bother going home some days after school, heading straight to my uncle's house to see Maverick. But he wouldn't be injured forever. Eventually, he'd return to school, to his friends… the team.

"Nothing will change, Cous."

"How do you do that?" My head snapped over to Kyle and he flashed me a knowing grin.

"It's one of my many superpowers."

When the Jeep pulled into the parking lot, Laurie was

already waiting for us. Kyle cut the engine and wasted no time going to his girlfriend. I watched them, a pang of jealousy vibrating in my chest.

"Kyle, put me down," Laurie's protests went unheard as my cousin swung her around, peppering her face with sloppy kisses.

"Guys, come on," I groaned, and Kyle stuck his hand out behind his back and flipped me off.

"Whatever," I called, walking toward the building. I didn't see the person behind me until it was too late.

"Watch it, bitch."

"Caitlin, nice to see you too." I kept my voice level despite my blood boiling, and went to move around her but her icy glare pinned me in place.

"How does it feel being his dirty little secret?"

"Excuse me?" My spine straightened.

"I said,"—she leaned in close—"how does it feel being his dirty little secret? I mean, come on, did you really think he'd want everyone to know about the two of you? You're nobody."

My teeth ground together behind my lips. I wanted to bite. To tell her she knew nothing. But I refused to bend. To play her games.

Caitlin's eyes narrowed, daring me to engage. But then Laurie and Kyle were by my side, flanking me. "Oh look, the cavalry has arrived," she drawled.

"Back off, Caitlin," Kyle warned but I stepped away from them and closer to Caitlin, trying to figure out her game. For the last week, she'd watched me. Accusatory eyes following me from class to class. But she hadn't made her move until now.

"What do you hate more, Caitlin? That he wants me— a *nobody*? Or that he no longer wants you? That he never wanted you in the first place?"

The smirk fell from her face, but anger flashed in her eyes. I didn't give her time to answer, shouldering past her and into the building. When Laurie and Kyle caught up to me, my heart raced in my chest so fast I felt lightheaded.

"What the fuck, Cous?"

"Kyle's right, Lo, don't give her an excuse."

I ripped my locker door open and started trading textbooks. "An excuse? Are you kidding me? She came after me or have you both forgotten that?" My eyes snapped to Laurie's. "If I remember rightly, you were plotting your own revenge only the other week."

"Lo, come on, you know we haven't forgotten, but she can make life very difficult for you and next year..." Laurie's voice trailed off as I slammed the door shut, my gaze settling on her face. The truth of what she was saying sinking into my chest.

"Maverick will be gone." My shoulders sagged with realisation.

"Cous." Kyle slung his arm around my shoulder. "She's just pissed Lions called her out last—"

Laurie shot him a wide-eyed look and he spluttered, choking on whatever he'd been about to say. I glanced between them. "What aren't you telling me?"

"Nothing, come on class awaits." Laurie tried to tug me down the hallway, but I was watching Kyle. He wouldn't meet my eyes.

"Kyle, what's going on?"

"I ... hmm... I. Aw, shit, babe." He shot his girlfriend a pleading look. "I can't lie to her."

"Kyle," Laurie breathed out. "Fine, fine." She shot him another incredulous glare and then focused her attention back on me. "Caitlin and Devon got into it at The Shack. Everyone saw it. She was saying some stuff and he just went off at her."

"Stuff? What stuff?"

"It doesn't matter." She slid her arm through mine.

"But Devon shut her down. He stood up for you, Lo."

"Me? She was talking about me?"

Of course she was.

Bitch.

"I should've throat punched her when I had the chance."

Kyle chuckled. "That's the spirit, Cous. Class calls. I'll see you two ladies later." He stole a kiss from Laurie, ruffled my hair, and disappeared down the hallway but not before turning back around and calling, "And, Cous? Behave!"

I was still seething about Caitlin. And Devon? I didn't know what to make of that. After trying to talk to me on the first day back, he hadn't tried again. But he defended me against Caitlin? Against the girl he'd wanted all along?

"Uh oh," Laurie leaned in, whispering and I twisted my face to hers.

"Uh oh, what?"

"You have that look."

"What look?"

"The look someone gets when they see a stray dog in need of rescue."

"No, I don't." I winced at the defensive edge to my voice and she chuckled under her breath, patting my hand.

"Sure, you don't. Just be careful. That is a mess you don't want to get in between. He's my friend and I kind of feel bad for him, but you're like family, so take my advice and stay away from Devon, Lo."

My mouth opened to reply—to tell her I didn't intend on going anywhere near him—but I snapped it shut at the last second, letting her warning swirl around my mind.

~

After Summer's birthday dinner, I headed straight to the pool house, much to Dad's disapproval. I paused in the doorway, watching Maverick as he slept. The gentle rise and fall of his bare chest. How the sculpted muscle rippled with each breath.

"Are you going to stand there all day?"

"I thought you were sleeping." I stepped further into the room and his darkened gaze snapped to mine as he pushed up on his elbows with a pained groan.

"How was the dinner?"

"It was... interesting. I thought Nick was going to throw up all over his pasta. Gentry, my dad, and Kyle were a little intense."

"Man, I would have paid to see that shit." He sighed flopping back onto his pillows.

"You need to heal, Maverick."

I'd missed him, but Rebecca insisted he stay home. Macey had spent the whole time throwing me daggers and somehow, I ended up sitting beside Beth, who sat next to her mom, which meant I had to use a six-year-old kid to evade Stella's attempts at polite conversation. The whole thing had been awkward and strained. But in true Stone-Prince style, no one mentioned it.

"No, I need to get the fuck out of here before I lose my mind."

Dropping into the chair, I kicked off my Converse and nudged my toes against his arm. His brows quirked up as he slid his hand over my feet, kneading gently. It felt so good I groaned.

"It won't be much longer and then you can get back to the team."

He shrugged, refusing to meet my gaze. "Doesn't matter. My fate is pretty much signed and sealed."

"What if there was another way?" I didn't want to bring it up before, not until I knew for sure that it could work.

But now I knew it was a real possibility, I just needed Maverick to see that.

"UCLA was my back up plan and he still managed to fuck it up." Maverick rolled onto his side with a pained groan. "There is no other way, Lo. You don't get it, my father, he's..."

"I get it." I lowered my feet, leaning toward him, propping my elbows on my knees. "But what if there was a way? Gentry thinks he can find a workaround in the contract, he just needs you to buy him some time, right?"

"Yeah, so?"

I rolled my eyes at his shitty attitude. Maverick was growing more and more agitated by the second.

"I did a little research and there's a bunch of colleges with rolling admissions. You could retake the SAT and—"

"London," his voice had an edge to it. A warning. It rippled through my bones like nails on a chalkboard.

"*Prince*," I shot back. "You can't let him win. You can't let him dictate your life. It's not fair. You're one of the best players in the state. Basketball is your dream. I was reading about Steinbeck University and they're a Division 1 team, Maverick." Kyle and Coach Callahan had explained to me that if Maverick wanted a shot at going pro he really needed to be competing at the highest level.

"Steinbeck University?" He shuffled upright and swung his legs to the side of mine. Our thighs brushed, and tiny sparks fired up my leg and into my stomach.

"Yeah. Their record isn't brilliant but with you they could have a great team. Kyle said—"

"Stone knows about this?"

"I had to ask someone for help. I don't know about these things."

"You did all this?" His hand scrubbed over his face. "For me?"

"You can't give up, Maverick. It's your dream. And any dream is worth fighting for." I rummaged in the bag at my feet and pulled out the envelope, handing it to

Maverick. He stared at it as if it was contagious.

"I... I don't know."

"Take it. Just think about it, please." I pushed it at him until his fingers curled around the paper. His eyes didn't leave the packet, but I saw uncertainty in his stare, felt the defeat radiating from him.

"The tests are..." he swallowed hard and it was the first time I realised what an issue this was for him.

Maverick Prince was infallible. Untouchable. He commanded the basketball court effortlessly. Ruled the school hallways with silent domination. But he had secrets.

And this one was perhaps his most unexpected.

"But the school can help. Coach Callahan and Miss Tamson are already on board, and I read Steinbeck has an excellent program for students who need extra support."

"Lo," he breathed out. His voice softer than before but still defensive.

I sat up and took his hands in mine. "I'm just saying, think about it. I can help. Kyle will pitch in. People want to help, Maverick. Maybe Coach Callahan can reach out to their coach?"

He stared at me as if seeing me for the first time. Confusion swirling in his inky depths.

"What?" I whispered, overwhelmed by the raw intensity in his eyes.

"I fucking love you." His hands ensnared my wrists, tugging me forward. I crashed against him, my hands flying to his chest.

"Maverick, what... what are you doing? I could hurt you." I stared at him through wide-eyes.

"If you pull away it'll hurt more." Notes of desperation lingered in his voice as his breath fanned my face. "I need you, Lo. Please."

He hated this—the powerlessness. But I was here. For

him.

I would always be here.

"Lie back." I commanded, pulling away slightly. Desire flashed in Maverick's hooded gaze as he shuffled back on the bed, stretching long legs out in front of him.

Without thinking too much about it, I stood up and started unbuttoning my shirt. His eyes followed me down, trailing over my skin. He didn't speak but I saw the effect. The quickening of his chest as it rose and fell. The way his Adam's apple bobbed. When the material slid off my body, my hands glided down to my jeans and I pushed them over my hips, wiggling out of the denim until I stood before him in only my underwear.

Maverick moved, hissing in pain, but I narrowed my eyes and said, "Lie. Still."

"Lo, you're killing me here."

And I was.

His resolve was slipping. It was right there, in how his fists pressed into his sides or how his jaw clenched tight, the muscle ticking rhythmically.

"Let me do this for you." I crawled forward, straddling his hips, my own heart hammering in my chest.

His hand shot out to steady me as I lowered down over him, but I caught it, shaking my head with a grin. "My show, Maverick."

"London." It was a growl. Low and throaty and a sign of how much it was killing him to relinquish his power. But I didn't let it deter me. I leaned down, careful not to put any pressure on his ribs and brushed my lips against his.

Chapter *Fifteen*

Maverick

She was going to be the death of me. But I could think of worse ways to go. Lo's lips danced over mine, her hips rolling over my rock-hard dick, grinding onto me.

"Fuck, Lo," I choked out and she grinned against my mouth, aware of exactly what she was doing.

"Maverick, stop trying to take control," she whispered as I tried again to hook my arms around her.

"London," I warned again. I didn't hand over power. It made me vulnerable. Weak. It made me feel fucking useless. I needed to feel in control.

At. All. Times.

But this was Lo. She wasn't out to hurt me or get one over me. She was here for me—*with* me.

Lo eased away from me, the sudden movement sending licks of cool air dancing across my chest. She stared down at me, her skin flushed with need. But something else was there. Grit. Fierce determination. My girl had a wicked glint in her eyes that had me groaning and my dick straining painfully against my shorts.

"My. Show," she said again, raising an eyebrow.

Fine.

She wanted to play it that way, I'd let her think it was all her show. I nodded slowly, swiping my thumb across my bottom lip as I watched her rise onto her knees giving her enough room to work my shorts down my legs. My dick sprang free, her fingertips grazing the tip. I thought I might explode right then. It had been too long—too fucking long—since I felt her wrapped around me. Warm and soft and perfect.

Lo sunk down on me and my head dropped back, my eyes shuttering, as I breathed out a long groan. She felt so good. Like soft velvet. And, for a moment, she erased all the pain radiating through my body.

But I needed more.

As if she heard my silent plea, Lo rolled her hips, setting a slow torturous pace. Long dark hair hung over her shoulders and I wanted nothing more than to bury my hands in it, but my muscles were like lead.

"Oh, fuck," fell from my lips as she moved again, and pleasure exploded through me. "Condom," I rasped out as an afterthought. "We need a con—"

"Pill, I'm on the pi—oh, God."

That was good enough for me. Now I'd felt her—*all* of her—there was no way I'd ever have her any other way. And I loved it.

I loved her.

Fuck, did I love her.

"Are you okay?" She paused, glazed eyes snapping to mine.

I stared up at her, unsure how to answer that because I wasn't okay. I was so fucking gone. Completely at her mercy. Lo owned me. Plain and simple. She had ever since that night on the beach. And I'd walked away.

I'd lost her once, but she was here now. She was mine, and I'd do everything in my power to keep it that way.

"Maverick?" Her voice softened, and I gave her a

wicked smirk.

"Show's over," I said somewhere between a groan and a growl. Reaching out, I clamped my hand around her waist. She gasped as I lifted her gently and pulled her back down, flexing my hips up at the same time. It hurt like a bitch. Indescribable pain rippling from my pectorals down to my groin but it was worth it.

Worth it to see Lo's eyes half-closed with pleasure, to hear her labored breaths and my name falling from her lips in a whispered prayer.

"Maverick, God," she panted, tracing her fingertips over my bruises. "More, Rick, I need more." Lo leaned forward, barely able to stay upright, lost to the sensations washing over her.

She needed this as much as I did. It was right now, like this, that all the bad shit—all the stuff with her dad, and the accident, and my dad, and our fucked-up families—disappeared. There was just the two of us.

And it was fucking perfect.

I flexed my hips again, changing the angle. My fingers dug into soft flesh, anchoring her on top of me. I could stay like this forever. Lo wrapped around me like a glove. One of my hands skated up her toned stomach and over her perfect tits. Her body shuddered, and I did it again. What I really wanted was to pull her down to me and lick and suck until she was writhing above me and screaming my name, but my pain threshold was already at breaking point.

Lo's moans turned into a string of whimpers as I went at her harder. Faster. Beads of sweat rolled down my forehead as I tried to push down the agony and focus on her.

Lo.

Lo.

Lo.

The world stilled, went quiet, and then shattered into stars as I came. Lo flopped down beside me as I tried to catch my breath. My gaze followed her. Flushed skin, eyes heavy with desire, I gulped down the rush of emotion in my chest.

"What?" Her voice washed over me.

"You."

She smiled, tracing patterns along the ridges of my stomach with her fingers. "Me?"

There was so much I wanted to tell her, to confess. But the words lodged in my throat. I reached for her, brushing her hair out of her face. "Thank you. I needed that."

A slow smirk tugged at her lips as she stared at me. And I swear, in that moment, it was like she could see into my soul.

"Will you think about it?"

"About what?" I played dumb, still riding the high of her body pressed against mine. Her moans. How she looked when she came apart around me.

"About Steinbeck University."

"Yeah, I'll think about it." I don't know who was more surprised I'd said it, me or her. But I wanted college. And I wanted basketball. Fuck, did I want basketball. It's all I'd ever wanted. From what little I knew about Steinbeck University, it was a good school but their team, *The Scorpions*, was a different story. They'd never made it past the sweet sixteen in their sixty years of Division I basketball and even then, they had only reached the finals a handful of times. They weren't a team known for molding players into pros. But it was closer to home. Closer to Lo. And it was all I had right now.

"If he finds out—" Darkness edged into my euphoria.

"He won't. He doesn't have to know. We can be careful. Maybe they'll even have a scholarship you can apply for."

It didn't matter. It was never about the money. Mom had trust funds in place for me and Macey, and Gentry would take care of Kyle and Summer. It was only ever about protecting them from my father. By letting him control me—my future—it kept them out of his claws. But if Gentry meant what he said; if he could find a way out of his contract with my father, maybe I had a shot at a future I wanted. A future I earned without his name or money or loaded threats.

"Maverick?" Lo brushed her nose across my shoulder. "What is it?"

"I want it, Lo. Steinbeck University and basketball, and you, and a future without being his puppet."

I wanted it so much I could taste it. But I wasn't foolish enough to think there wouldn't be a price to pay. Nothing in this life came free. And I knew my father which meant I knew things were about to get a whole lot worse before they got better.

~

"Didn't expect to see you up and about yet." Kyle shot me a questioning look and I went to reply, but Mom beat me to it.

"He's not supposed to be up and about yet." Her eyes narrowed, dropping to my arm which hung protectively over my side.

"I can't sit around any longer. I'm going out of my mind."

"Maverick," she sighed. "You need to heal. And if you're back at school, don't for one second doubt I don't think you'll be back on the court."

"I won't, I promise. But I can still watch; help Coach run plays. Be there for the team. I'm the captain, Mom, I should be there. Besides, Coach won't risk me getting injured any more than I already am." With regionals looming, I needed to be there.

131

She pinched her temples and I saw the stress etched in her features. Since our conversation about my father, she'd aged.

"I'll be fine."

"Of course he will, he has the lovely Lo to look after him; right, brother?" Macey appeared from behind me and made a beeline for the plate of bagels.

"May as well get over it, Mace. Didn't you get the memo? Prince and Lo are the real deal." He was joking but it wasn't helping things.

"Kyle," Mom said at the same time as I groaned, "Stone."

"Maverick doesn't date." She shot me a terse glare. "He hasn't even looked at anyone since Caitlin, and we all know how that ended. And you're trying to tell me this is any different? He'll screw her over, if she doesn't screw him over fi—"

"We get it, Mace. You don't like Lo and you don't like that I lied to you." I held her unforgiving gaze. "Look, I get it. I screwed up and I should have told you sooner. I'm sorry, okay? But Lo isn't going anywhere."

Mom let out a strained sigh, watching our exchange with trepidation. We'd always been a united front. It had always been Macey and me against the world. But not now. Not since the day I walked into the kitchen and saw Lo standing there. And part of me hated the distance between us, but my sister needed to know if she wanted to draw a line, I'd be on Lo's side every damn time.

"Okay, okay." Mom finally broke the stifling silence. "I have to get to work. I have an early meeting. Can I trust you all enough not to kill each other before breakfast?"

"Who's killing who?" Summer breezed into the room. Sixteen looked good on her. Although, something told me her new found confidence had more to do with Nick than her recent birthday.

"No one is killing anyone. Summer, since your older siblings can't agree to disagree, you're in charge. Okay?" My baby sister stared at Mom like she'd grown a second head. "It'll be fine. I'll see you later."

"She's joking, right?" Summer said as soon as Mom disappeared, and Kyle hopped down off the stool and ruffled her hair.

"What do you think?" he glanced between me and Macey and she scowled. "For as much as I want to stick around and watch this, I have shit to do. You need a ride?" he said to Summer and she shook her head.

"Nick's picking me up." Her eyes slid to mine, and I saw the hesitation there. She expected me to speak up— to have a reason as to why she couldn't ride with him. But I swallowed it down. He was a good guy. He loved her and even though I hated it—hated the very idea that she was involved with anyone—Lo was right, I had to learn to ease up where she was concerned.

"Macey?" Kyle arched his brow at her.

"Come on, Mace," I said. "You can still ride with me."

"Are you riding with Lo?"

I didn't answer. She knew.

"Give me ten minutes," she said to Kyle before storming out of the kitchen.

"Well, that went well." He came to stand beside me. "Want me to talk to her?"

"Nah." I rubbed my jaw. "She'll come around."

I hoped.

I had enough to deal with without the girls in my life fighting. But Macey had taken an instant dislike to Lo. My sister hated change. Wary of strangers, of their motives and hidden agendas, she trusted people less than I did. Or maybe she saw the way I watched Lo. The way I acted around her. Whatever it was, I'd have to deal with it eventually. But today was not that day.

Kyle clapped me on the back and barked a laugh. "Good luck with that one, Prince. I'll see you at school. You're good to drive?" He cast me a sideways glance and I nodded.

"Only one way to find out."

"Crazy sonofabitch," he murmured as he left the kitchen.

I loaded a plate with some fruit and a bagel and sat at the island. Summer joined me. "I'm sorry I missed your birthday."

She shrugged. "It's okay."

"It isn't," I said. "I messed up."

Summer met my eyes and gave me a sad smile. "Yeah, you did. I've never seen Mom like that, Rick. She was…" her voice trailed off, but the pain in her voice twisted my gut in a way I hadn't expected. "I heard Kyle say he and Lo dragged you out of there. Is it true?"

Lump in my throat, I nodded.

"I can't imagine…"

"Sum, come on, I'm fine. And it won't happen again." No matter how much the darkness ate away at my soul, I wouldn't step back in that ring. It was a promise I'd made not only to Lo but to myself.

"I love you, Maverick." Summer lifted her head, sitting tall. She might have been two and a half years younger than me, but in that moment, I felt small. "But if you hurt Lo, God help me I will never forgive you."

My mouth hung open as I tried to form words, but I had nothing.

I didn't ever want to hurt Lo. She was the one good thing in my life. I needed her the way I needed air. But Summer knew. She knew my MO. I pushed people away. When shit got too hard or things didn't go my way, I put up walls so high no one could break through.

And for as much as I wanted to tell her she was wrong—that she had nothing to worry about—I was

Maverick Prince. It was a title that came with expectations. I was son to Alec Prince and a pawn in his game. So, while I wanted nothing more than Steinbeck and basketball and a future with Lo, I wanted to protect her more.

Even if I ended up hurting her in the process.

Chapter Sixteen

Lo

"You're quiet?" Maverick flicked his gaze to me and I dropped my eyes to the floor.

"I'm just..." How did I even begin to explain this?

"What?" he snapped, and my head whipped up to his.

"Maverick," I ground out. "It's not like that. I'm just... We haven't done this yet. Not out in public."

"You don't want everyone to know?" Hurt lingered in his voice, wrapped up in anger.

"You're being ridiculous," I sighed.

"Am I? I thought this was what you wanted? Us, out in the open? No more secrets?"

"Seriously, you're acting like a complete arsehole. You know that's not how it is. I just..." The school came into view and my words died on my tongue. After my big speech in his bedroom last night, how could I explain that I was scared? That when we climbed out of his car, *together*, everything would change again? Imaginary lines would become very real. Us on one side. All of Maverick's enemies on the other.

He didn't answer as he steered the car into a free parking bay and cut the engine. This was always going to be an issue between us. Out here, in public, Maverick was someone else. He wasn't the fiercely loyal, protective, vulnerable boy, I'd spent the last ten days nursing back to full strength. The boy he let only me see.

Maverick's hand gripped the wheel as silence hung heavy between us. I waited. Letting my words sink in.

"I'm sorry." It was barely a whisper. But it was a start.

"It's okay." I twisted round to him. "This is new, for both of us. But the second we step out there, everything changes, Maverick. It's what I want, no more hiding, no more sneaking around, but it puts us both in the firing line. That's all it is. I'm scared. I wouldn't be human if I wasn't."

His face lifted to mine, his eyes saying everything he couldn't.

He understood.

He wished things were different.

He loved me.

I still hadn't told him. I couldn't. Not yet. But I felt it. Felt it all the way down to my soul. Maverick had the power to make me soar, but he also had the power to wreck me in the worst kind of way. The kind of way I didn't know if I'd come back from. That's why I didn't say the words he needed to hear. Because those words were the last line of my defense, and I needed to cling onto them for a little while longer.

"We don't have to do thi—" he started but I reached out for him, pressing my finger to his lips.

"Yeah, we do."

We met halfway, our lips colliding in a desperate kiss. Maverick's hand buried deep in my hair as his tongue explored my mouth and heat flashed in my stomach as memories from the night before flooded my brain.

I pressed a hand to his chest and breathed out, "Okay, we need to stop."

He dropped his head to mine, trying to catch his own breath. "Tonight?"

"Tonight." My lips curved up.

"How many hours?"

"About ten?"

"I won't survive," he said.

"Sure, you will. There's a saying, you know. Absence makes the heart grow fonder."

"It'll make something grow, that's for sure." Maverick gave me a smile that sent my pulse racing, and he broke away from our intimate position. "Come on, before they send Principal DeLauder out to get us."

We got out of his car and my worst fears were confirmed. The whole parking lot ground to a halt and I froze, rooted to the spot.

"Lo," Maverick said, irritation in his voice. When I still didn't move he barked, "Start walking, London." Once upon a time, his bossy growl would have pissed me off, but right now, it grounded me, and my legs started moving. When I reached him, he took my hand, outwardly unaffected by the way everyone watched us. But I felt the tension pouring from him.

"Okay?" He searched my eyes and I nodded still too overwhelmed to speak.

"Prince, over here," Luke yelled from where he was huddled with the rest of the guys. A couple of them looked surprised to see us together but Luke and Aaron seemed unfazed, wearing easy smiles.

"Hey, man. Good to see you up and about." Luke's eyes flashed to mine, a silent apology there. "It's nice to see you survived his cranky ass, Lo."

I smiled, but my mind was elsewhere. On the eyes burning into my back. The whispers floating on the gentle breeze.

Look at them.

He's too good for her.

Can you believe he wants her?

"Coach will shit a brick when he sees you," Aaron added.

"I think Coach is the least of his problems." Trey let out a low whistle as he flicked his head to the main building where crowds of kids gawked in our direction.

"Let them stare," was Maverick's only reply, and he and Luke went back to discussing the team and what had happened in his absence. His hand remained firmly around mine as if he never intended on letting go. But he would. In a minute, we'd have to walk through those doors and go to our separate classes.

And I didn't know if I was ready for that.

~

"I can't believe it's true. Maverick Prince doesn't date, like ever."

"But you saw what happened at Winter Formal; he came for her. I knew there was more to it. I mean, they're practically family, it's weird."

"It's not weird, it's gross." She fake gagged and my fingers tightened around the pen until the blood drained away. "I mean, she lived there for like three months."

The rap of my pen against the desk grew louder. But it did little to deter them. They knew I was sitting two rows in front. I was *right there*. Yet, they carried on their conversation as if I wasn't.

"Hey, Claire," Kyle's voice rose amongst the idle chatter. The girls stopped talking. Everyone did. Even the teacher sat a little straighter waiting to hear what Kyle Stone had to say. I wanted to disappear. For the ground to open up and swallow me whole. It was only second period. I had another four classes to survive and forever after today.

"Yes, Kyle?" the girl said with a saccharine lilt.

"Didn't you hook up with Brody Peters over the

weekend?"

"Yeah, so?"

"I wonder what his girlfriend thinks about that."

Her quiet gasps filled the room and I couldn't help but glance back. Her face was pale, her friend's eyes wide with shock as she tried to console the crushed girl beside her.

"Mr. Stone. That's quite enough, thank you. Class, back to it."

Kyle shot me a wide grin and I rolled my eyes. While I appreciated the save, he couldn't jump in every time someone said something he didn't like. I'd either have to find a way to deal with the whispers and stares or learn to ignore them.

When the bell rang, and we filed out of the classroom, Kyle caught up with me. "Are you okay?"

"I'm not sick, Kyle," I groaned, hugging my books close to my chest.

"I know that, but what they were saying... they're just jealous, Cous."

"I know." I narrowed my eyes at a couple of girls staring in our direction. "It's just intense, is all. I'm not used to being in the spotlight."

It had been bad enough being the new girl. A Stone-Prince by association. But this was a whole other league. I wasn't only one of them now. I was dating one of them.

He slung his arm around my shoulder with a throaty chuckle. "Well, you picked the wrong guy then, because Rick *is* the spotlight."

We rounded the corner and I saw it. Maverick. His friends. The way everyone gravitated around them. He was laughing with Luke and Aaron. From the wounded look on Trey's face, it was a joke at his expense. But when his eyes snapped to mine, everything melted away. He didn't move. Waiting to see what I'd do.

Kyle leaned in close. "Everyone knows, Cous. May as

well give them a show." I knew what he was saying—he'd said something similar before—but could I do it?

Could I be the girl Maverick needed me to be?

I inhaled a deep breath and started walking. One foot in front of the other until I arrived in front of him. "Hey," he said running a brisk hand over his head. "Are you okay?"

Without thinking about it, I curled my fist into his jersey and tugged him down, finding his lips. Some snarky comment spewed from Trey's mouth, but Luke and Aaron shut him down, and I was vaguely aware of them moving away, giving us space. But with the pound of my heart against my chest, and the tremble of my body with each brush of Maverick's tongue against mine, it was hard to concentrate. He fuelled me. Gave me strength. Made me stand taller.

"What was that for?" Maverick stared down at me as I broke away, wonder shining in his eyes.

I shrugged, ducking my head to hide the colour staining my cheeks. It had seemed like a good idea at the time, but now I wasn't so sure. "Everyone's looking, aren't they?" I said in a hushed voice and the corner of Maverick's mouth lifted in a smug smile.

"Wasn't that the point?" He lowered his head and tried to steal another kiss, but I leaned back staring into his intense eyes.

"Yeah." I swallowed. "I guess."

"You guess?" He raised his eyebrows. "I could always put my jersey on you."

"Your jersey?"

"Yeah, my number. Then everyone would know exactly who you belong to." His eyes flashed with something dark, *dangerous*, making my tummy clench violently.

"And how would everyone know who you belong to?"

"I think it's pretty obvious." Maverick looped his arm around my waist, drawing me closer. "You own me, Lo." His voice a husky rasp in my ear and a deep shiver rippled up my spine. "Now get to class before I drag you to the nearest empty room and show you exactly just what you do to me."

Part of me wanted to push him to make good on his word but we'd sparked enough rumours for the day. I pressed one more kiss to his lips, said goodbye, and wound through the streams of bodies with my head held high. When I reached my next class, I breathed a sigh of relief. Until a voice stopped me in my tracks.

"So, it's true then?"

I turned around, steeling myself to meet JB's scrutiny. He tilted his head to the side, stepping into my space. The hallway had emptied leaving me at his mercy.

"Shame, really. We could have had some fun."

"I think we both know that was never going to happen."

He stepped forward and I backtracked, keeping some distance between us. "Scared, Little Stone?" There was a warning in his voice, and the same ripple of unease I felt whenever he was around passed through me.

"This isn't about me, is it? It's about Maverick, about hurting Maverick." Surprise flashed across his face, but he quickly schooled his features, and I continued, "What happened between Caitlin and Maverick is between them. Let it go, JB."

Maybe I was overstepping the mark—poking my nose where it didn't need to be—but he'd made it his business to taunt me at every available opportunity. And I was done.

His nostrils flared as he regarded me. "I like you, Little Stone, more than I should, so a word of warning. Watch your back."

In a flash, he was gone but I was too stunned to

move. *Watch your back.* It sounded a lot like a threat but as I entered the classroom, something niggled me. Something about his voice, the hesitant inflection I thought I'd heard. But I had to be wrong. JB hated Maverick. I'd witnessed their animosity with my own eyes. He wanted to hurt him the way Maverick had hurt Caitlin. And now I was with him it made me the perfect victim. Maverick would lose his shit if JB so much as looked at me. So it made no sense that he'd try to warn me. And from who?

His sister?

Or something else entirely?

Chapter Seventeen

Maverick

"You good?" Luke asked when he reached our locker bank.

"Yeah, why?"

His eyes darted around the hallway. "Because I have it on good authority Holloway was talking to Lo earlier."

"What?" My voice was cold, the complete opposite of the heat running through my veins at the mention of his name.

"Yeah, apparently, he collared her before she headed into class, you know after she publicly kissed the shit out of you." He grinned, but it was lost on me. JB had approached Lo? If he so much as touched her...

"Do you know what he wanted?" I ground out, unable to disguise the tremor in my voice.

Luke's shoulder shrugged as he leaned back against the lockers. "I can take a stab in the dark, though."

"Yeah." Dragging a hand over my face, I released a long breath. This was the last thing I needed. Not now. Not when so much was hanging in the balance.

"So, what are we going to do about it?"

"We?" I raised an eyebrow.

"Well, yeah. You know he's been waiting for the right ammunition. And you just handed him Lo, on a silver platter."

This was one of the reasons I hadn't wanted to go public. To avoid her falling into the hands of my enemies. Namely JB Holloway.

"He won't do anything."

"You sure about that?"

"He doesn't want war. Not with graduation right around the corner." Even JB wasn't that foolish. He had plans. A football scholarship at San Diego State. He wouldn't risk it.

"Okay, man," Luke sighed, "if you're sure. But I've seen him watch her. He's itching to make you pay for Caitlin. You know that." My best friend gave me a pointed look, and a groan bubbled in my throat.

"Let me deal with Holloway. But I appreciate the heads up." Luke was one of the few people I trusted.

"Sure thing, and you know I've got Lo's back. The rest of the guys too. Trey likes to give you shit about her, but he doesn't mean anything by it."

"I want eyes on her, always. If I'm not with her, someone is watching her."

"Got it."

Lo was a junior. Our paths rarely crossed around school and I couldn't watch her twenty-four-seven. Kyle and Laurie knew the drill. They knew Caitlin could make life difficult for her if she wanted to. She'd already proved that with her little stunt at Winter Formal. But if Luke was right and JB was going to make a move to use her to hurt me... well, that couldn't happen.

"You need to be discreet," I said. "If she knows we're—"

His head shook, an amused smirk plastered on his face. "Jesus, you're whipped."

"Taffia," I warned, and he threw up his hands.

"Hey, it looks good on you. She's good for you. It's about time you had something good in your life. Just don't fuck it up."

I couldn't argue with that. But he didn't know Lo the way I did. If she knew I was having her watched by someone other than Kyle, she'd have my balls. But I was already risking her by just being with her. Caitlin wanted Lo out of the picture. There was a good chance JB wanted to use her to hurt me. And once my father found out about us—if he didn't already know—he'd use her against me.

Lo was my weakness. And it was only a matter of time before someone exploited that.

~

After my conversation with Luke, I headed straight for Coach's office. He'd told me to come by after last period, but when I knocked on the door and slipped inside, he was taking a call. *Take a seat,* he mouthed, and I dropped into the chair, scrubbing a hand over my face.

It had been a long day. I'd expected it to be bad—the stares and whispers and constant questions—but it had been intense. The lingering waves of pain hadn't helped my mood. Luke and the guys kept the piranhas from circling and our group went on lockdown for most of the day. Laurie and Kyle did the same with Lo, but I knew she'd had it rough in a couple of her classes. Kyle told me as much. Because where I was used to being in the limelight, used to the way people gravitated to me and mine, Lo wasn't.

Fuckers.

Why couldn't they just leave us alone? It wasn't like Lo had taken me off the market—I was never on it to begin with. Aside from Caitlin, I didn't date. Period. And before her, I'd rarely so much as looked at any of the girls from school and, if I had, they were a means to an end.

An itch to scratch. But I knew how their minds worked. Being with me painted a target on Lo's back and the line started behind Caitlin Holloway.

"Maverick, thanks for coming, son." Coach hung up his phone and spun his chair to face me. "I had an interesting chat with a Miss Stone last week." His mouth curved in a sly smile.

"You did, huh?" I leaned forward, rubbing my jaw, unsure of what to do with that.

Lo wanted me to pursue Steinbeck, I knew that, but truth was, I still hadn't decided what to do. I wasn't used to someone trying to railroad me. To take the decision out of my hands. That right was reserved solely for my father.

"Smart girl, I like her." His smile was genuine.

I like her too. Too much.

I held his unwavering expression, but I didn't say the words.

"I'm going to level with you, son. After all the work we put into UCLA, I don't want a repeat. I don't want to push you into this only to have your father screw things up at the last minute. But I'm not afraid of getting my hands a little dirty either. So I'm asking you right here, right now, what do you want, Maverick?"

"I—" The lump in my throat choked me and I stalled, feeling the prickle of anger in my bloodstream. I'd wanted UCLA with every fiber of my being. It was my dream for as long as I could remember. To play for Bruins. To wear blue and yellow.

"What. Do. You. Want?" Coach repeated, his eyes boring into me, pinning me to the spot. Anyone else and I would have looked away, refused to answer. But Coach Callahan knew me better than most people. He knew what basketball meant to me. What a life out of my father's clutches meant. He'd never had his blinders on where my father was concerned, but his hands were tied. Just like every other teacher in Wicked Bay High. They knew the deal—who I was, who my father was—but Coach was different because, in the end, when it mattered, he came through for me.

My hands balled into tight fists as I replayed the last few months over in my head. The hopes, the expectations... the bone crushing disappointment when I realized UCLA was no longer within reach. My father had his claws so far in me, I no longer knew where he ended and I started. The lines between us were blurred, messy and suffocating. But his dream wasn't mine. His future wasn't mine.

I was a Prince, but I didn't want *his* kingdom.

"I want basketball, Sir," I said. "I want it more than air."

Basketball was my life. It ran through my blood, kept my heart beating.

"I didn't hear you, Prince. What do you want?"

"Basketball, Sir," I said with more conviction, feeling the stir of something different—something that could chase away the darkness.

Fight against it.

"Good." He slammed his hands down on the desk and leaned forward. "Because I already made the call."

My eyes widened to saucers as an easy grin transformed his face. "No time like the present and it just so happens I have connections."

That didn't surprise me. He made it his business to have connections. This was good. It was more than I could have hoped for. But then Coach's expression turned grim again. "They're interested. Who wouldn't be? But, and it's a big one, I'm not sure I'll be able to pull the right strings to get them to ease off on your test scores."

Fuck. I raked a hand through my hair. "Did you... tell them?

"No. It's not my decision to make. But maybe it's time to own your shit, Maverick. It's dyslexia. It's not a death-sentence."

"I'll think about it." I said, a defensive edge in my voice.

"Well think quick, kid. You're going to need to pull this out of the bag with the SAT. I checked, and the test is in a few weeks. It will mean a lot of hard work. Are you up to that?"

I'd already sat the SAT twice to try to improve my score for UCLA. Standardized testing, and I had a rough history. Over the years, I'd learned to manage my dyslexia. To work around it and keep it under wraps. And as I got older, people became less interested in my grades and more interested in my game point average and whether I was partying over the weekend or not.

"I already spoke to Miss Tamson, and she's agreed to help again, discreetly, of course."

"Thank you, Sir, I appreciate it." More than he would ever know.

I got up to leave but his voice rooted me to the spot. "Look, Maverick, you're a good kid. One of the best players I've ever seen. You could go all the way, but you need to believe in yourself. And you need to fight for what's yours.

"You think I don't know what you get up to on a weekend? How you blow off steam? Son, I may be gray-haired and pushing the wrong side of fifty-five, but I'm not stupid. I've seen you walk into my locker room with a busted lip or bruised knuckles one too many times. And I've kept quiet because sometimes we gotta do what we gotta do, but this shit with your father, don't let it define you. You are not him, Maverick. Don't give him that kind of power. You hear me?"

"Yes, Sir."

"Good, now get out of here. You have a test to study for."

I gave him a tight nod and slipped out of his room, his words whirling around my mind. He didn't know the whole truth, but he'd deduced enough over the last couple of years. And he'd turned a blind eye to activities off the court because once my feet hit the hardwood, everything melted away and I became the guy I was always destined to be. Coach Callahan didn't look at me and see Alec Prince's son or the spoiled rich kid with an unhealthy anger living inside of him. He just saw me. And for the first time in a long time, I let myself believe that maybe it was my time to step out from under *his* shadow. To prove myself for me. Because Coach was right, somewhere between my father pinning me to that wall and right now, in this very moment, I'd lost a part of myself. And every day a little more of my soul fell away in oblivion. But I had things to fight for now. I had Lo. And Steinbeck. And basketball. I had a future that was my own.

I just had to reach out and take it.

Chapter Eighteen

Lo

"And he said he thought it could work?" I pushed open the door waiting for Maverick to catch me up.

"Yeah, he seemed positive, but I still don't know, Lo."

"Maverick," I sighed. "What's to think about, if it means—" My feet ground to a halt and he crashed straight into me, grunting with pain.

"Lo, sweetheart, I, hmm, I wasn't expecting you home." Dad's eyes bulged as he glanced between me and Maverick and then back to Stella who sat quietly at his side.

"What's going on?" I immediately went on high alert. Papers were scattered over the coffee table and Stella's eyes were red-rimmed and sore. "Is everything okay?" I raised an eyebrow.

"Nothing you need to worry about," he said shifting so that he sheltered Stella behind him. "Are you and Maverick staying?"

"We can study at the pool house. It's no problem, Uncle Rob," Maverick said. He didn't come around often, and he especially didn't come around when Dad was home.

Stella sniffled, breaking the awkward silence that had descended over us, and Dad mumbled something that sounded a lot like we could stay and hang out. But I said, "I'll just grab my things and we'll get out of your hair."

Whatever was wrong, it looked serious. Stella didn't meet my eyes, taking refuge behind my father's broad stature. Nor did she speak.

"Okay, kiddo." His eyes flashed with appreciation. "Maybe it's for the best."

"Wait for me in the car?" I said to Maverick, and he nodded, excusing himself as I went to my room and grabbed the books I needed. Not that I anticipated much studying to happen when we got to the pool house, but Dad didn't need to know that.

"That's me," I said when I returned to the living room. Dad glanced up, his arm tucked protectively around Stella's shoulder, and he offered me an apologetic smile.

"I have my phone if you need me." I hurried from the house, unsure of what to make of everything. Dad never brought Stella to the house. At least, not when I was around. If she was here, it could only mean whatever had happened wasn't good and my stomach hollowed.

"Everything okay?" Maverick said as I climbed inside the Audi.

"I don't know." I glanced over at the house. "That was weird, right? Did Stella seem like she'd been crying to you?"

He shrugged, backing the car out of the driveway. But my mind was already working overtime, imagining all the different scenarios that could lead to her sitting in my living room being consoled by my dad.

"Lo, stop over-thinking," Maverick's voice reached a place inside of me and I looked over at him.

"Things just settled down, what if—"

"You don't even know what's wrong yet. Don't jump to conclusions. It could be nothing."

Or it could be something.

Something that would disrupt the strange level of normal Dad and I had found over the last few weeks.

"Hey." Maverick's hands reached for my knee. "I'm sure everything is fine."

I gave him a little nod but didn't trust myself to reply. To say any of the things circling my mind.

"You can't flake out on me now, not when I have a test to study for."

"You mean…?"

A slow grin broke over his face. It was a rare sight. Infectious and blinding. Seeing Maverick happy was one of my favourite things.

"I want it more than anything. The idea of sitting the SAT again makes me want to puke," he admitted, unable to meet my gaze. "But I'll do it."

I slid my hand to his cheek, forcing him to look at me. "This is good, Maverick. This could change everything, and I'll help you. We all will."

"No," he said flatly. His face slipping back into its usual stone mask. "No one can know. If I want this to happen, he can't know, Lo. He can't—" His fists tightened on the wheel.

"Maverick," I coaxed him back to me, but he was gone. Lost to his demons; the hold his father had on him. His breathing turned shallow, short and sharp rasps, as his body vibrated. The anger radiating around him like a forcefield.

"Maverick, don't let him in. I'm here, I'm right here." My voice was soft. Calm. I reached out and laid a hand on his arm, but he didn't flinch. Maverick didn't take his empty glare off the road.

"I'm right here," I whispered, trying to reach him, to bring him back.

This was why he fought. I understood now. Alec Prince had power over Maverick. The deep ingrained vicious kind. The kind that ate away at your soul until there was nothing left. Fighting made him feel strong again; for those few minutes when he was in the ring he was in control. I'd promised to be his anchor now. But what if I couldn't? What if he needed the pain and hurt? What if he needed the feel of his fist driving into bone and soft tissue?

Maverick had promised me no more fighting, but what if it was a promise he couldn't keep?

What if my plan didn't work out?

What then?

~

"I can't do this." The book in Maverick's hand flew across his room, landing with a thud, and he dragged a hand down his face. "It doesn't make sense."

"Sure, it does," I sighed shifting off the bed to retrieve the textbook. "You already sat the SAT twice. You can do it and remember Miss Tamson said to concentrate on your strengths. Focus on the math questions and then you won't have to score so high on the critical reading section."

"You don't understand," he ground out, tugging his hair with his fingers, his eyes darting around me but refusing to meet mine.

"So, tell me." I sat back on the bed, crossing my legs in front of me and waited. I was learning that you couldn't push Maverick. He had to do things in his own time. In his own way. And he was right; I knew nothing much about dyslexia. I knew it affected a person's ability to read and write. That words got muddled. But that was it. I didn't know what it was like to live with that.

Maverick scrubbed his hand over his hair again and

then down his face. Finally, he met my intense gaze and said, "Dad refused to believe there was anything wrong. I was a bright kid. Eager to learn. But I struggled with reading and writing. I'd get so frustrated when I couldn't spell a word or forgot a word's meaning when I thought I had it locked down. Mom and Dad had only been divorced a year. It was rough, on everyone. I think my teachers thought I was rebelling or something. But eventually, they called my parents in. They wanted to have me assessed. Dad wouldn't hear of it. No child of his had a learning disability. Mom tried to talk him around, but he wouldn't listen.

"I was seven. My parents were divorced, my father, the man I idolized, had a new family, and I hated the man trying to replace him. I was in a bad place, Lo. I didn't want something to be wrong with me and I couldn't bear the thought of my dad being disappointed with me. So I promised to try harder. I was good at maths. Numbers came easy. Words not so much. And I already loved basketball. I applied myself. Studied harder. Played harder. I got Macey to help me with homework. It wasn't the ideas I struggled with, it was writing them down. I'd get confused or forget what it was I wanted to write and then I'd get frustrated and the letters and words would blur together on the page. So, she became my scribe."

"You covered it up." I said, my heart breaking for the boy who had hidden this part of himself for so long.

"I tried. My grades suffered but by the time I got to junior high, I was breaking records on the court and people started paying less attention to my performance in class. Besides, I was Maverick Prince, son of the one of the richest, most powerful men in Wicked Bay, no one was going to question my intelligence. Or lack of it."

"Maverick," I scolded, hating the self-deprecation in his voice.

He reached for my leg, hooking it over his. "I wasn't dumb, Lo. I answered questions in class. Did my homework. Copied notes from my friends. I scraped by. I think it was easier for my teachers to believe I was just another kid more interested in sport than learning. A lazy student unwilling to push himself. That they weren't failing me; I was failing myself. But then everything changed."

His walls slammed down.

"You found out the truth about your dad."

"I'd always been a frustrated kid, but something changed that year, when I realized Alec Prince wasn't who I thought he was. I mean, I wasn't blind. I knew he was a cold-hearted business man, you didn't get to where he was without it. But he loved me and Macey, Alex and Elle. And he raised Will, Maxine's son, like his own. He was a good man, a good father. It was like finding out the truth opened this vortex in my chest. I had all this anger building inside of me. And I didn't know what to do with it.

"Basketball was my safe place, the only time I felt free. And it showed. The more bitter I became about life, the more I resented my father, Gentry and myself, and the better I played. Coach started to talk about college scholarships and the future. But I had this dark cloud looming over my head."

I uncurled my other leg and slipped it over his, shuffling forward until we were almost chest to chest. Maverick looked so pained. So defeated. I wanted to take it all away. To absorb the darkness that lingered over him. But I knew he needed this, to get it out in the open. Even if he disagreed. My mum always said a problem shared was a problem halved.

"When he called me into his office to talk about college, things were at breaking point between us and I could barely stand to be around him. He sat me down and presented me with an application to East Bay. We hadn't talked about it since the day I agreed to date Caitlin. He just assumed it was a done deal, that he had me where he wanted me. Because that's his MO, whatever Alec Prince wants, he gets. I laughed in his face, asked him how the hell he thought his dyslexic son was going to manage to major in business and administration and do you know what he said? He looked me dead in the eyes and said, 'Maverick, you are a Prince and Prince's succeed.' Like it was that fucking simple. Like that wasn't all I'd been trying to do since fourth grade.

"When I didn't answer, when I didn't tell him I'd make it work, he slammed his fist down on the desk, straightened his tie, and said, 'It doesn't matter, it's been taken care of'." Maverick let out a bitter laugh. "Because that's what I was to him, a problem to fix. I'm eighteen, Lo. Eleven years later, and he still won't acknowledge it. He'd rather buy my way into college than accept the truth because in his eyes I'm a failure. Because my disability makes me weak."

"Maverick," my voice cracked, and I reached for him, but he caught my wrist, suspending it in the space between us.

"Don't." The vulnerability in his voice almost broke me. "I can't. Not yet."

"You are not a failure and you are not weak. You're one of the strongest people I know. Everything you've done, everything you've shouldered. You have spent your whole life putting others first. But this is your future. Not his. Don't let him take that from you. Promise me you won't let him take that from you?"

I didn't realise I was crying until Maverick's thumb slid over my cheek catching the teardrop. "What did I do to deserve you?" he whispered, closing the space between us, his mouth hovering over mine.

I leaned into the kiss. Trying to show him that love wasn't something deserved, it just was. I didn't love Maverick because he was a Prince or a star basketball player or because the boys at Wicked Bay wanted to be him and the girls wanted to date him. I'd fallen in love with him because he was a good person. Underneath his hard exterior and high walls, he was just a boy fighting his own demons while putting those around him first.

And I wanted to tell him—God, did I want to tell him—but something held me back. Even now, after he'd told me everything, I was still holding back.

Chapter Nineteen

Maverick

I let myself believe the lie.

That was my first mistake.

As I sat opposite my father, watching as he shuffled papers with deep lines of concentration around his eyes, I realized my second mistake.

I shouldn't have come.

But when he'd called and asked—*demanded*—I go straight to his house after school, I knew my time with Lo was up.

Alec Prince was calling in his *favor*.

"I trust you're healed now?" He didn't look up. Apparently, I didn't deserve his eyes, his scrutiny.

"Yeah, I'm good."

"How many times have I told you, fighting is a poor man's sport?"

I pressed my lips together, rolling my tongue behind my teeth, and glared at him.

"Well, don't you have anything to say for yourself?"

He was pushing me. Testing me. And I hated him all the more for it.

"It won't happen again," I replied flatly.

It seemed to pacify him as he went back to his papers. This was all part of the show. His bravado. Alec Prince waited for no one and yet, he'd make you wait a lifetime. Just because he could. Because this room was his ring, and I was an unworthy opponent.

I shifted in the chair. Hands clasped in front of me. Focusing on my breathing.

In. Out.

In. Out.

Lo was waiting for me at the house, determined to ride this thing out. But I knew when I walked out of here, nothing would be the same. Even though we'd made promises, even though Lo looked me in the eyes and told me she wouldn't let him come between us, we both knew the truth.

And it killed me.

After what felt like an eternity, my father finally leaned back in his chair and studied me. "I need you to do something for me."

And there it was. No small talk. No lead in. Just straight to the point.

"I'm listening." The words came out strangled as I pictured Lo's face. Her eyes. Soft lips begging to be kissed. Smooth skin begging to be touched.

"Negotiations with Gavin Holloway are back on the table. Turns out, he needs me as much as I need him. But he's playing hard to get. Needs a little something to sweeten the deal."

My pulse thumped against my skull as the room zeroed in around me.

I couldn't think... Speak... I couldn't see past the red haze filling my vision.

"Maverick?"

"No," the word flew from my mouth before I could stop it.

"No?" He tilted his head with a raised eyebrow. "You don't even know what I need from you, yet."

But I did.

There was only one thing Gavin Holloway wanted, and that was to make his daughter—the rotten apple of his eye—happy.

Smug satisfaction flickered over my father's face as he watched everything fall into place in front of my eyes. "Miss Holloway is a nice girl, Son. Good stock. She'd make you very ha—"

"Anything but that." I stuttered. But he had me right where he wanted me. Thanks to my mother's mistakes I was in an impossible situation. With a heavy sigh, I added, "Please."

"Don't beg, Son. It's unbecoming for a Prince."

My skin bristled, my blood boiling in my veins.

A Prince.

That's what I was.

A Prince.

His son.

I couldn't escape the name bestowed on me even if it meant sacrificing the one good thing in my life. The *only* good thing right now. Because even though Lo was strong, she wouldn't survive this. She wouldn't just sit by and watch as I played puppet for my father.

"I have it on good authority you and the Stone girl, Louise was it, are dating?"

"Eloise." I bared my teeth. "Her name is Eloise."

"It doesn't matter. This doesn't concern her. And I'm sure she understands your *relationship* is finite. Soon you'll be off to college; you'll have more important things to think about than your high school girlfriend waiting for you. The world is your oyster, Maverick. If you embrace everything that I am offering you that is."

The glint in his eye told me my father knew he had me

l. a. cotton

in the palm of his hand. It was the one thing he always bet on—my loyalty to Mom. To protecting my family.

"What exactly do you need me to do?"

"You know how much Miss Holloway has always loved accompanying her father to business functions. An astute young woman, indeed. But it would look so much better to have a Prince on her arm, don't you think? To present a united front to investors. To give Gavin the nudge he needs to make the right decision."

"No dates outside of business. No pretending we're together. We are not together." Each word cracked my heart wide open until it was a gaping bloody hole in my chest.

"Maverick, be reasonable. I need Mr. Holloway to believe you're at least open to the idea of making his only daughter happy."

"She wants me? This is how she gets me. I'm with Lo. I love Lo."

He scoffed as if the idea was ridiculous. "Love, what do you know of love? You're eighteen. You have your whole life ahead of you."

My fingers slid over the edge of the chair, biting into the leather.

"As soon as the formal offer from East Bay arrives, you will accept. You will accompany Miss Holloway as and when required." He paused, his eyes narrowing into slits. I could do this. There were three and a half months left until graduation. All I needed was to sit tight, retake the SAT, and go with Caitlin to a few business functions.

I could do it.

For Mom. For Macey. For Stone and Associates.

For Lo.

If it meant a future with Lo—one that included Steinbeck and basketball—I could do it.

"Fine."

My father's mouth twisted into an ugly smile. "Good.

I'll see to it that Gavin knows we are on the same page."

With nothing else to say to him, I stood up and moved for the door, but he wasn't done.

That was my third mistake.

"And Maverick," his voice was smooth. Too. Fucking. Smooth. I turned slowly, my eyes sliding to his. "I assume I can trust you to do the right thing where Miss Stone is concerned?"

It wasn't a question, and I held his gaze for another second before storming out of his office and slamming the door behind me. The sound echoed off the walls, vibrating deep in my chest.

"Alec, what on earth? Oh, Maverick, I didn't realize you were here." My father's wife Maxine peeked around one of the doors, tucking bottle blonde hair behind her ear. "Is everything okay?"

My eyes bore into hers as I tried to rein in my anger.

In. Out.

In. Out.

"Maverick?" she crooned when I didn't answer. But I had nothing. Nothing she wanted to hear. So I kept walking, right past her and out of the house.

His house.

His kingdom.

The kingdom that, in the end, would suck my soul dry.

~

The letters started to blur together. Dancing on the screen. Jumbling in front of my eyes. And what should have taken me seconds to read, took a few minutes to make sense.

Lo: How did it go?

Lo: Where are you?

Lo: Maverick, please

It didn't happen often with text, but the pounding in my skull didn't help. My cell bleeped again, and I almost didn't want to read it because deep down, I was waiting for her to realize.

To realize I wasn't worth it.

But it wasn't Lo and for a moment, I could breathe again.

Kyle: What the fuck happened?

Of course, she went to Kyle.

Kyle: If I have to drag your sorry ass out of that ring again, so help me God...

Squeezing my eyes shut, I counted down from ten, inhaling a long breath before I opened them again. Slowly, my vision cleared, and I re-read each text before replying to Kyle.

Maverick: I'm fine. I just need time.

Kyle: And what should I tell Lo?

I tipped my head back feeling the sea breeze lick my skin. After leaving my father's, I'd wanted to go straight to the warehouse. I craved it: the pain, the burst of adrenaline, but I'd promised her. And even if it was the only promise I could keep, I would. So I drove to the Bay and parked up. Now I was sat on the hood of my car, watching the waves roll to shore. It was peaceful. Calm. Nothing like the storm raging inside me.

Maverick: I don't know. Just buy me some time.

Please.

Kyle: One hour. I'll give you one hour and then I will hunt you down and beat your sorry ass myself.

A faint smile tugged at my lips. Kyle might have been Wicked Bay's best running back, but he couldn't take me. I just needed to catch my breath. To steel myself for the next few months. It didn't surprise me he wanted me to end things with Lo, but I had no intention of walking away.

Not now.

Not ever.

This thing could ruin us. It probably would; but at least I'd know it wasn't because I walked away.

A couple down by the sea caught my eye. The guy hugged the girl to his chest, his arms wrapped around her waist, head tucked onto her shoulder as they watched the sunset. And jealousy struck me. Right in the heart. The one still in tatters at my father's demands. My gaze moved past them, over to the spot where I'd first met Lo. She was different back then. Innocent. Warm. Young. She tried to hide her nerves that night, but I noticed the way her pulse raced when I reached out, brushing the hair from her face. How her fingers trembled against mine as I kissed her. It was obvious she'd never been touched. It's why after watching her fall apart around my fingers, I stole one more kiss and left. Because I'd wanted more.

I'd wanted so much more with her.

It didn't make sense. She was a stranger. And I was angry, confused and high on the adrenaline cursing through my veins. But something about her calmed me, anchored me. And I wanted more … I wanted to lose myself in her.

It felt like a dream now. She wasn't the same girl and

fuck knows, I wasn't the same guy. But the pull between us was still there, and it was stronger than ever. My pocket vibrated yanking me back to the present, and I slid my phone out, letting my eyes pore over every word.

Lo: Whatever happened we'll get through it. I'm here, Maverick. I'm right here.

She said that now. But she didn't know that when I went back to her, I'd drive a wedge between us so deep that I was sure all the promises in the world wouldn't hold us together.

~

The second I walked into the pool house, I saw it. The visible sag of her shoulders. The relief as it washed over her features. Lo had expected me to come back hurt. Or worse, she hadn't expected me to come back at all.

And it stung. That she didn't believe I could change, that I'd break my promise not to fight again. But I didn't blame her. How could I when I was about to deliver the blow that would change everything?

"Thank God," she breathed out as she came over, drinking me in. Big eyes sliding over my face and down to my knuckles.

"I'm sorry."

Lo pressed against me, burying her face into my chest and my arms went around her waist. Time and time again, people told me how much it had affected her seeing me after my last fight, but she was so strong, it was easy to forget.

Easy to pretend it never happened, that she hadn't seen me at my worst.

I allowed myself a minute, to soak her up and imprint the feel of her in my arms. It couldn't last. As soon as the words left my mouth, whatever was growing between us would be tainted. Overshadowed by my father's demands.

"I was worried," her voice was muffled, and I curved one hand around her neck, dropping a kiss on her head.

"I'm fine."

Lo eased away, staring up at me. "What happened?"

"He knows… about us."

The color drained from her face, but my strong brave girl rolled back her shoulders, standing a little taller. "We knew he'd find out. It doesn't change anything."

"There's more…" I swallowed over the lump in my throat and Lo's eyes went flat. She was already pulling away. She might not have meant it, but I felt it.

I was losing her.

And I hadn't even told her everything yet.

"Go on," she said coolly.

"He wants me to smooth things over with Caitlin."

Lo shucked out of my arms and inched back. "No. No way."

"Lo." I stepped forward, reaching for her, the shredded pieces of my heart in my mouth.

"No, Maverick. No. Anything but that. Anything but her." Tears filled her eyes. "He can't…" The words died on her lips. Because she knew the truth.

He could.

And he had.

"I'm sorry." I dragged my hand over my head and clutched the back of my neck. Whenever I felt out of control, unable to rein in my emotions, I fought. But I made a promise and as much as I wanted to step into that ring and feel the sting of some faceless guy's fist against my bones, I wanted Lo more. So I pushed it down. Forced all of the bad shit, the rage and the explosive energy in my chest away. It didn't disappear. It lived in me. Under the surface. Simmering in my veins. But I had control.

With Lo in my corner, I didn't have to succumb to it

anymore.

"I told him it's strictly business."

It didn't matter; we both knew that. Caitlin would use the situation to her advantage, find ways to force me to spend time with her.

"If she so much as touches you..." Fire burned in Lo's eyes, but I was stuck on the part where she said, *'if she touches you'.*

"You mean..." No. It was too much to ask of her. To expect her to stand on the sidelines while I played happy families with Caitlin and her father.

Lo's gaze hardened. "I mean it, Maverick. If she so much as touches you, I won't be held responsible for my actions." Her whole body trembled, and I went to her, pulling her into my arms. There was so much I wanted to say but I couldn't find the words. Lo's fingers twisted into my t-shirt and I closed my eyes letting myself pretend for a little while longer.

Chapter Twenty

Lo

Maverick took me for milkshakes. After dropping the latest bombshell, he'd kissed me and insisted we go out. One last night of normal. I couldn't refuse his wicked smirk even if his eyes told a different story. He was worried this would push me too far. I saw it every time he looked at me, felt it every time his fingers grazed my skin. He thought this was it.

The end.

But I meant what I'd said. Nothing would come between us—not even Alec Prince and Caitlin Holloway. So, for much as my blood boiled at even the thought of her breathing the same air as him, I would survive. For Maverick. Because no one had ever stood up for him before. No one ever put him first. He was always protecting others, shouldering a burden that shouldn't have been his to carry.

"What?" he nudged my foot under the table and I blinked over at him.

"Just thinking."

"Sounds dangerous." He studied me, dark stormy eyes

searching my face for answers.

I slurped on my strawberry shake, holding his gaze. "I'm plotting all the ways I can kill her."

Maverick slammed his fist to his chest, spluttering and gasping for breath. "Jesus, Lo."

My shoulders shrugged as I spun the straw in the glass. "I mean it. If she touches you…"

"Lo, come on," he lowered his voice, leaning forward. "You can trust me."

"It's not you I'm worried about."

"One night. I thought we agreed one night before the shit hits the fan?"

"I'm fine."

"You sound fine," he shot back, his brows pinched together.

"I want you to promise me something. If she tries anything, you'll tell me. No secrets, Maverick. You don't need to protect me from the truth. I can handle it."

His hand slid across the Formica table and encased mine. "I love you. *You*, Lo. This doesn't change anything. It's a means to an end. A game we have to play."

I felt his words. The conviction in his voice. But when I parted my lips to tell him, the words died. Again. When I did say them, I didn't want them to feel like goodbye. I wanted them to feel like forever.

Head tilted to one side, I forced a smile. "I suppose there'll be rules we have to stick to?"

Maverick dragged his hand over his face. "Do we really have to do this now? I can think of better things to be doing." Hunger flashed in his inky depths, a direct line to my stomach.

"There you are," a voice said, and we both looked over at the door. I sighed, the connection between us broken, for now. Frustration vibrated from Maverick as Kyle and Laurie made their way over to us.

"Do I even want to know how you found us?"

Kyle tried to look offended, but his lips tugged up in a smile. "I have my ways."

"I told him you probably didn't want to be interrupted," Laurie added as she slid in beside me.

"Is everything okay?" Kyle arched his eyebrow at me as he sat down, and I pressed my lips into a flat line, giving him a small shake of my head. He twisted around to Maverick and silently questioned him.

"Okay, why do I feel like I'm the only one not a part of this conversation?" Laurie let out a strained laugh.

"It's nothing." I bumped her with my shoulder. "We already ate but we can hang out for a while."

"I need food, I'm starving because someone,"—she grabbed a menu and thrust it in Kyle's direction—"kept me waiting, to watch the hockey game."

"Babe, it was an important game."

"Whatever," she grumbled, dropping her eyes to the menu. "Like it isn't enough I already have to compete with football. Ooh, the chicken burger sounds so good."

Kyle and Maverick continued their silent conversation while Laurie scanned the menu. In some ways, their arrival was a welcomed distraction. But it was only delaying the inevitable, the moment Maverick laid down new rules for our relationship. Alec Prince had inserted himself between us. Just as Maverick said he would. And he'd brought Caitlin Holloway along for the ride.

"Lo?"

"Huh." I blinked at Laurie who stared at me with a strange expression on her face.

"Seriously, I was talking to you for like two minutes. Are you sure you're okay?

"Fine, I'm—"

"Tell them."

Our heads snapped up to Maverick's. "Wh-what?" I choked out, unsure if I heard him right.

"They should know. It's okay." He nodded. "Tell them."

"I—"

"Will someone please tell us what the hell is going on?"

I looked at Maverick, a million thoughts running through my mind. He was usually so closed off. So untouchable.

"I saw my father today." Silence descended over our booth and I glanced around, relieved we'd chosen one tucked away at the back of the diner. There was no one else close by. No ears wagging in our direction. When I looked at Maverick again, his eyes were fixed on me. He was about to tell Kyle and Laurie one thing, but he was telling me another.

He loved me.

He hated this.

And he wanted to make sure I was okay.

~

"Hey, how are you holding up?" Laurie dropped into the chair beside me. After Maverick filled her and Kyle in on his conversation with his father, we'd headed back to her house.

"Okay, I guess."

"I can't..." she hesitated. "I mean, I knew he was a piece of work, but this is... wow. I'm speechless."

"You must never tell anyone, Laurie."

Maverick had skirted over the things she didn't need to know—things no one needed to know about his toxic relationship with his father—but it made things easier if she knew just enough for me to not have to keep evading her questions.

"I wouldn't, I swear."

With a nod, I tipped my head back and stared up at the blanket of stars. Her garden was peaceful. The twinkle of the fairy lights and moonlight shimmering on the water cast the whole place in a soft silver hue. The boys were somewhere in the house, drinking beer, doing boy things. I'd wanted some air. Some time to stop and catch a breath.

"He would never hurt you, Lo. You know that, right?"

"I know." And I did. But it didn't mean I wouldn't get hurt.

"He's completely in love with you. I mean, I didn't really see it before. He's usually so closed off. But something's changed. I saw it that night we played Monopoly in the pool house. The way he watched you." There was a sadness to her voice I didn't understand.

"Laurie?" I met her eyes. "What's going on?"

"Nothing. I'm fine. Besides, we're not talking about me, we're talking about you."

Silence settled between us. I watched the stars. Laurie was lost in her own thoughts. After a few minutes, she shuffled. "What will you do, Lo?"

"Whatever he needs me to."

"You haven't told him yet, have you?"

"Told him what?" I followed her line of sight to where Maverick and Kyle were, in the kitchen.

"That you love him too."

"No."

"Why not?"

"I don't know."

"Liar." She laughed quietly as we watched them—our boyfriends. They were so different. Light and dark. Fun and serious. But they were also similar. Loyal. Protective. Infuriating at times.

"Do you think about what will happen after Maverick graduates?"

"Not really." We'd barely survived the last few weeks. Summer seemed like a lifetime away. "Why, do you?"

"Do I think about what will happen when Maverick

graduates? Not really." She smiled around her words and I leaned over and batted her arm.

"Laurie."

"Kyle wants to play football, obviously. And he will. He'll get a scholarship and go off to college and do amazing things with his life."

"And what about you Laurie Davison? What's in your future?"

She groaned, kicking long legs out in front of her. "Honestly? I haven't got a clue."

"Well, that's okay, isn't it?" I didn't know either. Between the accident, the move, and Maverick, there wasn't much time for thinking about the future. About what I wanted to do with my life.

"Yeah, but don't you ever worry you'll get left behind?"

I sat forward and twisted to face her. "Where is this all coming from? Did something happen betwe—"

"No, no." Panic flooded her face. "I just, oh, I don't know. Ignore me. It's nothing. I'm just feeling the pressure, that's all."

"Kyle loves you, Laurie. Whatever his future looks like, you're in it."

A faint smile tugged at her lips just as Kyle and Maverick joined us. He tugged her up and slid onto the seat, pulling her down with him and nuzzling her neck. If Laurie had doubts, they were wrong. Kyle loved her.

"Hey." Maverick loomed over me and offered me his hand. "Ready to leave?"

Nodding, I let him pull me up. "We'll see you tomorrow." The word stuck in my throat as he wrapped his arms around my waist and leaned down to capture my lips.

Tomorrow, tomorrow, tomorrow.

I wanted to freeze time. To stay in this moment forever. Because I knew when tomorrow rolled around, things would change.

Again.

~

"Kyle's here," Dad's voice filtered down the hallway as I dragged a hairbrush through my hair ignoring the sting of hurt in my stomach.

'Kyle's here', he'd said, not 'Maverick's here'.

I knew he wouldn't be. What Alec Prince demanded, Alec Prince got. And he wanted Maverick to 'cool things' with me so he could sweeten up Gavin Holloway. I should have seen it coming after Caitlin collared me at school. She was too smug not to know something was about to go down. But I was too focused on how to help Maverick, I didn't even stop to consider *this*.

"Lo, he's waiting."

"Coming, Dad. I'm coming." I grabbed my bag, hoisted it over my shoulder and headed out. Dad was in the kitchen, sipping his coffee, poring over a stack of papers. Did he know? About Alec's ties to the company? His easy smile suggested he didn't. But before moving to Wicked Bay, I'd never once saw the hint of another woman in his eyes either. And, although the thought bothered me, I realised my father was also a master at keeping secrets.

"Everything okay?"

"Sure, Dad."

"Breakfast on the go." He flicked his head to the banana and carton of juice and I smiled.

"Thanks."

"I'll be—"

"Late. Got it," I called as I reached the front door. "I won't wait up."

Outside, Kyle's Jeep taunted me, but I stuffed it down. I'd promised Maverick. Promised myself, I could do this.

"Hey." I climbed inside and buckled up.

"This is bullshit, you know that, right?"

"Kyle." A heavy sigh slipped from my lips. "What choice does he have?"

"I don't know, but this is bullshit." He slammed his hand down on the wheel, the crack of skin against rubber reverberating around us. "I can't believe Rebecca and my dad are okay with this."

"It's a mess."

"It's bullshit."

"You already said that."

"No jokes, Cous. Not right now."

He'd played it cool in front of Laurie last night. We both had. It made life easier for Kyle and me now she knew the basics, but we'd still have to keep some things from her.

We rode to school in heavy silence. I didn't like seeing Kyle so uptight and brooding. It didn't suit him. Usually a ray of sunshine, today he was all storm clouds and thunder. But when the Jeep turned into the school parking lot and my gaze landed on Maverick with his friends, my mood darkened too.

"Hey." Kyle cut the engine and turned to me. "Remember, this is just a game, Cous. It isn't real. The two of you, that's real. What goes on out there,"—he flicked his head to the window—"doesn't matter. Okay?"

I gulped, dragging my eyes from Maverick to my cousin. "Just don't let me do something stupid, like kill her in cold blood."

"Deal." His frown morphed into an amused smile.

We climbed out and made our way toward school as kids watched. Their stares and whispers chased me, nipping at my heels, but I kept my head held high. Only today I wasn't envied, I was pitied. Because I just became the girl cast aside by Maverick Prince.

His eyes followed me. But I didn't look. Caitlin stared at me across the lawn, victory glittering in her eyes, but I didn't take the bait. Instead, I carried on walking. Talking to Kyle as if nothing was different. As if everything was exactly the same. Because he was right.

I knew the truth.

And that's all that mattered.

Chapter Twenty-One

Maverick

"Fuck, I missed you." I pulled Lo closer, tracing my tongue down her neck, sucking and biting, feeling my dick stir to life.

"Maverick, we're supposed to be studying." She pressed her hand into my chest shoving hard.

"Spoilsport." I slipped my arm around her waist and hugged Lo closer, breathing her in, refusing to let her go.

Two weeks of stolen glances and sneaking around sucked. Watching the guys at school watch her, working up the courage to ask her out. I'd lasted a couple of days before I shut it down. Just because they thought I wasn't with her anymore, didn't mean she wasn't still mine.

And no one touched what belonged to a Prince.

Maybe it was a jerk move—getting the guys to spread the word she was off limits—but if it meant I wouldn't get arrested for beating the shit out of my classmates every time they so much as looked in Lo's direction, it was worth it.

"Come on, the SAT is in two weeks." Lo slipped out of my grasp and made a beeline for the desk. I flopped down on my bed, plotting ways to get her over here. But when her eyes met mine, bright with determination, I sat up, grumbling under my breath.

True to her word, Lo had stuck by me. Playing by the rules. In public, at school and games and parties, we were back to being step-cousins. Family. But behind closed doors, nothing had changed. Well, nothing except Lo's insistence I study for the SAT.

"Fine," I huffed. "Let's study. But you know I work so much better with positive reinforcement."

"You do, huh?" Her lips curved in amusement and I pouted, letting my eyes run down the length of her body. A body I knew almost as well as my own.

"Maverick," she snapped. "Eyes up here, buddy."

"Buddy?" My brows shot up, and she chuckled. Smooth and easy, her laugh was one of my favorite sounds lately.

"Okay." Lo leaned forward. "How about for every ten questions you answer, you get a kiss?"

"Just a kiss?" I tilted my head, swiping my thumb across my bottom lip, a move I knew drove Lo crazy. A move I knew would have her begging for me.

"Maverick." Her voice was breathy, the skin along her neck blushed. I inched closer until my lips were hovering close to hers.

"You were saying?" It came out low, husky, and Lo swallowed, her eyes glazed with desire.

"I... hmm..."

My lips barely touched hers before I tore away and threw myself back on the bed, unable to stop the rumble of laughter in my chest. Lo sighed, throwing me a stern glare. "Not funny, Prince."

"I thought it was pretty funny."

"Ten questions. Now."

"Yes, boss."

We worked in easy silence, used to the routine now.

Lo knew short sessions were better for me before the words blurred together and the letters became muddled. My girl had slaved away familiarizing herself with the SAT and the types of questions they asked. She'd even asked Miss Tamson for some old papers. Lo went above and beyond. But she didn't need to. Just her being here, believing in me, was all I needed. Between the two of them and Coach Callahan's regular words of encouragement, even I began to believe I could do it.

Forty-minutes later, I was done. "That's it." I threw the pen down and shoved the stack of papers away from me rubbing my temples trying to ease the dull ache. "I can't do anymore. It doesn't make sense."

"Yes, it does," Lo's voice was soft. We'd been here before, more than once. "You're just tired. You need a break."

"No, I need you."

"Maverick."

"Come on, Lo. We've been at this every day for the last two weeks. You know I can't work at your pace."

"No." She placed down her textbook and strode over to the bed. Then she was climbing over me, straddling my legs. I slid my hands up her thighs but Lo snagged my hands, holding them in place. "You can do this. If you need a break, take a break. If you need some help, ask. But don't quit, Maverick. You're a Prince, and Princes' don't quit."

"You sound like him."

She flashed me a harsh glare, and I used her irritation to my advantage, slipping out of her hold and running my hands up the curves of her waist.

"Okay, we take a break. Just a quick one." Lo leaned down, ghosting her lips over mine and I groaned. Fuck, she tasted good. Like vanilla and strawberries. I moved to deepen the kiss, but she hovered out of reach, smiling down at me.

"My dad and Stella are going out of town at the weekend, I thought you could stay over. If you wanted?"

I went rigid at Lo's words. I'd been trying to find a way to tell her, but things were good between us. I didn't want to rock the boat. And I was a coward. Worried about what this would do to her.

To us.

"Maverick?" She searched my eyes. "What is it?"

"I, hmm, shit this isn't how I wanted to do this."

"Do what?" Her body recoiled, the small action burning through me.

"My father called a couple of days ago. There's this thing this weekend..." I swallowed, forcing myself to maintain eye contact despite the words almost choking me.

"Thing? What thing?"

"A business thing. With Gavin Holloway..."

Lo went still, her eyes boring into mine. We were close, our bodies touching, but I felt the distance grow between us. "When were you going to tell me?"

"Lo, it's not li—" She was gone. Off the bed and out of the room. I heard the bathroom door slam, the sound vibrating deep inside my chest. My head sank back into the pillows.

Fuck.

I hated this. Hated that the one person I wanted to break free from still held so much power over me. Over my relationship with Lo. *'A means to an end'*, I'd called it, but part of me wondered if it would be the end of us. Because if our roles were reversed, I would have lost my shit at the very idea of Lo rocking up to some business dinner with another guy. I wouldn't have been able to stand it: the jealousy, the soul crushing pain at the idea of someone else even breathing the same air as her. Yet, here I was, asking her to do the one thing I knew would push me over the edge if it were me in her shoes.

I was a selfish bastard.

The worst kind.

Lo deserved more. She deserved better than me. Better than my father's games.

Scrubbing a hand over my face, I let out a frustrated groan before pushing off the bed and going to the bathroom. Greeted with the door, I tested the handle. It clicked open, and I slipped inside. Lo met my eyes in the mirror but she didn't speak. She didn't need to. Anger rolled off her in ferocious waves. But I was willing to brave the storm if it meant touching her. Soaking up her comfort. Reassuring her that she was the only person I wanted. Now. Tomorrow. And all the days after that.

Eyes locked on hers, I approached slowly until I was right behind her. Lo's hands were braced on the counter, knuckles white with frustration. I reached for her, ghosting my hand up her spine, brushing her hair off her shoulder to reveal smooth skin. Her eyes fluttered shut, but I said, "Look at me, London."

Surprise flared in her gaze. She hated when I called her that, but I could handle feisty Lo. I could handle the girl who had given me a run for my money during her first few weeks in Wicked Bay. I could handle the push and pull between us.

I couldn't handle *this*.

Pressing closer, I wrapped my other arm around her waist pulling her flush against me. Soft and hard. Rough and smooth. "I was going to tell you, I promise," I whispered into the curve of Lo's neck, and her pulse fluttered wildly while my fingers glided down between the valley of her tits. Heat flashed in my stomach and I pressed harder, showing her what she did to me.

Lo fought back a soft moan. "I thought I could do it," she choked. "I thought I could be okay with this, but now I'm not sure…"

I spun her around and slammed my lips down ending the conversation, sliding my hands down to her thighs and lifting her onto the edge of the counter.

This was all I needed. Her. Us. Desperate kisses and shallow breaths.

As long as I had this, I could walk on water. I could do whatever my father demanded. Because my future was only worth fighting for if Lo was in it.

I couldn't lose her.

Not over him.

Not over this.

"I love you," I said between needy kisses. "I love you, I love you."

She had to know. She had to feel it. To sense it.

Silence met my words but Lo didn't pull away either. She kissed me harder, her fingers digging into my shoulders. How things had reversed. Four months ago, she'd been the one desperate for my touch, but now I couldn't get enough. I'd bled out in front of her, literally, and she still couldn't say the words I needed to hear.

I dragged my hand down her body, pressing and kneading until I reached the juncture of her thighs. Breaking the kiss, I stared at her. Cheeks flushed. Eyes half-mast. Lo watched me as I pressed the heel of my palm against her warmth.

"Oh God," she panted.

"Only you, Lo," I reminded her as if I was the one in control. As if I held her heart in the palm of my hand. But I didn't.

She owned me.

Every broken fucked up little piece.

Her eyes told me what I needed to know. She felt it too. She just couldn't say it. Something was holding her back and for as much as it stung, I wanted her to protect herself. To keep those words locked away until this shitstorm blew over. Until she knew, without doubt, that I was in. All in. Because the idea of hurting her, of breaking her heart, killed me. And I knew it wouldn't only be her in tatters.

I wouldn't survive it either.

"Kiss me," she whispered.

And I did. Deep and slow, exploring her mouth with my tongue. I would have climbed inside her if I could have. My fingers dug into her ass, dragging her closer to me until her legs were wrapped around my waist.

"Too many clothes." She swallowed my words as I lifted her off the counter and set her down on the floor, my hands wasting no time undressing her.

Her hoodie went first. Then her t-shirt. My jersey was next. Jeans. Until there was a pile of clothes at our feet and nothing separating us but our underwear.

"You look a little bit dirty," I said raking my eyes down her body at the inches upon inches of smooth milky skin.

"I do, huh?"

My hungry gaze landed on Lo's wide-eyes and I smirked. "Oh yeah. I think we need to get you cleaned up." I took her hand and pulled her toward the shower.

"Maverick, we're supposed to be studying."

"Shower. Then study." I reached in and turned on the jets. We hadn't done this yet. But now I'd thought of it, I couldn't unthink it. Lo. Wet and soapy. Skin on skin. Her pressed up against the tiles while I—

Her hand glided over my junk and I almost came right there. "Jesus, Lo," I hissed, and she giggled. We made quick work of stripping off the rest of our clothes and then we were stumbling into the shower unwilling to come up for air.

I chased the water over her body with my fingers, my tongue, while my fingers slid between her legs, warm and wet and tight. Fuck. This was going to be over quicker than I planned if she kept up her whimpers and moans.

"Maverick... Maverick... Rick..." Lo chanted. Over and over. As I explored every inch of her. "I need..." Her teeth dragged over her lip.

"What? What do you need?" I lowered my face to hers, crowding her against the tiles, cupping her jaw as the water rained down on us.

Lo's eyes flickered open. Heavy with lust. Glittering with what I wanted to believe was love. "You, I need..." I hooked my fingers inside her, rubbing my thumb over her clit, slamming my lips to hers, swallowing the string of moans. Her whole body coiled tight as she clung to me, and I knew she was close.

"Hold tight," I whispered into her ear as I withdrew my fingers and hitched Lo's legs around my waist, pressing her back against the wall. Her arms wound around my neck while I worked to get us in position and then I eased inside of her, slowly, inch by inch until I could feel nothing but her. Think nothing but her.

Her.

Her.

Her.

Chapter Twenty-Two

Lo

"Is it true?" Laurie dropped down beside me as I picked at my salad.

"Is what true?"

She leaned in close, whispering, "That Maverick is taking Caitlin to some party tomorrow?"

I went back to my lunch, pushing the green wilted leaves around my plate.

"Lo." Her elbow nudged my side.

"What?" I snapped, my wide gaze meeting hers. "What do you want me to say?"

"I—" The colour drained from her face. "Crap, I'm sorry. I just heard some girls talking in the bathroom and I…"

"You what?"

"I shouldn't have said anything, sorry."

"Ugh. It's fine." My eyes flicked over to Caitlin and her friends. "I just…" The words died on my lips leaving a sour taste on my tongue. "I don't want to know. So, whatever you hear, whatever you might see, I don't want to know. Got it?"

"And you're okay with that? I mean, if it were me, and

I had to watch Kyle with some other girl." She shuddered, the reality of her words hanging between us.

"It's better this way." After Maverick pulled me into the shower and made love to me, I asked him to promise we'd leave her at the door. I didn't want to talk about her… them. I didn't want to know the details. Did he place his hand on the small of her back? Did he pick her up from her house?

I wanted to know nothing.

Not unless she tried to make a move and then I wouldn't be held responsible for my actions. Even though I knew it would eat away at me like a slow poison infiltrating my veins, I knew how he felt about me. I knew he loved me. That's what I would focus on.

Him.

Me.

Us.

Laurie slurped her juice and tipped the cup in my direction. "You're a stronger girl than me, Lo. He's lucky to have you."

Lips pressed together, I gave her a small nod of appreciation.

"Okay." She placed the cup down and grinned, a sparkle of mischief in her eyes. "We should go out Saturday. Keep your mind off things."

"I don't know."

"You really want to stay home and obsess over what they're doing?"

No. I didn't.

God, I didn't.

"Okay, I'm in."

A squeal of excitement slipped from her lips. "This is perfect. Girl's night. I'll text Autumn and we can make plans."

"Nothing too crazy, Laurie." The last thing I needed

was to be faced with temptation. It wouldn't end well.

But then my gaze landed on Caitlin again and a flash of white hot jealousy burned through me. My fingers curled around the edge of the chair, biting against the plastic. As if she felt me watching, her eyes slid to mine, and her lips curved in a smug smile.

"Lo, what's wro— Oh. Maybe you should…"

The buzz of anger drowned out my friend's voice. Caitlin knew what she was doing. She thought this lame attempt at getting her claws back into Maverick was going to work. But she'd underestimated one thing.

Me.

~

"All good, Cous?" Kyle slung his arm over my shoulder and yelled over the music. I nodded, taking another sip of beer. Girls night had turned into a party at one of Kyle's teammates. Although the football season was officially over, the guys still trained together. Partied together. Caused general mayhem in the hallways at school.

"You know he's only doing this because he has to, right?" Kyle's voice dropped an octave as he leaned in close. "He would never—"

I slammed my hand against his chest and said, "Stop. I'm fine. Okay? Everything is fine."

His eyes said he didn't believe me, but he gave me an easy smile before warning me to behave. Kyle slipped away, disappearing into the crowd of people.

"Was that my boyfriend?" Laurie said coming up beside me.

"Yeah. You haven't seen him yet?"

"I'll see him later, he knows the rule on girls' night." She linked her arm through mine and steered me over to Autumn and a couple of other girls from our class. I found it an odd thing to say given girls' night had never stopped Kyle from stealing Laurie away before.

I listened to their conversation. What boys were here. Who was hooking up with who. Who wanted to hook up with who. I smiled in the right places and added my two cents here and there, but my mind was elsewhere. Specifically, the business dinner at The Coastal, an upmarket hotel and restaurant downtown. True to our words, I hadn't asked Maverick anything about tonight, and he'd offered nothing. But I overheard Dad talking on the phone with Stella about it when he thought I wasn't listening. He'd been more than suspicious when I told him we'd cooled things off. But he didn't push. He never pushed. Probably scared of tipping me over the deep end again.

"Oh, I love this one," one of the girls—Amber, I think—shrieked with delight. "Come on, let's dance."

They started moving toward the reception room where a DJ was set up. But Laurie paused when she realised I wasn't following. "Lo?" she said over her shoulder.

"Go, I'll be right there. I need to find the bathroom first."

"You sure?"

"Yeah, go."

"Okay, but come straight back. It's down the hall, last door on the left."

I gave her a weak smile, downed the rest of my beer, and went in search of the bathroom. A couple of boys smiled at me as I passed them. It happened more often since everyone thought Maverick had cast me aside. But I didn't use my name to win any popularity contests at school. I kept my head down, worked hard in class, and stayed out of the spotlight.

And for the most part, it worked.

But I was still a mystery. An enigma. And I'd been Maverick's girlfriend—if only for a brief moment in time.

It gave girls an excuse to hate me and boys a reason to want me. Outside the bathroom, I gripped the handle and pushed just as the door swung open and I stumbled straight into someone.

"Shit, sorry." I steadied myself only to be met with a deep scowl. "Macey?"

"Really, Lo? Could you be any lamer?"

"Whatever, are you done? I need to pee."

She went to move and then paused, a strange expression crossing her face. "What's Maverick doing, Lo?"

My brows knitted together. It was the last thing I expected to come from her mouth. "Excuse me?" I choked out only to be met with a heavy sigh.

"I know he's up to something. He's with her tonight, isn't he? Caitlin? She's been telling everyone who'll listen that they're back together."

I stared at her, pushing down the flare of anger in my stomach, unsure of what she wanted. She'd barely spoken two words to me since Christmas. And even fewer before then.

"Fine. I get it. I've been a bitch. Don't take it personally. It's not you, it's everyone."

Okay then.

"And yeah, maybe I didn't like that he wanted you. That he pushed me out, for you. That's how I know he's up to something. Maverick has never acted the way he does with you. Never. And he hates Caitlin."

"Maybe you should ask him," I said, still in shock we were having this conversation.

"I've tried, but he shut me out. It's because of him, isn't it?"

She didn't need to explain, I knew exactly who she was referring to. "I really think you should talk to Mave—" But Macey cut me off.

"Don't let him do this, Lo. I know my brother and I

know he probably thinks he's doing what needs to be done, but you can't play by his rules and win. No one can."

"I…"

Macey was gone leaving me standing there, gaping after her. I closed the door and turned the lock. Bracing my hands on the ceramic sink, I drew in a couple of deep breaths. Macey was jealous. Summer and Kyle told me as much, and in a strange way, I got it. Until I arrived on the scene, it had been her and Maverick. The two of them against the rest of the world. But the desperation in her voice had thrown me for a loop.

When I was done, I rinsed my hands and steeled myself for whatever was on the other side of the door, but when I yanked it open and saw Devon standing there, I felt like I was stuck in the middle of a nightmare.

"Hey." He dragged a hand through his shaggy hair.

"I'm done, it's all yours." I went to move around him. It was our game lately. I dodged him in the hallways at school. He sat away from me in the couple of classes we shared.

"Lo, wait," he called after me and maybe it was the beer or my run in with Macey or the unspoken apology in his eyes every time I looked at him, but this time I didn't walk away. I turned around and released a deep sigh. "Yeah?"

"I—" he hesitated clearly stunned that I was still standing here. "Sorry, I'm sorry. I really screwed up."

"Yeah, you did."

"I just, shit, this isn't easy, and it's kind of loud." He glanced around. It was quieter down this end of the house, but the thump of the music still reverberated off the walls. "Can we go somewhere and talk?"

"I don't think so, Devon."

"Right, sorry."

"Laurie told me you stuck up for me, with Caitlin?"

"Yeah, hmm, I…"

"Thanks, I appreciate it." I smiled, and it wasn't forced or strained. Because I was grateful. He'd hurt me, sure. But I suspected it was more about getting the girl and hurting Maverick. I'd been collateral damage, caught in the crossfire.

"See you around, Devon."

His mouth opened to reply, but I spun on my heels and this time, I did walk away. But I felt lighter somehow. Things would never be the same between us but maybe, one day, we could be friends again.

~

"Fuck, how much did she drink?" Kyle eyed the drunk girl beside me, his brows knitted together.

"Don't look at me," I said. "I didn't force her to drink all those jello shots. Is everything okay with you two? She seemed… I don't know. On a mission to get wasted." The more I thought about it, Laurie had been acting weird for a while.

Kyle grumbled something under his breath as he manoeuvred the Jeep out of the line of cars parked alongside the house.

"Kyle, what's going on?" Laurie hiccupped before snuggling in closer and I smoothed her hair out of my face. "This is me, if something's wrong—"

"Nothing's wrong. I'm taking heat from Coach about my college applications and there's all this stuff with you and…" his voice trailed off.

"Whoa, don't blame me for you acting like a dick."

"I'll take care of it." His eyes flickered to the lifeless girl pressed against me.

"Hurt her and I'll kick your arse."

His smooth chuckle filled the Jeep. "Like you could take me."

I raised an eyebrow and stuck my tongue out at him

just as we pulled up outside my house. Untangling Laurie from my arms, I laid her against the window.

"You'll be okay getting her home?"

"Yeah, it's a good thing her mom and dad are away again."

"I'll text you tomorrow." I went to push open the door when his voice gave me pause.

"Lo, this shit with Mave—never mind." My eyes followed whatever it was that had caught his eye. Maverick stood outside my door, hands shoved deep in his pockets. He looked so handsome in the dark jeans and shirt. It reminded me of Winter Formal. But then I remembered where he'd been, why he was dressed like that and all my lust fuelled thoughts fell away.

"Will you be okay?" I barely heard Kyle's question over the thud of my pulse in my ears.

"Yeah. I'll text you tomorrow." Warm air brushed my skin as I climbed out, doing little to calm my racing heart. Relief and anger swirled together, rushing through my veins, stealing my breath as I walked up the driveway to my house.

To Maverick.

"Hey," he said rocking on the balls of his feet, eyes planted firmly on the ground.

"Hi." I dug out my key and slid it into the lock. It clicked open, but I didn't push the door. "What are you doing here?"

He gaze snapped to mine, and he gave me a look that said 'Really, Lo', but I didn't take the bait, waiting for him to explain himself. "I just needed to see you, but I can go?" Uncertainty lingered in his voice, touching a place deep inside of me.

"Stay," I whispered. "You can stay."

Because despite my anger. The pain carved in my chest. I couldn't tell him no.

I never could.

Chapter Twenty-Three

Maverick

The second we stepped inside Lo's house and the door clicked shut behind us, it was like I could finally breathe. Hooking an arm around her, I pulled Lo back into my chest, nuzzling her neck. "I missed you." My voice muffled in her hair.

She smelled of smoke and beer.

She smelled like a party.

"You were out?" I said, and she stilled.

"You didn't know?"

"Kyle texted and said you were okay, that's all."

"We went to the football team's party. It was Laurie's idea." Her voice was flat, and I turned her in my arms, taking in her torn expression.

"What's wrong?"

Her brow raised, lips drawn into a thin line.

"Okay, dumb question. But I'm here now, and your dad's not." And I needed her. Fuck, did I need her.

Three hours mixing with my father's business associates, playing in his world. I needed to erase it all. Not to mention the lingering stench of Caitlin's perfume.

Her fake smiles and high-pitched laughter that set my hair on end.

"I need a drink." Lo shirked out of my hold and stormed down the hallway with a slight sway. I dragged a hand down my face with a groan. I'd wondered what I would find when I showed up here. All night, I'd played over the possible scenarios in my head. Would she run into my arms, relieved to have me back in one piece, or slam the door in my face?

I guess we were somewhere in the middle.

And it would have to do. Because being here was better than being there: playing the puppet, letting him pull my strings. Adrenaline rushed through me, the familiar spike of anger looking for a way out. I craned my neck from side to side, trying to work out the kinks. Trying to push down the storm.

Three deep breaths and I moved down the hallway after Lo. She could run but she couldn't hide. The second I stepped in the kitchen, my eyes found her, drinking in the sight of her clutching the glass like it was her life supply.

"Say the word and I'll tell you everything," I said. "I'll give you the whole play-by-play if it'll make you feel better."

"Don't." Her eyes shuttered as she let out a shaky breath.

I wanted to touch her. God, did I want to touch her, to reach out and make her see there was only her.

Only ever her.

"London," I growled, and her eyes widened, flashing with contempt.

"Fuck you." A mask slammed down over her face, but it wouldn't keep me out.

Nothing would keep me out.

"You can shout at me." I walked toward her slowly. "Call me all the names under the sun. Hit me. Hurt me."

Lo moved back, keeping distance between us, but I was quicker. My body almost slammed into hers, sending the water splashing over the rim of the glass. I crowded her against the counter, staring down at her. "You can hate me and wish you never got messed up in my fucked-up life. I'll take it. I'll take it all. But you can't leave me, Lo. You promised."

Her eyes glazed over and soft full lips parted on a soft sigh. "I hate this," she whispered. "I hate imagining her with you."

I lowered my face until my mouth was hovering over hers. "So don't. Imagine me. Us. Imagine me kissing you. Holding you. Imagine me inside of you. Loving you."

She swallowed, the sound piercing the thick silence, and she swayed again. Lo was drunk. Maybe not wasted, but she'd been drinking and like a pussy, part of me hoped it was the reason for her acting like this.

But deep down, I knew it wasn't.

"When your mind goes there, imagine this." My hand slid along her neck, burying itself in her hair. "Me. Standing here, telling you how much I love you. Showing you how much I love you." A shudder ripped through her and I leaned in licking a trail from her collarbone to the soft skin underneath her ear. "Only you, Lo."

I wanted nothing more than to scoop her up and carry her caveman style to the bedroom. But I was exhausted and Lo looked ready to collapse. So I took the glass from her and placed it on the counter, slipped my hand into hers and guided us down the hallway to the bedroom. Then I stripped the clothes from her body and helped her into bed.

"Stay with me?" She pulled the covers up around her body and I moved closer, reaching down to brush the stray hairs from her face.

"Not tonight. You need sleep and if I stay we both

know that won't happen."

Lo pouted, her bottom lip begging to be kissed. But I resisted, stuffing down all my desires and needs and said, "Good night, Lo."

She was asleep before I got to the door.

~

I should have gone straight home. When Selina's text came through, I should have told her I was sorry. That I couldn't babysit her brother.

But I didn't.

I was too wired. Leaving Lo was the right thing to do. She was angry, tired and a little bit drunk; throw sex into the mix and I knew things could turn sour. But now I had all this pent-up energy and nowhere to use it. So when the text came through, I got in my car and drove.

The warehouse loomed in the distance, lit up by a couple of floodlights. Cars lined the perimeter. And as I drew nearer, the beast inside me stirred. It had been almost a month since I last fought. My bruises were healed. The pain barely noticeable anymore. But I missed it. Fuck, did I miss the sting. The jarring bite of agony. The adrenaline pumping through my veins.

The high.

But I'd made a promise, and I had no intentions of breaking it. But just because I'd promised not to step in the ring, didn't mean I couldn't watch. Like an addict stalking a bottle of vodka or a junkie lingering in a stoner's smoke. Just one taste.

One. More. Taste.

The second I entered the place, my blood sizzled. It was busy. The crowd already fired up and thirsty for blood. I'd grabbed my spare hoodie out of the trunk and slipped it over my body, leaving the hood up. But a couple of guys noticed me, tipping their heads in respect. I cut through them, positioning myself as near to the ring as possible. Two guys were going at it, fists smacking.

Heads cracking. Bone crunching.

Thirst exploded in my chest and heat flashed through me, forming beads of sweat across my forehead. I wanted in. I wanted to make it stop. To rain my fists down on some faceless opponent, imagining it was *him*.

"Prince?" Someone yelled over the noise and I turned to see Dex bouncing on his feet, shoulders pitching to the side with each crack coming from the ring. He looked as wired as I felt. A junkie itching for their next hit.

"Hey, man," I said lifting my chin before fixing my hardened gaze back on the ring.

"Didn't expect to see you here." He moved closer. "I thought you were done after what went down last time."

"I am done," I ground out.

"Looks like it, man." He slapped me on the back and I bristled, folding my arms over my chest. He laughed, deep and coarse, and it only fueled my agitation. When he noticed my worsening mood, he laughed.

"Easy, Prince. I'm just pushing your buttons. I don't blame you for stepping away. Wish I could sometimes, but we both know it's not going to happen." Realization flashed in his eyes. "Wait, did Selina... of course she fucking did. She needs to learn when to—"

"She's worried."

He puffed out his chest. "Yeah, well she doesn't need to be. I've got this, man."

One of the guys went down and the room exploded. The crowd jostled, shoving us forward, but when they caught a glimpse of Dex's blue-tinged mohawk they backed off, mumbling apologies.

"Listen, I got to go get ready. Stick around, we'll catch a drink afterward." He scratched his jaw.

I opened my mouth to tell him to be careful, to watch his back. To remember he had Selina to think about. But he was too far gone, and no fighter wanted to hear those words seconds before a match. So I gave him a tight nod and watched as he slipped into the crowd.

Dex was a live-wire, carrying a darkness not even I could comprehend. He'd lost his girlfriend. The person he loved. If anything ever happened to Lo… I couldn't even go there. It was a place I wouldn't return from. Bobby and the security guys hauled the lifeless guy off the cold ground and dragged him to the back room. *She saw you like that*, my conscience whispered. Only I'd been worse. Blood everywhere. Eyes swollen shut. Barely conscious. And Lo hadn't run, she'd stuck by me. Visited me every day while I healed.

The thought gutted me. Punched me in the chest, sucking the air clean from my lungs. She'd been standing right here, watching as I destroyed myself. And she was still here. Without a second thought, I turned around, slid my phone out of my pocket and melted into the sea of bodies. As I texted Selina, I ignored my name being called. Ignored the flashes of recognition on guys faces. I ignored it all. I was done. I didn't need this anymore. I had the one thing I needed.

The *only* thing I needed.

And I was going to fight whatever bullshit my father or Caitlin or JB threw at me because she was worth it.

Lo was worth every agonizing second.

~

"I enjoyed the other night."

I slammed my locker, glaring down at Caitlin. "You're in the way. Move."

"Come on, Maverick, do you need to be so grumpy? It was fun, wasn't it? Just like old times." She trailed her finger up my arm and I snatched it away, glancing around the hallway. Caitlin mumbled something under her breath, rolling her eyes. "Don't worry, she isn't here. I saw her walking to class with Devon."

"Lio—" I slammed my lips shut. She was baiting me,

and I was falling for it. "Move, Caitlin, before I make you move."

"Is it wrong I like the sound of that?" she purred like a strangled cat. It was no doubt supposed to sound sexy and seductive, instead it grated on me like nails against a blackboard. Everything about her rubbed me the wrong way. And I hated that I'd ever allowed myself to be manipulated into a relationship with her. Hated that she knew my most intimate parts, my secrets.

"Look, this thing, you and me, it's business. Nothing more. The sooner you accept that, the better."

Anger flashed in her eyes but then it was gone, a smug smile tugging at her lips. "There's a gala this weekend. Daddy got us tickets."

My fist clenched, and I inhaled deeply before I did something stupid. Something I couldn't take back. "Fine."

"Pick me up at seven?"

"Whatever. I need to go." I shouldered past her and ducked down the hallway. When I rounded the corner, Kyle saw me and came straight over.

"What happened?"

"Caitlin."

"Shit."

"Yeah, shit. Listen, I can't do this here. Too many ears. Was she—" The words died on my tongue. Of course she wasn't okay. She'd been distant yesterday when she'd come over to study. She played a good game. Her kisses felt the same, her touch, even the way she pushed and challenged me. But I knew her better, and I knew she wasn't there with me. Not really.

Lo was pushing me out. She was letting them win.

"I'm worried about her." Kyle's mouth down-turned at the corners.

"I know. Me too. Just keep an eye on her, okay?"

He nodded, and I saw he wanted to say more. But he knew as much as I did, I had no choice but to see this thing through until the end. It was the only way to put shit with my father behind me once and for all.

"You know I will." He held my stare saying everything I needed to hear.

"I have to go see Coach. Text me later."

"Consider it done." Kyle clapped me on the back and then he was gone.

As I made my way out of the building and to the gym, Caitlin's words played in my head. I knew she was lying. Lions had tried more than once to talk to Lo and every time she'd brushed him off. It burned that she hadn't told me herself, but I got it. She didn't want to run to me every time something happened. But lucky for me, I had eyes and ears everywhere and not much got past me.

Not where Lo was concerned.

Chapter Twenty-Four

Lo

Another week passed. Another weekend of waiting around, trying not to imagine what they were doing. It was slowly killing me. But I couldn't tell Maverick that. He needed me to be strong, to get through this. So I did. I spent hours at the pool house studying with him, poring over past test questions. At least by the time I came to sit my own SAT, I'd be more than prepared. But it was little consolation for the constant ache in my heart. The burning jealousy I felt every time I saw Caitlin around school.

She played up to it, of course. Spreading rumours she and Maverick were back together but taking things slow. Every time I heard a whisper in the hallway or girls talking in the bathroom, another little piece of me died.

"Lo, earth to Lo," Laurie nudged me, and I blinked at her.

"Huh?"

"I said, come on, we don't want to miss anything." She slipped her arm through mine and guided us through the gathering crowds to our seats. My stomach knotted tightly as my eyes found Maverick as he stretched with his teammates. It was his first full game since the fight. Coach let him play two quarters in the last game, but he struggled. We all saw it. But he looked strong today as he flexed his arms above his head and out to his sides. My eyes followed the lines of his muscle. Smooth and sculpted.

"You have a little drool." Laurie mocked, and I cast her a sideways snarl. She chuckled but then her smile slipped. "Ugh. Bitch alert."

The cheerleaders ran out onto the court. Caitlin stood front and center. Her skirt too short and her top too tight and her smile too fucking smug. I groaned.

"He hasn't even looked in her direction. You have nothing to—Oh, shit."

Anger ignited in my stomach as I watched Caitlin bounce over to the boys as they warmed up. "If she even thinks about tou—" My hand flew to Laurie's, crushing it in my fingers as Caitlin got right in Maverick's face, cunning and victory oozing from her.

"She wouldn't dare," Laurie choked. "He wouldn't…"

Everything slowed.

Slowly.

Slow.

Slo—

Time stopped.

It was like watching a car crash happen in front of your eyes and being unable to stop it. She went up on her tiptoes, pressing herself against him, her lips inches away from his face.

"Prince, get over here," Coach Callahan boomed, and Maverick brushed past Caitlin sending a bolt of relief through me.

"She was going to do it, she was going to ki—"

"Laurie," I hissed aware of all the people around us.

"Anyway, where's Kyle? He's late."

Her brows knitted together. "You tell me. He said he'd meet us here," she said, her voice bitter.

It wasn't the first time I'd noticed it, and I wanted to push. To find out what was going on, but it was awkward. She was my best friend and Kyle was family. I didn't want to end up between them. Not when I needed them both.

"I'm here, if you need to talk." I held her conflicted gaze, letting her know she could come to me. That whenever she was ready, I'd be here.

"I'm fine. Everything's fine," she replied a little too quickly.

Music blared through the speakers and the cheerleaders got into formation for their opening act, but my eyes were focused on the huddle of players in red and white. Maverick stood out. Dark hair mussed over his eyes as he listened to Coach Callahan bark out orders, tapping the clipboard in his hands.

"So, explain it again." I turned to Laurie. "They have to win their next three games to go to the regional finals and then win those games to play in the State Championship?"

She nodded, a broad smile on her face. "Last year, they made it to the regionals but lost out to Roosevelt."

"Right, got it, I think."

"Just pray they win. Anything less and Maverick's shot at taking home a Championship before graduation is dust."

"Win, right," I mumbled, my eyes searching him out again. The teams were moving into position and Maverick faced off against a giant.

Laurie shoulder checked me. "It'll be fine and then tonight, we'll celebrate. You are still coming to the party, aren't you?"

"I—"

"Lo, you have to come. I know it's hard right now," she lowered her voice. "But he'd want you there. He needs you there."

I swallowed the reply on the tip of my tongue, pressing my lips together. Laurie rolled her eyes at me, but the whistle blew and Maverick leapt off the ground swinging his arm for the ball.

And everything else melted away.

~

"And where the hell were you?" Laurie slammed her hands into Kyle's chest and he staggered back, throwing his hands up to avoid another onslaught.

"I got held up, I'm sorry."

"Held up? You missed Maverick's first game back..." Laurie launched into a verbal assault and I studied Kyle. His brows were pinched together. Shoulders tight. He was hiding something alright. But I'd have to wait to ask.

"We missed you," I added, making a beeline for his Jeep.

"I got here as fast as I could. They won?"

"If you'd have shown up, you'd know," Laurie snapped, storming off with her arms across her chest.

"I guess I deserve that." He fell into step beside me.

"I don't want to pry, Kyle, but is everything okay?"

"Cous,"—he slung his arm over my shoulder guiding me to the door—"everything is peachy keen."

"Peachy keen? Who says that?"

"Me. I say it. Got a problem with that?" He smirked, the usual mischievous glint back in his eye.

"You're insufferable."

"I think the word you're looking for is awesome. I'm awesome."

We clambered into the Jeep, Laurie up front and me in the back. Kyle turned up the radio, drowning out his girlfriend's voice as she went on about how he'd stood her up, let his stepbrother down. Whatever was going on with the two of them, I hoped it passed soon.

My phone vibrated, and I dug it out of my pocket.

Maverick: I'll find you later. Wait for me.

Lo: What if I don't want to be found?

Maverick: Later...

A shiver passed through me. But then I remembered Caitlin and her little stunt on court. I didn't doubt it was because she knew I'd be in the audience. Because she wanted to rub it in my face. Maverick hadn't evaded her, but he hadn't encouraged her either. He'd just played his part. Indifferent. Unaffected.

With me he wasn't like that. He was warm and tactile, and he let me in. Maverick let me see the boy no one else got to. And I had to remember that.

Every time Caitlin tried to break me, I had to remember that.

~

Trey's house was on the beach, but it was smaller than Brendon Palmer's. Less glitzy. I liked it. Kids streamed in and out, drinking from red cups; the buzz of the team's win crackling in the air. But there was something about being here, with the basketball team, that settled my nerves. They were Maverick's friends. His teammates. And although Maverick hadn't said anything to me, I had a sneaky suspicion they knew enough to be allies. I'd caught Luke and Aaron watching me more than once. Their gazes following me around school, the knowing look Luke sent me whenever our eyes met. And while part of me, the part used to looking out for myself, wanted to be annoyed at Maverick's overprotectiveness, the other part kind of liked it.

"Are you ready to forgive me?" Kyle pouted at Laurie, looping his arm around her waist. "Or should I go find the guys and get wasted?"

"Jerk." She batted at his chest but soon melted into his touch and I grumbled, "Guess I'll go find a drink."

"Lo, wait," Laurie's voice was drowned out by Kyle's mouth.

"Give us ten minutes and we'll find you."

"Whatever," I called back as I entered the house.

"Autumn, thank Go—Oh."

Her face blanched as I realised she was with Liam… and Devon. "Hmm, hi, Lo."

"We'll go get drinks, babe. Hey, Lo." Liam tipped his head and then yanked a sheepish Devon off down the hallway.

"I am so sorry," Autumn rushed out as soon as they were gone. "Liam's been going on and on about Devon. I felt bad for him and before I knew it we were here. Together. Do you hate me?"

"It's cool." I shrugged.

"Are you sure because when Laurie finds out—"

"Don't worry about Laurie." Something told me she had enough of her own crap to deal with.

"So, we're good?"

I smiled. "We're fine. Come on, I need a drink." I really needed three… or four… or a bottle of vodka, but I wouldn't. Because I was sensible Lo now, and I didn't let myself give in to the cravings.

We found the boys in a big open plan kitchen. Liam handed Autumn a drink, and she eyed it suspiciously.

"It's just beer. There's a keg, see?" He flicked his head over to the counter. "Lo, you want?"

I nodded, and he disappeared. When he returned, he gave me a cup. "Thanks," I said trying to avoid looking at Devon. It was weird. Since the party the other week, I'd hardly seen him at school, either that or he was avoiding me.

"There you are," Kyle's voice floated over to us and my eyes rolled. Awkward just elevated to downright uncomfortable.

"Kyle." Warning hung in my voice as I shot him a terse glare.

"Hey, guys," Laurie seemed unaffected by the tension as she moved around us to get a drink. But Kyle didn't follow. He stepped up beside me, eyes fixed on Devon. I elbowed him in the ribs and he spluttered.

"Be nice," I hissed.

"Me?" he mouthed.

"Maybe I should go," Devon said. "I'll catch up with you later." He shared a look with Liam and then was gone, disappearing out of the back door.

"Stay here." I thrust my cup at Kyle and went after him.

"Devon, wait up," I called after him as he cut across the yard and down the path leading to the beach. "Devon, come on."

I don't know why it was so important to me that he stop—why I even went after him in the first place—but here I was, jogging in his direction.

"Dev—"

He swung around, his shoulders sagging with defeat. "What, Lo?"

"I—"

"You should go back inside." He flicked his head to the house behind me. Music drifted down to us, floating on the warm sea air.

"I wanted to make sure you were okay."

"Me?" He quirked up his eyebrow. "I'm fine."

People were saying that a lot lately. Devon. Laurie. Kyle.

Me.

But it was a lie. He wasn't fine. And neither were my cousin and best friend. And I was so far from fine it was a joke. Maybe that's why I followed him. Maybe that's why I was standing here, pleading with him to give me the truth. Because I was tired of the games and secrets. Of keeping up pretences.

"Devon, please."

"Fuck, Lo. What do you want from me?"

My gaze dropped to the sand beneath his feet.

"Just go back inside."

"I'm sorry," the words poured out.

"Sorry? What could you possibly have to be sorry for?" He dragged a hand down his face as I peeked up at him.

"I don't know." I shrugged. "It just felt like the right thing to say."

"You know what I did... with Caitlin. I never wanted to hurt you Lo. She can be pretty convincing when she wants to be, and I wanted to hurt Prince and—"

"You wanted her back."

"Yeah, pathetic, I know."

My lips curved with a strained smiled. "You can't help who you love, Devon."

Understanding passed over his rugged face. "What about you? It can't be easy since—"

"That is a conversation for another day."

"I am sorry, Lo. For everything, I know I fucked things up between us." Something caught his eye over my shoulder and a wall slammed down over his face. "I need to get out of here, I shouldn't have come. See you around, Lo."

"Bye." I watched him go, calling out at the last second, "And Devon, don't be a stranger."

Surprised flashed in his eyes and then he was gone., swallowed by the inky night. I turned to make my way back to the house and saw the reason for his sudden change of mood. Caitlin and her friends stood at the edge of Trey's garden, laughing and joking. Completely oblivious to the pain she caused—continued to cause. She was toxic. An infectious disease that plagued thoughts and got under your skin. Anger speared through me. I was so sick of her bullshit. Her smug smirk every time her eyes collided with mine across the hallway at school.

Head held high, shoulders back, I walked right past them. They didn't notice me, too wrapped up in their own lives. I wanted nothing more than to do *something*. Something to knock her down a peg or two. But I couldn't. I had to play the game, to let her think she'd won.

And it killed me.

I went back into the house and found the bathroom. I just needed a minute, to collect my thoughts, to calm my racing pulse. When I stepped back into the hallway I didn't see Caitlin before it was too late. Her shoulder collided with mine, sending pain ricocheting through my bone and I staggered back.

"What the f—"

"You're pathetic," she hissed, her eyes wild and set right on me. "Maybe I should give you a list of all my exes since sloppy seconds seems to be your style." Caitlin stepped closer, taking the air between us with her. Out of the corner of my eye I could see we were alone in the quiet hallway at the back of the house. "It's no surprise he came crawling back. I mean, why would he want a fake when he can have the real thing? We're supposed to be together and not you or anybody else will get in the way of that."

I smashed my lips together, scared of what might come out and she snarled, "Well?" She tilted her head, staring at me. "Don't you have anything to say?"

"You're a bitch," slipped from my lips before I could stop myself.

"That's all you have?" She raised an eyebrow, amusement dancing in her eyes.

"Caitlin," a deep voice said, and her gaze snapped over to the shadows crawling along the wall.

"JB, what are you doing here?"

"Making sure you don't do anything you'll regret." His voice was low, and I felt his eyes on me as he entered our space, but I didn't look.

I daren't.

"Oh, come on, we're just having a chat. Girl's time, right, Lo?"

She leaned in closer, smirking around her words. Peppermint breath danced over my face and I balked. But I still couldn't move. I wouldn't give her the satisfaction.

"I'll think of you like this, all sad and pathetic, when Maverick fucks me tonight." Her voice was low, only for my ears. And my fists clenched at my sides, but I couldn't stop the sharp intake of breath at her words.

Her lies.

Because Maverick would never—he wouldn't. He hated Caitlin almost as much as I did. But he had been there before, and she did know his body the way I did. And the thought made me sick to my stomach.

"Caitlin," JB growled and her head snapped to his again and I did something I never expected.

I ran.

Slipping past Caitlin, I ran until I spilled out into the yard and didn't stop until I was secreted away alongside the double garage adjoining the house. The crushing sensation in my chest made it hard to breathe, and I knew I needed to get out of here.

From her.

From JB.

From these games and lies.

Before *I* did something I would regret.

I started toward the gate, my hand clutching my phone ready to call a taxi, but before I could dial, a hand grabbed mine pulling me further into the darkness. "Got you."

My heart thumped against my chest as I found myself lost in Maverick's assessing gaze. "You scared the shit out of me," I breathed, trying to play it cool. But it was too late. His eyes searched my face.

"What's wrong? What happened?"

"I'm not doing this," I sighed tearing my face away from him, a storm of emotion sweeping through me.

"You're angry; did something happen? Did someone say something?"

I schooled my expression, trying to ignore Caitlin's words on replay in my head.

When he fucks me later.

When he fucks me.

Fucks me...

"Lo, you need to start talking." Maverick reached for me, but I dodged his hand, confusion and irritation swirling in his hard eyes. But I knew if he touched me, if he so much as grazed my skin, I'd crumble.

And I couldn't crumble. Not here. Not now.

"I'm tired," I whispered over the lump in my throat. "I just want to go home."

"Don't go, please. I've been waiting all day to do this." He leaned down, capturing my lips before I could escape, stealing the air from my lungs and all thoughts of Caitlin from my mind. My hand slipped to his jersey, twisting into the lightweight material, pulling him closer.

And just like that I came undone.

"She tried to kiss you," I whispered into his mouth as my tongue tangled with his, needy and desperate, swallowing the words I really wanted to say.

Did you fuck her?
Did you?
Did you?
Did you?

"Never," he replied, his hands on my waist. My shoulders. In my hair.

God, I wanted him. I wanted to shove Caitlin and her games out of my mind and lose myself in him. To reassure myself that it was me he wanted. Not her.

Never her.

But her words taunted me, refusing to stop flashing through my mind.

"Stop," I panted, the words almost painful to say. "We need to stop."

"No," he ground out biting my bottom lip, tugging it gently, chasing the sting with his tongue.

I summoned enough willpower to break away. Maverick groaned, running a brisk hand through his shower-damp hair. "Let's go back to the pool house." Lust and love danced in his eyes, and my body, my heart, screamed at me to say yes. To sneak off with him under darkness. But I was the strong one.

I had to be the strong one.

"You know we can't. They came to party with you, to celebrate with you. You should go."

His fingers slipped into the loop of my jeans, tugging me closer. "Don't do this. I need you."

Even if Caitlin hadn't planted the seed of doubt, my answer would have been the same. We couldn't get sloppy now. Not with so much hanging in the balance. But she had... and I couldn't unhear her words. And it was like a wall between us.

"Go," I whispered again unable to meet his gaze. But he didn't move. He didn't even flinch. "Fine. If you can't do the right thing, I will."

And I walked away, telling myself it was because I

wouldn't let Maverick ruin his life—his future—for me. And absolutely nothing to do with Caitlin.

Chapter Twenty-Five

Maverick

We stepped into the building and the whole place erupted. Trey and Aaron lapped it up; the cheers, the attention. But I wasn't in the mood. It had been two long assed weeks. Four games in nine days, not to mention the SAT, and our regional game over the weekend had been brutal. We'd trailed for the first three quarters, only to pull back a lucky couple of shots in the fourth. My brain was Jell-O and every muscle in my body ached, the burn deep and relentless.

But it was more than that.

It was Lo.

She was buried so fucking deep, and I'd hardly laid eyes on her since Trey's party. Since the night she walked away from me. Sure, she was there when it mattered—to wish me luck before the SAT and again, before the team left for our game at Long Beach State—but she wasn't present. She didn't brush her fingers against mine to reassure us both that we were okay, and her eyes didn't sparkle their usual fire. The distance between us felt more than ever and I didn't know how to fix it.

A couple of guys pounced on me, desperate for details of the game, but I hooked an arm around Luke's neck dragging him into the conversation, creating a buffer. A diversion so I could slip away and head to my locker. But I hadn't made it ten steps when someone stepped in front of me.

"I'm trying to figure out what your game is." JB eyed me suspiciously and my spine straightened. Everyone was gathered around the team, listening to Trey relive the moment I sank the ball to take us to the State Championship. It had been a long time coming and, if we won, would be the highlight of my career so far.

And I wanted it.

Fuck, did I want it.

The need to win coursed through me. But with this shit with my dad and Caitlin and the hard-eyed guy standing in front of me... I wanted it to stop.

The pressure...

The expectation...

The responsibility.

I wanted one second to catch my breath, and I knew the only person who could make that happen was the one person I couldn't run to. Not yet, at least.

"If you have something to say, say it, or else get the fuck out of my way." I raised my brow, the thin thread of control inside me one sharp yank away from snapping.

JB stepped forward, putting us shoulder to shoulder and leaned down. "You think you're so slick, walking around the place like you can do no fucking wrong. I don't know what game you're playing but leave my sister out of it."

My lips mashed together, fists balled at my sides, as he shouldered past me, and I forced the simmering anger down, counting down from ten. On zero, I sucked in a sharp breath and kept on walking.

He didn't know.

He couldn't.

Yet, he knew *something*. In the end, we weren't that different, him and me. We both looked out for our own. Protected what was ours. But where Caitlin was concerned, he had no fucking clue. She was the one with the power in this situation. With her sharp claws and vicious smile. Caitlin was an actress, the best of her kind, and she had the men in her family wrapped around her little finger. And because I couldn't come clean and tell him the truth, I had to accept I was the bad guy in his eyes.

I probably always would be.

"There you are." Her voice sent me on high alert. *Not here. Not now.* I traded my books and closed my locker, turning slowly. "Caitlin."

"Congratulations, Rick. I didn't get to say it after the game. Or at the party."

Because I'd avoided her like the plague; slipping out unnoticed, I'd gone home.

"I guess this means we'll be travelling to Sacramento together over the weekend?"

"I'll be with the team, Caitlin. You know that." My eyes darted around her, praying Lo didn't choose this exact moment to walk into school.

"No, silly. I mean we'll be there. *Together.* A whole weekend away. We should—"

"Prince, where the hell did you get to?" Luke shot me a questioning look and relief washed over me. Caitlin immediately backed up at the arrival of the guys, eyes darting between us like a skittish animal. She knew the guys didn't like her much. Not after witnessing how she used her relationship with me last year to her advantage.

"I guess we'll talk later." Her lips tugged up in a suggestive smile and then she was gone, swallowed by the morning crowd.

I tipped my head back against the locker bank and let out a long breath.

"She's so hot for you, Pri—"

My eyes snapped to Trey's, and he swallowed whatever bullshit was about to come from his mouth. I knew how it looked to them. On the one hand, I had them looking out for Lo and on the other, I was spending time with Caitlin.

It didn't look good.

But it's all they were getting, all they could know, for now.

"Come on, class calls." Luke tipped his head in the direction we needed. But when I pushed off the lockers, my heart almost exploded out of my chest. Lo was there.

Right. Fucking. There.

I hadn't seen her across the hallway, shielded by a group of kids. But there she was. Eyes narrowed on me. On where Caitlin had stood only seconds earlier. And I knew she'd seen us.

Luke called my name again, and I grumbled, "Coming." But I couldn't take my eyes off her. I couldn't stop silently asking her to stay with me. To ride this thing out to the end. To make her see what she just witnessed meant nothing. That it was all part of the game.

A show.

Lo broke away first, and fuck, if it didn't hurt, and all I could do was watch as she caught up to Laurie and Autumn and disappeared around the corner.

I pulled out my cell phone.

Maverick: I love you.

I waited... and waited. But she didn't reply.

~

The week dragged. Each day the weight on my

shoulders seemed to intensify until I felt like I would crumple under the pressure. Like there was no way I'd be able to drag my sorry ass out of bed the next morning.

But I did.

I needed to do something. To feel like I was in control. Before Lo, I would have stepped into the ring. Expended all the energy flowing through me on beating some faceless guy into a bloody pulp.

"You have that look," Stone bounded into the kitchen and eyed me knowingly.

"What look?"

"The one where you're five seconds from doing something really fucking stupid."

"She's killing me." I dragged a hand down my face, scrubbing my jaw.

There. I'd said it.

My stepbrother paused, the cereal box mid-tilt. "She's killing you?" His eyebrows quirked up. "Well, now you know how she feels."

"Fuck you."

"Nice, real nice, Prince. Lash out at the one person who gives a shit whether the two of you make it through this or not."

"Through what?" Summer came into the room and when neither of us answered she glanced from him to me and back again. "Fine. Cut the youngest sibling out again. I'm so sick of your bullshit. First you call things off with Lo and now you're hanging around Caitlin again. Who are you right now?" She grabbed an apple and stormed out.

"When did baby sis get all grown up?" he said, craning his head around the door to watch Summer's disappearing form.

"It was bound to happen one day," I grumbled, trying to push her words out of my mind, and he laughed, spluttering a mouthful of Rice Krispies at me.

"You're a pig."

"But you love me." He flashed me a wide grin. "So, what's the plan?"

"Plan?"

"You're slow this morning, Prince. You'd better play better than this on Saturday or you'll be coming home a loser. And no one likes a loser." His eyebrows danced, and I wanted nothing more than to reach over and rip them from his face.

"I don't know." I rubbed my temples and then an idea hit me. "She should come."

Confusion flashed in his eyes. "Hmm, not quite what I meant."

"No, this is perfect. Lo should come to Sacramento. You'll all be there, and I need her there. It's the perfect cover and after the game we can hang out, just the two of us."

"The whole team, Caitlin, and her little dog too?"

Shit. He had a point. But it could work. We could steal some time together. Somehow. Someway.

"Rick, think this through, man. I know you mean well, but I don't know if that's going to work."

It would.

Because it had to.

"What will work?" Macey breezed into the room and the temperature dropped a few degrees. She was still freezing me out and it had only gotten worse since she asked me about Caitlin and I shut her out. But it was the only way to protect her—to keep her out of our father's claws. The less she knew, the better.

For everyone.

"Nothing you need to worry your pretty little head with, sis." Kyle grinned, but Macey's eyes narrowed with a look that would leave most guys shaking in their boots.

"Bite me, *bro*."

"Someone's delightful this morning," he mumbled,

shoving another spoonful of cereal into his mouth.

Macey leaned back against the counter. "Well, what do you expect when I have to live with you two?"

"Hmm, Mace." Kyle jabbed the spoon at her. "Rick kind of moved into the pool house or did you miss that memo?"

"Jerk."

"Bitch," he coughed.

Her hard eyes settled on me, daring me to intervene, but I didn't. "You," she hissed. "Ready to tell me the truth?"

I rolled my lips together and stared back at her.

"Fine. I'm out of here."

"Always a pleasure, Mace. Always a ple—"

"Stone," I barked, levelling him with the same look I'd just subjected Macey too. "She's just pissed at me."

"Because you're shutting her out."

It wasn't a question.

"It's for her own good."

"Yeah, yeah. Keep telling yourself that." He went back to his cereal and I let out a frustrated sigh.

I knew Macey would come around when she finally learned the truth. I only hoped it would all be worth it.

~

"Are you nervous?" Lo glanced up at me from the bed as I threw another jersey into my duffel bag.

I raised my eyebrow at her and smirked. "You have seen me play, right?"

She balled up her paper and launched it at me. I ducked, and it bounced off the wall behind me.

"You're so arrogant."

"And you're stubborn," I shot back. "Come. It's two nights, max. It's the biggest game of my career. I need you there."

"Maverick," she shifted onto her ass and crossed her legs in front of her. My eyes slid over her tank, the curve

222

of her chest and heat speared through me.

"You need to pack."

"I can do it later." I stalked toward her.

"No, you need to be at school in an hour."

"They'll wait." If Lo refused to come, I'd need something to get me by. Forty-eight hours without holding her, touching her... it would seem like a lifetime.

Lo scooched up the bed, pressing her back into the headboard. "I can't. I have a thing."

"A thing? You have a thing? Are you fucking kidding me?"

"Actually." She sat taller. "I'm not. Laurie is—"

"You're blowing me off for Laurie?"

Irritation flashed over her face and she rolled her eyes. "I am not blowing you off for anyone. But I don't find the idea of being there as Lo, your *cousin*, all that exciting."

Ouch.

"You wouldn't be there as only my—"

"Yes, I would. And it's okay, Maverick. It's just how it has to be for now, I get it. But don't ask me to do this... to be there... with her."

"Fine." I turned my back on her, giving myself a second. Unwilling to let her see my disappointment, the frustration pinching my brows. I got it, I did. And maybe it was unfair to ask her to do it. To come and be there in the crowd: watching me, supporting me. But this was the biggest game of my life and she wasn't going to be there.

She was *choosing* not to be there.

And despite my head knowing why, my heart had a real fucking hard time accepting it.

Chapter Twenty-Six

Lo

"Ugh. I can't believe it's almost summer." Laurie tilted her face into the sun's rays while I slid my sunglasses over my face blocking out the light.

"Things seem better, with you and Kyle?" I glanced over at her and she shrugged.

"I guess. He's more... present. But I think that's because he finally decided on a school."

"The University of Southern California, right?" I'd heard him talking to Uncle Gentry and Rebecca about it.

"Yeah. Coach Munford says he has a real shot and he's already on their scout's radar."

"And have you decided?"

Her shaky laughter filled our quiet corner of the lawn. "Miss Tamson said my grades are good enough for USC. But do I really want to follow my boyfriend to college?"

"And what does he say about this?"

"He wants me to go."

"That's good, right?"

"It is, but..."

From the torn expression on her face, I knew I was still missing something. "There's a but in this scenario?" I asked.

"Oh, I don't know." A sigh rolled off her lips. "I love Kyle. I look into my future and see blond haired babies running around in number thirteen jerseys. But we're young. How many high school sweethearts make it?"

I opened my mouth, but nothing came out. She was right. When she put it like that, it did sound… ambitious.

"No one's saying just because you go to USC your life is set in stone, Laurie."

"I know that. But what if I follow him to college and he realizes there's more to life?"

"More to life… you mean what if he realises he wants to sow his wild oats?"

"Bingo."

"Laurie, Kyle lov—"

"Loves me now. He loves me now, Lo. Who knows what he'll feel when he leaves for college. And I know he's been keeping something from me."

My head snapped up to hers. "You don't think he's been…" I couldn't even say the word; the idea was so un-Kyle.

"I found a text."

"What do you mean, you found a text?"

"I wasn't snooping or anything. He was taking a shower and his cell started going off, so I picked it up to take the call and I saw it."

"What did it say?"

"You can't ignore me forever."

"Was there a name?"

"It wasn't saved in his contacts." She grimaced.

"Did you ask him about it?"

"And start World War Three? No, I didn't ask him about it. It could be nothing…"

Or it could be something.

But another girl?

I didn't buy it.

"Besides, it's been too long to bring it up now," she added, hurt lingering in her voice.

"Kyle isn't cheating, Laurie."

"How can you be so sure?"

"Because I know him, and he wouldn't do that to you."

She twisted and looked at me with her big honest eyes. "But how well do we ever really know someone?"

Maverick flashed into my mind. There'd been a time when I didn't know him—not the real him. But he'd wanted me to believe the façade. Needed me to believe it.

"Lo?"

"Huh?" I blinked at my friend and she frowned.

"I said, how are things with Maverick and *all that*?"

"I—" I stared at her, the words stuck in my throat, wondering how I even begun to explain. Because I knew she wouldn't understand, she wouldn't get it.

And roles reversed, I probably wouldn't either.

"Sorry, that was a dumb thing to ask. I know it can't be easy. But we'll have a good weekend, you won't even know he's gone."

"You could have gone." I knew Kyle had asked her to go with him and my Uncle and Aunt.

"And miss out on all the fun we'll have?"

"Laurie," I sighed. It wasn't that I didn't appreciate her support. I did. But I didn't need babysitting. Maverick would only be gone for two nights.

Two nights with her.

My lips mashed together as I forced down the bitter words bubbling up my throat.

"Don't let your mind even go there." Laurie eyed me knowingly. "He would never—"

"I know." I had no reason to doubt Maverick.

None.

But Caitlin was a whole other story because her words,

her lies, had cut deep.

"Crap, what time is it? I said noticing Laurie's watch. "I need to go."

"Go? Go where?"

"I have an appointment with Miss Tamson."

"Ahh, the whole 'your future is bright speech'. Good luck with that." She smirked, and I flipped her off before grabbing my bag and heading back into school.

Her door was ajar, and I stuck my head into her room.

"Come in, Lo," Miss Tamson beckoned me inside.

"You wanted to talk to me about something?" I took a seat and she leaned back in her chair, her kind gaze assessing me.

"I heard Maverick pulled it off? You must be very proud."

"I am," I said.

He'd improved his score in the SAT and decided to be honest about his dyslexia in his application to Steinbeck, but he still hadn't heard from them.

"And how is everything else?"

I shrugged, unsure of what to say. Like Coach Callahan, she knew more than most because we'd needed her help. But she didn't know enough to fully understand.

"Lo, I'm not blind." She smiled warmly. "I see things, hear things. I won't pry. Whatever is going on with Maverick and Mr. Prince, well it's none of my business, but I wanted to check in with you. See how you're doing? None of this can be easy?"

"I—" My throat tightened. "I'm okay."

Her smile slipped. "You can talk to me, Lo. I'm not here to judge."

I picked at the hem of my t-shirt not really knowing where she was going with all of this.

"You've been here a while now and junior year is almost over. I know we agreed in our last meeting to wait until after the summer to think about college, but I've taken a look at your grades and I think the sooner you start thinking about your future, the better."

"I—" The colour drained from my face as my chest tightened.

"Lo?"

"I haven't really thought about it," I choked out.

"I expected as much. Which is why I pulled some information together for you." She leaned forward and slid a thick folder toward me.

"What is this?" I fingered the packet as if it was infected with a contagious disease.

"Some colleges you might want to take a look at. Mostly in-state, a couple further afield. Your teachers all report you have a natural flare for the Arts. Maybe that's something you could pursue?"

"I appreciate the help, Miss Tamson, I really do, but I haven't thought much about college yet."

Maybe I'd take a year out or get a job or volunteer. It wouldn't be the end of the world if I didn't start college straight after graduation. Besides, it was still fifteen months away.

"Can I ask you something?"

"I guess."

"What's stopping you?"

"Excuse me?" My eyebrows knitted together.

"You're a bright girl, Lo. You arrived in a new town, started a new high school, and applied yourself with little issue. Your grades are far above average for an international transfer student and your teachers have been more than impressed with your work ethic. Honestly, with your GPA and a good SAT score in the autumn you could have your pick of schools. So, I'll ask you again, what's stopping you?"

I stared at her, all kind eyes and warm smile. Miss Tamson was the kind of person you wanted to tell all your secrets to. Which worked in her favour since she was the school's guidance counsellor. But I didn't have the answers she was looking for.

Not right now.

Expectation lingered in her eyes, so I did the only thing I knew would get her off my back. "Thanks, I'll take a look." I clasped the packet to me and forced a smile. Her whole face lit up with victory. But I knew I wouldn't open it.

Not today.

I stood to leave, and she said, "We'll talk again soon."

When she'd want answers.

When I'd have to make decisions about my future.

Whether I wanted to or not.

~

"Do you wish you were there?" Laurie eyed me sideways before shovelling a handful of popcorn into her mouth.

"Yeah."

The guilt I felt from telling Maverick I wouldn't go to Sacramento was coiled so tightly around my heart it hurt. But I couldn't be there and pretend. It was too much to ask.

Too much to bear.

Her phone vibrated, and she snatched it off the table, colour flooding her cheeks as she read the text message.

"My annoying cousin by any chance?"

"I—hmm…"

"Laurie?"

Her face was bright red as she slipped her phone in her hoodie pocket.

"Who was that?"

"No one."

"Laurie," I warned, not liking where this was going.

"Fine." She flopped back into the big cushions. "It's

Jared."

"Jared? As in Devon's friend Jared?"

"Yeah. He keeps texting me."

"I…" My mouth snapped shut as I tried to process. "Let me get this straight, you've been worried about Kyle possibly cheating and you're texting another guy?"

"No. No!" Her voice went shrill. "It isn't like that. I would never…"

"Laurie, you better start talking. Now."

"He's always had a thing for me. You saw how he was that day at the beach last year. But he knows I love Kyle. He's only…"

"A dog?"

"Ugh. I don't know. Kyle has been acting so weird and Jared saw—"

"What? What did he see?"

"He saw us fighting at school. Kyle stormed off and I was upset. He came over and asked me if I was okay."

"You need to stay away from him, Laurie. You're playing a dangerous game."

Kyle might have been keeping things from her, but he wasn't cheating. He wouldn't. He didn't deserve… well, whatever this was.

"I would never cheat on Kyle, Lo. But Jared is…"

"A dog," I snapped.

"It's not like that." Her eyes bore into mine. "I promise. He's a… friend."

"And does Kyle know about your new *friend*?" I raised an eyebrow and Laurie dropped her head, telling me all I needed to know.

"That's not fair," she whispered. "You know how Kyle gets. Maverick's the same. It's suffocating sometimes. And he's shutting me out. Whatever's happening with him, he won't tell me. Jared cares. That's all."

Oh, I didn't doubt Jared cared—about getting in

Laurie's pants.

"Look, Laurie," I softened my voice. "I know he's acting weird. I know you're worried, but talk to him. Do you really want to make things worse by giving him reason to think you're going behind his back?"

"You're right. I know you're right. And despite what you might think, I haven't been leading Jared on. He knows I love Kyle. He knows I want to work things out with him. I'll tell him,"—she snatched her phone back out of her hoodie—"I'll tell him right now, I can't text him anymore."

"Good." I folded my arms across my chest and watched as she sent the message.

When she was done her voice squeaked, "You won't tell Kyle, right?"

"No," I said. "But I won't lie either. If he asks me, I'll tell him the truth."

"That's fair, I guess. Gosh, I don't know what's going on with me lately."

"I do." I nudged her with my shoulder. "You love him."

"Yeah." She let out a strangled laugh. "And it's driving me crazy."

"Hey, who said it was easy?"

"Oh, this is it." Laurie clapped her hands together focusing on the screen. "Here they come."

I watched, waiting to catch a glimpse of Maverick. Hoping to avoid seeing Caitlin. And my eyes slid sideways to my friend again. Maybe I'd been too harsh on her. She loved Kyle. She wouldn't stray. But she wasn't wrong.

Love was enough to drive you insane.

Chapter Twenty-Seven

Maverick

"This is it..." Coach Callahan started. The locker room was silent, all eyes trained on him. Our mentor. Our leader. "I want you to go out there and play with the heart and strength I know you have. Don't let them intimidate you. Don't let them make you think you don't belong here. You earned it. Every single one of you. Now come on, hands in."

One by one we joined the circle, the air humming with anticipation. Luke shot me a sly smirk as we put our hands in, shoulder-to-shoulder, teammate-to-teammate. This was it. Our final game. Our last shot at glory.

And I wasn't walking off that court until we were crowned victorious.

I could feel it in my veins. The thirst. The adrenaline. There was no other feeling like it.

None.

"Okay, Wreckers on three," Coach's voice rang out loud and clear and we all counted with him, our voices growing louder with every number until our hoots and hollers filled the room, reverberating off the lockers and benches, walls and ceiling.

"I think I'm going to puke," Trey announced, and Coach snapped, "Not on my watch, Berrick, out on the court in five."

The guys started filtering out of the room, but I rushed back to my bag and dug out my cell phone.

"Prince, do we have a problem?"

"No problem, Sir." I glanced over my shoulder. "I'll be right out."

Coach eyed the phone in my hand, readjusting his red and white ball cap. "Make it quick."

"Yes, Sir."

I slid my finger over the screen and breathed a sigh of relief when I saw her name.

Lo: I know I'm not there and I know you probably hate me right now, but you've got this, Maverick. I'm with Laurie watching the game live... I'm right there with you.

Energy thrummed through me as I texted her back.

Maverick: For real? You're watching?

Lo: I wouldn't miss it for the world

Undefined emotion swirled in my chest as my cell bleeped again with another incoming text

Lo: Go Wreckers

I threw my head back with laughter, and fuck, if it didn't feel good. I'd wanted Lo out there in the crowd, more than anything. But knowing she was watching was the next best thing. I slipped it back inside my bag and took a couple of deep breaths, centering myself and went after my team.

The noise was deafening, the lights blinding. The Golden 1 Centre was at capacity and my eyes searched for our supporters, the sea of red and white easy to spot against the wall of blue and white of our opponents.

"It's something else, huh?" Luke clapped me on the back as we made our way over to Coach and the rest of the team, adrenaline pumping through me. The cheer squads were already entertaining the crowds but none of that interested me. I was here for one reason and one reason only.

Because basketball was a part of who I was.

I'd always known I had a gift. From the second I picked up a ball, it felt natural; as easy as breathing. But I'd spent so long using the game as an escape to cover up my struggles in class that when I played, I played to prove a point. To show everyone I was good enough.

Good at *something*.

And it worked. People sat up and paid notice: at my performance, my records on the court. And I hid behind it. Since my father sat in that office and refused to acknowledge what my principal was saying, I used basketball to prove my worth.

But I didn't need to do that anymore. Because I wasn't a failure. My learning disability didn't define me, and it wasn't going to stop me going after what I wanted. Coach Callahan and Miss Tamson showed me that.

Lo showed me that.

And the future I wanted—the one I'd carved out for myself—was so close I could almost taste it.

~

"Prince, get over here." Coach Callahan motioned for me to join him and I squeezed Luke's shoulder leaving him to the celebrations. Things had gotten a little crazy after the final buzzer sounded and the locker room had definitely seen better days, but we were riding the high of victory.

"Yes, Coach?" I ran a hand through my damp hair.

"You did good out there, son, real damn good. I'm proud of you, Maverick." He grabbed my hand and shook it hard.

"Thank you, Sir."

"I've coached basketball for a long time, kid. Too long. And I like to think I can recognize real talent from a flash in the pan. You've got it, Maverick. It's right there inside you. Don't let anyone ever tell you different. Work hard and play harder and you could go all the way, son. I truly believe that."

"I— I don't know what to say, Sir."

"Ahh, get over there and enjoy the celebrations. You deserve it."

I gave him a thankful nod and re-joined my teammates. They cheered as I approached, and Luke and Aaron hooked their arms around my neck, dragging me forward. "Time to honor our captain, Prince."

"Oh no you don't—"

Too late. Someone ripped off my shorts, and they shoved me hard into the freezing cold shower jets and I shrieked like a girl, cupping my junk.

"You'd better all get the fuck in here," I hissed acclimatizing to the ice-cold water.

They rushed me. Water spraying. Dicks flapping everywhere. It was crude and rude and too much naked guy skin for my liking, but it was tradition. And I wasn't about to ruin their fun. They deserved it.

We deserved it.

After we were dried and changed, we headed out to meet our families and friends who had made the journey to support us. Kyle and Mom were the first ones through the gathered crowd.

"You were wonderful, baby." Mom pulled me into her arms, hiding her tear-stained eyes.

Kyle caught my eye and mouthed, *"So emotional".* "Come on, Momma P, share the love." Kyle untangled her from my arms and handed her off to Gentry who held out his hand for me. "Congratulations, Son."

"Thanks."

Summer and Macey appeared, and I locked eyes with my sister. The grudge—the hurt of my betrayal—was still there, written all over her face, but to my surprise she came and wrapped an arm around my waist, hugging me. "I'm proud of you, Maverick."

"Thanks, and I'm sorry," I whispered. "But this is something I have to do."

"I know." She slipped away and made her excuses, insisting she needed to find the rest of the girls. But I knew Macey and there was a long way to go before she forgave me and Mom.

"You played amazingly," Summer said around a wide smile, and still riding the high, I yanked her into my arms.

"Thank you. And I'm sorry. For everything. I'll do better, I promise."

Surprise shone in her eyes as she pulled away. Summer was pissed with me over Lo, and I didn't blame her. But there was something about this moment. I felt the shift. Only for my heart to sink when I realized Lo really wasn't here.

"You know it was too much to ask of her," Kyle leaned in, keeping his voice low and I swallowed over the lump in my throat.

"I know."

"Here." He held out his cell phone, and I scanned the stream of messages. It took a few seconds for my eyes to adjust. For the words to form.

"She…"

"The whole damn game." Kyle slipped his cell phone

back in his pocket, his mouth twisted in a smirk. "She couldn't be here, but she didn't want to miss a single thing."

Lo had sent Kyle text after text: a running commentary of her thoughts and feelings as she watched the game.

"You should call her. Make it right."

"I'm never going to stop owing you, am I?"

"It's cool; one day I'll cash in." He winked and slung his arm around Summer's shoulder guiding her back to Mom and Gentry.

"I'll see you guys at the restaurant, okay?" They nodded, and I slid my hand into my pocket. Celebrations could wait. I had a call to make.

I snuck back into the arena and slipped into one of the benches. It was empty except for a few staff cleaning. An hour ago, it had been crazy. The noise, the announcements, the music. The whole thing was a blur. Now it was peaceful. The calm after the storm.

"Maverick?" Lo's voice filled the line, and I closed my eyes, soaking up the sound.

"Hey."

"You won, you did it. Congratulations."

"God, I miss you."

She laughed. "You're supposed to be celebrating. Laurie said there'd probably be a dinner and then a party?"

"I needed to hear your voice."

"I watched. At one point, Laurie threatened to call the police, I squeezed her hand so tight. It was amazing. You were amazing."

"I want to take you somewhere."

"What? Are you drunk? Because you sound a little weird." The excitement in her voice softened, and I dragged a hand down my face picturing her.

"As soon as we can make it work, I want us to go somewhere. Just the two of us. Okay?"

"Okay," she murmured. "But are you sure you're okay? You sound—"

"I'm fine. I just… Fuck, I miss you."

"You'll be home tomorrow. It's okay to enjoy this, Maverick. You deserve to relax and celebrate. I'm so proud of you."

I didn't want to celebrate. I just wanted her. But she had a point. The team would be waiting, and they would want to celebrate. Our families and friends too.

"I'll text you later," I breathed out not wanting to hang up.

"You'd better, Champ."

"Keep talking like that and I'll be catching the first flight out of here."

Her soft laughter filled the line, and I said goodbye, forcing myself to end the call.

Tomorrow.

Tomorrow, I could hold her. Kiss her. Lose myself in her.

I just had to get through the next few hours.

~

"Speech, speech, speech." The guys looked at me expectantly. The restaurant was deserted now, and from the looks the staff were throwing in our direction, we'd overstayed our welcome.

"Come on, you guys, we need to get out of—"

"No excuses, Prince," Luke called, and I shot him a narrowed glare.

"Speech, already," Trey added, and I stood up, setting our group off in a fit of hoots and hollers. Coach winked, flicking his head toward the middle of our area.

I cleared my throat, nervous energy bouncing in my stomach. "I don't do this, you should all know that by now. But today was my final day leading this team and what a fucking day it was."

Tables rattled and feet stamped. The whole place came alive at my words and I rolled back my shoulders, standing a little taller. These guys were my friends—my teammates. They didn't want an elaborate speech, and that's what I loved about them. They saw me for my strengths and accepted me for my weaknesses.

"On behalf of the team, I want to thank you, Coach Callahan. Without your guidance and leadership, we wouldn't be here today." My throat tightened, and I avoided glancing over to where he sat. "Playing alongside all of you has been a privilege. Even you, Berrick." I smirked at Trey and he flipped me off. "And I couldn't think of a better way to see out high school." I raised my glass in the air. "To us. State Champions of twenty-seventeen."

I slid back into my seat. Luke grinned at me and I said, "What?"

"You should totally join the debate club at East Bay, public speaking comes so nat—"

"Fucker." I reached over and yanked him into a headlock, ignoring his pleas. When I'd ruined his perfectly styled hair, I shoved him away and raised an eyebrow, "You were saying?"

Coach stood up. "Okay, listen up. It's straight back to the hotel and I don't want any complaints landing on my door tomorrow, got it?"

"Got it, Coach," we murmured as he went to settle the check.

It was only a short walk back to the hotel and as soon as Coach's door closed, the guys made their way to Trey's room. He and Aaron and a couple of the other guys had interconnecting rooms, and it was decided that's where we'd celebrate or commiserate tonight. When I finally got to their door, the music filtered into the long hallway.

"You might want to keep that down," I said as I stepped inside.

"Don't be such a pussy," Trey called from behind one of the cheerleaders. I scanned the rooms for Macey but there was no sign of my sister. It didn't surprise me, she'd been quiet over dinner, leaving with the rest of my family.

"Great game, Maverick."

"Caitlin." I nodded at her before moving further down the hallway. *Show my face and then get the hell out of here*, that was the plan.

Caitlin had other ideas. Slipping around me, she cut me off before I could get into the room. I walked backward keeping a safe distance between us. With glassy eyes and a sloppy grin on her face, she looked buzzed. My eyes darted around Trey's room. A couple of the guys were drinking. But it wasn't out of control. Not with Coach Callahan down the hall.

"Maybe you should call it a night," I said, and she frowned.

"But I've been waiting for you..." she stepped closer forcing me to back up until I hit the wall and had nowhere else to go. Her fingers glided down my arm as she stared up at me through her lashes with come-fuck-me eyes.

Shit.

"We were good together, Maverick. We can still be good together."

"Caitlin," my voice was cold. "This isn't happening. Not here or anywhere else. Got it?"

Hurt flashed across her face but quickly morphed to anger. "I'm only messing around, Rick, you don't have to be so serious all the time."

I looked to my friends for support, but the fuckers were all too busy having fun. So I did the only thing I could think of, shoved past her and got the hell out of there.

Chapter Twenty-Eight

Lo

"I'm in here."

"Hey, Dad." I bound into the kitchen and threw my bag down on the table.

"That bad, huh?" He looked up from his stack of papers.

"Just another day of 'your future is bright' crap."

He let out a wry laugh. "That'll be you next year, kiddo."

Didn't I know it?

After my meeting with Miss Tamson, I couldn't get the future out of my mind. The packet she'd given me lay on my desk, taunting me every time I walked into my bedroom, daring me to open it. But I wasn't ready. I couldn't explain it or put it into words... I just wasn't ready to go there.

"Listen, sweetheart, there's something—" His phone vibrated, and he scanned the screen. "I need to take this."

"Sure thing, Dad." I helped myself to some cookies from the cupboard and headed to my room. Seconds later, he appeared around the doorway, deep lines creasing his eyes.

"Everything okay?" I asked, and he flashed me a smile, but it felt forced.

"Yeah, I need to pop out. Stella is—"

"It's fine. What did you want to tell me?"

Eyes narrowed, he let out a weary sigh. "Nothing that can't wait."

"Sure, okay."

"I'll see you later?"

I shrugged. "I'm not sure what I'm doing yet."

"Okay, I'll leave some money in the usual place. In case you want to order in or go out." He seemed distracted, but that made two of us.

Dad went to leave but at the last second, I said, "Say hi to Stella and Beth for me."

Surprise flashed in his eyes and then a smile split his face. "Sure will, kiddo."

He looked like he'd won the lottery.

It wasn't much, not really, but it was a start.

When he was gone, I finished my snack and lay back on my bed, staring up at the ceiling. I'd almost survived my first year at Wicked Bay High. Another two months and it would be over. Then I had a year to decide what to do with the rest of my life. Although, in reality, it was much less time than that. People would expect me to start senior year with a plan.

My phone bleeped pulling me from my thoughts.

Maverick: I'm at your back door

A smile tugged at the corner of my lips and I climbed off the bed to go let him in. "This is unexpected," I said as the door swung open. His eyes drank me in, the way they always did.

"I missed you."

"I missed you, too."

Maverick slipped passed me and I closed the door. "How did you know my dad was out?"

"I didn't. I was driving by and saw his truck was gone."

"You were driving by?" I raised an eyebrow and a rumble of laughter built in his chest.

"I hoped he was gone. Guess my luck was in."

I studied his face. The dark circles around his eyes and lines across his forehead. He was tired. Worn down. It had been a crazy few weeks. The SAT, this thing with his father and Caitlin, not to mention the State Championship game.

"Any news from Gentry?"

Lips pressed in a flat line he shook his head. Time was running out. We hadn't talked about what would happen if Gentry's guy couldn't find a loophole, but the clock was ticking.

"Maybe we should talk about—"

"No," he said running a brisk hand over his head.

"Maverick, come on. Graduation is in eight weeks. Time is running—"

"I said no." He stalked toward me until there was a sliver of space between us. "They'll figure it out. They have to." His eyes held mine, silently telling me everything he couldn't say. "They have to find a way."

I reached for his hand, tangling our fingers together. Maverick played his part well but if people looked closely, past his cool exterior, they'd see the cracks. They'd see he was just a boy with the weight of the world on his shoulders. And he was one second away from being crushed under the pressure.

Slipping my arms around his waist, I buried my face against his chest, not daring myself to speak.

"I got in," his voice was so quiet, muffled by my hair, I barely heard it.

"What did you say?" I pulled away and stared up into his eyes.

"I got in, the letter was waiting for me when I got home."

"You got in?" I breathed. This was everything. Maverick's shot at basketball, at a future he wanted.

A future he deserved.

I raised up on my tiptoes, pressing my lips to his, showing him how proud I was of him. "You deserve this, Maverick. You deserve it so damn much." He swallowed my words, his tongue parting my lips, swirling with my own. And I felt the urgency in his kiss, the desperation. But most of all, I felt the relief flowing out of him and into me.

He got in. Not because his father was an alumnus or donor. Not because Coach Callahan pulled the right strings. Because he worked hard and went after it. Even with the odds stacked against him, Maverick didn't give up.

Breaking the kiss, I eased back and smiled up at him. "This is it, your ticket to freedom."

We just needed Gentry to come through. But I understood the conviction in Maverick's voice now, when he'd arrived. He didn't want to consider Gentry's plan wouldn't work because it had to.

"They'll figure it out," I said with a half-smile as he tucked me back into his chest.

Not because I believed it.

But because right now, in this moment, Maverick needed to hear it.

~

"Seriously, Prince, you can't just let someone else win?" Kyle threw his cards down, grumbling a string of cuss words under his breath.

"You're such a sore loser, babe," Laurie stroked his hair the way you would a wounded puppy and shot me an

244

amused look. I laughed, relieved to see they seemed to be back to their usual back and forth. She promised me she was done texting Jared and from the way she and Kyle had been looking at one another tonight, they seemed good.

Maverick slipped his arm around my shoulder and pulled me closer. "What time is it?"

"Like eight," Nick said.

"I'm going to order pizza." Maverick pulled me up with him.

"This is nice," I said as we went to the small kitchen counter while he dug out a menu. After coming over to the house to tell me about his acceptance letter, Maverick had surprised me by saying he wanted to celebrate.

"Yeah, all we need now is for Macey to hook up with someone," he smirked.

"When hell freezes over," I grumbled, and he said, "She'll come around."

"We'll see."

I wasn't expecting that day to come anytime soon. She might have cared about her brother but since collaring me at the party, Macey had made next to no effort to talk to me again.

Maverick ordered pizza, and I went to join the others, but his hand caught me, and he hooked his fingers through my belt loops. I arched my eyebrow at him and his eyes darkened, a challenge there, causing shivers to roll up my spine. When he hung up, his voice turned husky. "Where do you think you're going?"

"Back to the others."

"Two minutes." He leaned in and I swallowed.

"Maver—"

His lips came down hard on mine as he yanked me flush against his body. My hands slipped under his t-shirt running over the taut muscle, exploring and touching.

"Seriously, guys, I don't know how much more of this my eyes can take," Kyle's voice boomed, and I laughed, dropping my face into the crook of Maverick's neck.

"I think it's cute," Summer shouted. She'd been angry at me for all of two-minutes, when I finally came clean to her about me and Maverick. She knew there was more to it but unlike Macey, she knew Maverick wouldn't shut her out unless it was for a good reason.

"Cute? It's fucking disgusting. They're practically dry humping."

"Stone," Maverick warned over my head.

"You're only jealous, babe."

"Jealous? I'll show you jeal—"

"Kyle, you disgusting pig," Laurie's shrieks filled the pool house followed by Summer and Nick's laughter, and I craned my head back, trying to see what was going on.

"Come on," Maverick's voice was low in my ear as he curled his body over mine. "I guess I'll have to share you until they go, which is when by the way?"

I playfully punched his arm, stealing one more kiss. "It was your idea to invite them."

"I'm an idiot," he mumbled as I led him back to the others.

We'd been playing cards for the last hour, but Kyle was right, Maverick wiped the floor with us. Nick was the only one who came close to beating him. But it was fun. More than that, it felt normal.

When the pizza arrived, Kyle put on a film and the six of us ate and chatted and laughed. It was the most normal my life had been in weeks. And hope blossomed in my chest. But then, out of nowhere, Nick said, "So have you guys made plans for prom yet?"

Summer elbowed him in the ribs and he spluttered, "What?" Confusion shining in his eyes.

"Nick," she hissed, and realisation flooded his face.

"My bad... I... shit, I really put my foot in it, didn't

I?" He looked from me to Maverick and then raked a hand through his messy hair, averting his gaze. Awkward silence descended over us.

Summer gave me a sympathetic smile while Laurie's mouth hung open like a fish. Even Kyle had no witty reply, and the silent boy beside me went rigid, anger radiating from him. He got up and stalked away.

And just like that the bubble burst.

"Shit, Lo, I'm sor—"

"Don't worry about it, Nick." I offered him a weak smile as I went after Maverick. There weren't many places to hide in the pool house and I found him sitting on the edge of his bed, eyes fixated on the carpet.

"Mav—"

"Don't."

"It's fine," I said going to him.

"Nothing about this is fine," he whispered finally meeting my eyes as I sat in the chair I'd sat in so many times when I helped him study for the SAT.

"You got in, Maverick. Steinbeck chose you. This is a huge deal. I won't let them ruin it. Not tonight." My fingers danced over his arm. "You deserve to celebrate. You deserve one night of normal."

His eyes stayed on mine. Dark and hard. Two intense inky pools pulling me in, holding me captive.

"It shouldn't be like this."

"But it is." He flinched, but I went on. "And I can live with it. If all this means you get your shot at a future you want, I can live with it."

"I love you, Lo. I love you so fucking much it scares the shit out of me. If I lose—"

"You're not losing me. I'm right here." I leaned in closer, ghosting my nose across his cheek. He turned and our lips hovered millimetres apart.

"I won't lose you." The conviction in his voice

stunned me. But then he was kissing me, sweeping me away in his touch, and I gave over. Because even though I knew the road was only going to get harder, Maverick was right. I wasn't going anywhere.

Chapter Twenty-Nine

Maverick

I eyed Lo as I headed out of Wicked Bay and pulled onto the highway. We needed this. Time away from my father and Caitlin. The shit with her Dad and Stella.

We needed space to remember how good things could be between us.

Fucking Nick and his big mouth. I knew the kid didn't mean it. He was tangled up in a web of lies and secrets he didn't understand, but everything came crashing down the second the question about prom left his mouth. Lo tried to reassure me it was okay but nothing about this mess was okay.

"Where are we going?" she finally broke the silence, and I replied around a smirk, "You'll see."

Kyle had pushed for this time away as much as I had. He was worried about her.

We both were.

After that night, we'd spent another week of pretending, of walking the school hallways trying not search one another out. I'd told Lo I couldn't lose her, and she'd promised she wasn't going anywhere, that she was right here with me, but words only held so much power. I needed to hold her. To touch her. To lose myself in her. So much I ached for it.

For her.

So I made a split decision. It wasn't easy. We needed our parents to buy our cover stories. As far as Mom and Gentry were concerned, I was staying at Luke's for the night and Lo was over at Laurie's. It was a risk, but one worth taking.

"It won't take us long," I added, and she flashed me a strained smile. Because despite how much we clung onto the hope everything would work out, time was running away, and Gentry was no closer to a solution.

But that's what tonight was about, finding one another again. Of reminding ourselves of what we were fighting for. With only six weeks left before graduation, we'd come too far to let him win.

Forty minutes later, Lo straightened in her seat. "Hollywood? You brought me to Hollywood?" Her eyes widened on a soft gasp, taking everything in.

"Yes and no," I said following the GPS to our hotel. "This traffic is insane." If we wanted to make the show, we'd need to hurry.

"This is... just when I think my life can't get any stranger, it does."

"Strange? That's not quite the reaction I was hoping for."

She threw me an amused look. "You know what I mean. This isn't real life, Maverick. Not for me."

"But it is, Lo. Your life is in Wicked Bay now."

She settled her gaze back on the sights. I'd been here enough times not to be wowed anymore. But seeing the sparkle in Lo's eyes was worth it.

I just hoped she enjoyed the rest of the night.

~

Lo stared at the door, her eyes wide. Confusion

imprinted on her soft features. "Lo?" I said, and she took a couple of steps back. Retreating.

Beats didn't look like much from the outside, but it was one of the best live music venues in the whole of LA.

"I- I can't go in there." Her hand hovered in front of her as if she was physically protecting herself.

"But, this is the surprise." I raked a hand over my head feeling as confused as she looked. "I got tickets to see Three Steps Back, they're pretty awesome."

"I- I'm sorry." Her arms shot out, wrapping around her waist. "I can't do it, Maverick."

"What? I don't—"

And then it hit me like a wrecking ball.

I'd fucked up.

"The accident..." my voice trailed off.

"Can we just go, please?" Her eyes were skittish, glazed with unshed tears I knew she was fighting to hold back, and people were starting to stare. I went to her and wrapped an arm around her. "Come on, let's go."

Fuck, how could I have gotten it so wrong?

Her discomfort in crowds. How she'd come off the ride at Disney, pale and terrified.

We walked back to the hotel in awkward silence. Surrounded by dazzling lights and the noise of downtown LA, I'd never felt more helpless. Lo had disappeared into herself, lost to her memories of what she'd survived.

When Gentry got the call about the accident, he'd told us all, but he hadn't gone into detail. Lo's mom and brother died. She suffered life threatening injuries resulting in a long stay in the hospital. That's as much as we got. Back then, they weren't real people to me. It was tragic, and it affected Gentry the way it would any brother who found out his sister-in-law and nephew were gone, but they weren't real to me—or so I thought.

Now all I could see was the girl I loved, hurt. Laying in some sterile bed, hooked up to machines and tubes. A deep shudder rolled through me. I'd never pushed her about what happened. But whatever Lo had experienced left deep scars, and not just physical ones.

The hotel came into view and I went ahead, holding the door open for her. She didn't make eye contact as she slipped inside and waited for me to guide us to our room. As soon as the door closed behind us, Lo disappeared into the bathroom. I paced, rubbing the back of my neck, wondering what the hell to do.

Was she having a panic attack?

Did I need to call someone?

Jesus, how had this blown up so epically? *Because you're a fuck-up, Prince,* my father's voice echoed in my head. It was funny how once, he'd been the person who lifted me up and made me want to be better. Now he was the person who made me doubt myself. The devil on my shoulder. Taunting and teasing.

"Lo?" I rapped my knuckles on the door, pressing my ear to the wood.

"I just need a minute."

A minute.

I could give her that.

But when five minutes had passed, and I'd burned a hole in the carpet from pacing, I knocked again. "L—" The door swung open and Lo stood there.

"I'm hungry, shall we order room service?"

What. The. Actual. Fuck?

I stared at her, searching her face for any signs she'd been crying. But all I saw was Lo's indifferent mask. The one she usually reserved for family dinners with Stella.

"Lo…"

"Maverick." She folded her arms over her chest, building her walls higher. But if she thought she could keep me out, she was wrong.

So fucking wrong.

I straightened, filling the doorway, refusing to let her through. There was no way in hell we were just going to pretend that didn't just happen. I'd given her time, I'd waited for her to open up to me, but watching her go into herself like that freaked the shit out of me. I couldn't just forget that.

Not again.

"What happened back there?" My voice was hard, and anger flashed in her eyes. I didn't blame her. I was being a dick. But sometimes it was the only way I knew how to reach her. When she still didn't respond, my head dropped, the fight leaving me. I could own the court. Trample over some of the best defensive players in the state. But I couldn't find a way to reach my girlfriend.

"What's the matter?"

My head snapped up, our eyes colliding. "You're asking me what's the matter?"

"You have this look…"

"I don't know how to do this, Lo."

"Do what?" her voice was soft.

"Be who you need me to be."

"I just need you, Maverick." She leaned into me, letting me wrap my arms around her. We were both broken. Worn down by our pasts and our messy presents. But here, like this, everything made sense.

"Come on." I led us to the bed. "Let's feed you. And then we talk."

She didn't answer but I could have sworn I felt the small movement of a nod.

We ordered room service. Lo only picked at the plates. Her hunger disappeared the second the food was delivered. But it eased the tension, and we ate in comfort, sticking to safe topics. We didn't mention Caitlin, or my father, or Lo's freak out. It wasn't exactly what I had planned for our night in LA, but I'd take it.

"I'm sorry." Lo said as I cleaned the plates away.

"Sorry?" I stalked back to the bed and sat on the edge.

"For earlier. I ruined your plans."

"It's my fault. I should have realized, should've known..."

"Maverick, it isn't your fault. It's not something I talk about. Ever."

"I know, and I get it, I do. But talking might help you deal with it."

"I write things down. In the journal you gave me." Her eyes dropped away. "It helps to sort through my feelings. It's been over a year, you know..."

"Shit, Lo, I'm so sorry."

"It's okay." She shrugged, the small movement cutting me in two. "It's not something I want to celebrate, but it's made everything seem... I don't know, more somehow."

"Hey, hey. Come here." I kicked my legs up and shuffled back up the bed to sit beside her. "I'm right here. Whenever you're ready."

"I just... I haven't really ever dealt with it." Lo lifted her face and what I saw crushed my chest. She was hurting—Lo was still hurting so much and I'd been too preoccupied to notice.

Silence enveloped us and after a few minutes I thought she might never talk. But then she started, her voice barely a whisper.

"It was my brother's idea. We'd been talking about our regrets over dinner one night and Mum said she regretted not hearing more live music. Elliot was a doer and before the night was over, he'd convinced me and Mum to go to this local venue with him. They had live mic nights, jam sessions, that kind of thing. Dad thought we were mad. But it was always hard to say no to Elliot.

"It was busy. The band playing was a local favourite. Mum was so excited, it was nice to see her happy. Things between her and Dad had been strained. They didn't tell us, but we saw it."

I reached for her hand and rested it between our legs. "What happened?"

"Everything was fine, at first. The band was great. The crowd was amped. I slipped away to go to the toilet but there was a queue. I was washing my hands when I heard the first screams."

Lo's body trembled, and I smoothed circles over her hand. Grounding her.

"I ran back into the room and it was chaos. Smoke ... there was so much smoke. I'd been gone less than ten minutes. I didn't understand what had happened, but people were running, screaming... and the smell.

"Then I saw it, the fire behind the stage. I couldn't see them. People were rushing for the doors, pushing and shoving and screaming. But I couldn't leave them, I couldn't..."

"It's okay." I pressed a kiss to her head. "You don't have to... it's okay."

Lo dragged a deep breath into her lungs, stifling back her tears. "The fire spread quickly. Too quickly. It was an old building, a lot of the wood was... the smoke was unbearable, I could barely breathe, but I couldn't see them and..."

She broke down. In a hotel in downtown LA my brave strong girl let her walls down. And although I knew it would help her in the long run, I couldn't imagine how she felt reliving it.

"I'm so sorry, Lo. I'm so sorry," I shifted, dropping my arm around her shoulder and pulling her into me. Her soft sobs filled the room.

After her tears slowed, Lo untangled herself from my

chest, pushing damp hair from her face.

"That was the last time I ever saw them. Laughing. Dancing... Happy. I can't..."

"Ssh, come here."

Lo settled beside me. Heartache radiating from her. She'd lost so much. Survived so much. She was strong, I didn't doubt that. But it was a front. A mask for the pain she carried with her every second of every day.

But she had people. She had her dad, and Kyle, and Summer, and Laurie.

She had me.

And I'd spend a lifetime trying to make her happy, if she let me.

I leaned down, tilting her face to mine and brushed my lips over hers, reassuring her that I was right here. Silently promising that I would never knowingly hurt her. I would protect her and keep her safe. And most of all that I would love her. Scars and all.

Chapter *Thirty*

Lo

Something changed after LA. The night I bared the deepest darkest corners of my soul to Maverick. I'd never relived the events of that night to anyone. Not Dad, not my counsellor, or the many doctors I'd seen during my time in hospital. I could never find the words... to verbalise my last moments with Mum and Elliot. It was as if part of me decided forgetting—drowning out the memories with drugs and alcohol—was easier.

I realised now; it was probably what drew me to Maverick. The need to know the darkest parts of his soul. To soothe them. Because just being with him, with someone who understood me, even if he didn't realise how much, soothed some part of me.

We were both broken, but together, we were whole.

It was also part of the reason I decided that regardless of what happened with his father, I would stick by him. I'd survived losing a parent and a brother. Survived a horrific accident. And I'd survived my own demons.

I could survive Alec Prince and Caitlin Holloway.

In the end, it was that simple.

And as Maverick had loved me that night, whispering promises in my ear, I realised something else. I didn't have to stay silent. I could fight for us too, the way Maverick thought he was fighting for us. It might not make a difference, or maybe it would.

But I wouldn't know unless I tried.

"Lo, you still with me, sweetheart?" Dad's voice snapped me out of my daydream and I blinked over at him. "I just need to swing by and show my face and then we can head out, okay?"

It was bad enough we were meeting Stella and Beth for dinner, but now Dad had dropped this on me last minute.

"I can stay in the car, right?" Eyeing the hotel, I looked down at my jeans and favourite t-shirt.

He noticed and chuckled. "It's only half an hour, tops. Come on, humour your old man."

"And what exactly is it again?"

"Just a drinks reception for some investors. Nothing too intimidating. I need to say hello, shake a few hands. There'll be champagne and canapés?"

"Canapés?" I raised an eyebrow, and he rolled his eyes.

"Come on, the sooner we get in there, the sooner we can leave."

With a heavy sigh, I followed Dad out of the truck and toward the building. He looked good in his tailored trousers, navy shirt and black tie. And for as much as it still hurt, I was past denying the reason for the new man standing beside me.

"I appreciate this, kiddo. You know that, right?"

"I know, Dad," I said as we slipped into the hotel lobby. I also knew he wasn't referring to this, here.

It wasn't the first time he'd asked me to dine with him

and Stella, but every time I had an excuse. Every time, I threw my walls up and pushed away his new life. But it had been almost nine months. She wasn't going away, and I was tired of being alone in the house. And ever since stumbling across her sobbing in my father's arms, I couldn't help but feel sorry for her. Dad told me enough that I knew Beth's father was giving her problems. Still, I didn't probe, and he didn't give away more than he should.

My eyes swept over the lobby: brushed copper and rich mahogany paneling, abstract art fixed to the wall in neat rows. It oozed money, and I felt like a fish out of water.

"Don't look so worried, it's just drinks."

He kept saying that but who did 'just drinks' in a place like this?

In the confines of our modest house, it was easy to forget Dad's associations. Even at school, or with Maverick at the pool house, I was blinkered to just how wealthy my extended family were. My name—being a Stone—hadn't changed me. I was still just a girl trying to survive each day. To figure out how to fit in this new life.

"Smiles on," Dad whispered around an amused grin as he pushed open an ornate wooden door. The room, a private bar, was set up with shaker style tables, and men in suits far more expensive than Dad's, milled about chatting and laughing. A couple of immaculate waitresses floated about serving plates of tiny sandwiches and small pastries.

"Fancy," I mumbled, trailing after him as he made a beeline for Gentry.

"Ahh and here he is," my uncle clapped eyes on us and beamed. "Robert, get over here and meet Lance."

Dad slipped away from me without so much as a backward glance and I made for the bar, pulling up a stool. "Drink?" the bartender asked, and I nodded.

He slid a flute of champagne over to me and gave me a sly wink. "You look like you need it."

"Thanks." I sipped the drink, bubbles fizzing in my mouth, popping as they slid down my throat. Spinning on the stool, I took in the room. Dad and Gentry's laughter echoed around the high ceilings. My uncle had the men hanging off his every word while Dad smiled and nodded, hands jammed deep in his pockets. He was the quieter brother, but he didn't look out of place. He looked happy... at home. And even after all this time, it made my stomach drop.

Thirty-minutes and my second glass of champagne later, Dad showed no signs of saying his goodbyes any time soon.

"One more then I'm cutting you off," Wesley, as I discovered the bartender was called, refilled the crystal flute.

"Thanks." My lips pressed into a thin line and I grimaced.

"How old are you? Wait." He frowned. "Don't answer that. I don't want to lose my job for supplying alcohol to minors."

That earned him a weak smile as I twirled the stem in my hands. I already felt the flow of expensive champagne in my veins. It wasn't enough to get me drunk, but it helped. Took the edge off.

"Alec, Gavin, good to see—"

My blood turned to ice as I slowly turned. Alec Prince approached a stiff looking Uncle Gentry, accompanied by another man. Blond hair peppered with grey, he was tall and broad, with the same unforgiving expression as Alec Prince. But my eyes ran right over him to the other two people with them.

I spun back around to Wesley and deep lines crinkled his eyes. "I'm going to lose my job, aren't I?"

My gaze fixed on the neat line of bottles arranged on the shelf behind him and I choked out, "I'm really sorry to do this to you, but I'm going to need something stronger. Much stronger."

~

"Sorry, I'm sorry," Dad rushed out with a strained smile as he slunk into the stool beside me, loosening his tie. "I didn't expect it to take so long."

"Can I get you something to drink, Mr. Stone?"

"I'll have a—" His eyes narrowed on me, on the empty glass in front of me. "Have you been drinking?"

"You said there was champagne, I thought you meant..." I shrugged, trying to keep my voice even, trying to disguise the storm raging inside me.

"I cut her off at two, Mr. Stone," Wesley added, shooting me a discreet glower.

"It's fine." Dad studied me, and I forced a smile. "I shouldn't have left you so long. We didn't expect for Alec... never mind. We should really get going before Stella sends a search party."

I rose from the stool on unsteady legs. The two vodka and lemonades Wesley had slipped me did little to ease my surprise when my gaze landed on Maverick and Caitlin. Her hand curled possessively around his arm. How her fingers tightened when she noticed me sitting there. The smug flash of fucking delight in her eyes. But I didn't really want to get Wesley fired and I couldn't afford to embarrass myself in front of Dad and his business partners. Or cause a scene in front of Alec Prince. So I steeled myself, turned my back to them and sipped my drinks, all while plotting a thousand ways to kill Caitlin Holloway in cold blood.

But it was too late, my efforts fruitless. Maverick's eyes burned into my back the whole time I sat there, nursing my drink. Silently questioning what I was doing here, silently asking me to look at him. But I didn't.

I couldn't.

That was the rule.

My rule.

It had been hard enough knowing they were in Sacramento together. I didn't want to have to see it, to feel it. When he got back, and he found out he'd been accepted into Steinbeck, I thought the tide was changing. I thought it was a sign that everything would work out. But I should have known fate was a cruel bitch, and she'd decided to shove it right in front of my eyes catching me completely unawares.

"Lo, are you ready?"

"Yes, yes." I blinked at Dad, smiling, all teeth and bitterness on my tongue. My eyes travelled the room. Maverick and Caitlin were with their fathers, talking, laughing—looking very together. She shuffled closer, pressing into his side as if she felt me watching.

"I'm sorry," Dad said in a low voice. "I had no idea they'd—"

"It's fine," I said. "Let's go. I'm starving."

It was a lie. Dinner would choke me, but he didn't need to know that. He didn't need to know I was one second away from grabbing the nearest glass of bubbly and drowning Caitlin in it. Or maybe I'd go for Alec. He was, after all, the reason for all of this.

For this lie.

This fucking sham.

Just when I thought I was getting a grip on it, the rug was pulled out from under my feet and my world crashed down around me.

I managed to croak out a goodbye to Uncle Gentry and then I was out of there. Marching toward the door, and fresh air.

"Are you sure you're okay?" Dad said as he caught up to me, fumbling with his keys.

"Starving."

"If you say so," he mumbled as he rounded the truck and climbed inside. He knew me well enough to know I wasn't okay. But he wouldn't push. Because that's what we did. We avoided. We lived in suffocating silence. Besides, he probably thought I was still hung up on Maverick.

He didn't know the truth.

Because that was another rule.

As I climbed inside, my phone bleeped, and my heart lurched into my mouth, my palms clammy, as I slipped it out and read the incoming text.

Maverick: I'm sorry. Shit, I'm so sorry. Where are you headed? Give me twenty and I'll be there. Just say the word Lo, and I'll be there.

Shutting it off, I slid it back into my pocket.

"Laurie?" Dad asked, and I nodded.

"Yeah."

"I'm glad you have her, kiddo."

"Sure, Dad." *Sure.*

I dropped my head back and closed my eyes but all I could see was Caitlin. Caitlin pressed against Maverick. Her pretty, manicured hand possessively on his arm. Over the top glossy smile aimed in his direction, beaming at him as if he hung the fucking moon. Her moon. Perfectly styled hair, designer clothes and make up a model would be proud of. She embodied money. Wore it like a second skin. And for as much as I hated to admit it—for as much as it made me want to puke all over Dad's leather seats—they looked good together.

My fists clenched at my sides until my nails bit into my skin, as I tried to rein in the anger building in my chest. They might have looked good together, but he was mine.

Maverick was mine.

He'd made promises to me.

He loved *me*.

But Gentry still needed time. *'Close'*, he'd told Maverick the last time he asked. He was close to finding a workaround for cutting all ties with Alec. But time was something we didn't have. Because although I'd made a promise, although I'd played by the rules, I was losing myself.

Slowly, little piece by little broken piece, this whole thing was eating me alive.

My phone vibrated again, and I debated ignoring it. Just for a little while. But I couldn't do it. Even though I willed my hand to stop, it didn't listen.

Maverick: I love you. You, Lo. Don't forget that.

I hadn't forgotten.

I just didn't know if it was enough anymore.

~

Kyle: Cous, come on. Answer the damn phone

Kyle: Lo…

Kyle: Do you want him to end up arrested for breaking and entering?

Lo: Not fair, Kyle. I just need some time.

Kyle: How much time?

Lo: Kyle!!!

Kyle: Fine, I'm going to cover for you. But don't make me regret it. Take your time and then

FUCKING CALL HIM

Lo: Fine!

Kyle: Fine!

Kyle: I love you, Cous. You know that, right?

Lo: I know. Now leave me alone

My fingers lingered over the screen. It had been hours since I saw Maverick at the hotel. I'd gone to dinner with Dad and Stella and somehow survived two hours of painful conversation while they fawned over one another. At one point, I thought Beth was going to puke all over her spaghetti at the sight of my dad kissing her mom. We ended up playing eye spy. At first, I hadn't wanted to like her. What she represented. But it was hard to deny she was cute, and I saw a lot of myself in her. She was lost. Trying to keep up appearances. To process what was going on around her. But for as much as we'd found common ground, I still didn't look at her and see my sister.

My stepsister.

Because from the way Dad and Stella were headed, it was a real possibility. They were sickeningly in love. And he'd already become a huge part of Beth's life.

My phone vibrated again, and I half expected to see Maverick's name flash across the screen. But it didn't.

Kyle: Operation distract the Prince has commenced. You have an hour. Two tops.

Lo: My hero.

God, he was relentless. I knew he meant well. I knew he didn't want to see Maverick do something stupid. But I needed time. No one said this would be easy, but seeing them together... seeing her touch him. It stirred something in me. And, in that split second, I understood why Maverick fought. Why he stepped into that ring at the risk of ending up hurt, or worse.

He wanted it to stop.

Just for a second, he wanted it to stop.

The lies... The games... The pressure.

But this was real life. It was messy and raw and real and sometimes it hurt so much you didn't think you'd be able to carry on. You couldn't fight your way out of the hard times, you just had to ride them out and hope you survived. So I would allow myself an hour. Sixty minutes to hurt and sulk and wallow in pity at how horrible my life was, and then I'd brush myself off, paint on a smile, and pretend everything was fine.

Even if it wasn't.

Even if I didn't know how much more I had left to give.

Chapter Thirty-One

Maverick

"No way, no fucking way."

"Watch your mouth," Dad hissed down the line as I paced back and forth, dragging my fingers over my scalp, letting the bite of pain ground me.

"I've played by your rules, turned up at every event you asked, but prom is mine."

And, if I gave two shits about the dance, which I didn't, there was only one girl I'd be there with.

"So you can ask the Stone girl and flaunt your sordid relationship in front of everyone? Do you think I don't know you're still seeing her? I saw the way you looked at her at Valencia. Jesus, Maverick, I thought you'd have at least half a brain. The obvious choice is Caitlin. Besides, it's already arranged. Gavin has taken care of everything. You'll attend with Caitlin, and JB and his date, and then we'll celebrate on Sunday."

"Celebrate?" With JB? Not likely.

"Gavin and I agreed on a deal. We sign the papers, Monday."

Gentry's man needed to work fast because time was

running out. Prom was next weekend, graduation the week after that. If they couldn't figure it out soon, my future was over. And all this, the last four months, was for nothing.

"I have to go," I rushed out, feeling anger spear through me.

"Don't let me down, Maverick. Once the papers are signed and sealed, I don't care if you spit on the girl and throw her to the wolves."

My lips mashed together to stop me saying something I might regret. Caitlin was a bitch, the worst kind, but even she didn't deserve my father's harsh words. The line went dead, and I threw my cell down on the bed. All those years I spent worshipping him. Seeking his approval.

What a fucking joke.

He was rotten to the core. Toxic. And he poisoned everything and everyone around him. It wasn't any wonder Maxine was out of town so much. Why their kids were barely ever home. I pitied them. But if they knew the things I knew, surely they would have run far, far away from Alec Prince.

My eyes flickered to my cell. It taunted me. Daring me to call Lo, to ask her to come over and ease the storm stirring in my chest, but it wasn't fair to her. To keep dragging her deeper and deeper in this mess.

When she found out about prom... well, I didn't want to add another crack into our already fragile relationship. It had been almost three weeks since she saw me and Caitlin with Gavin and my father at Valencia. Something changed that day. She'd promised to stand by me, to ride out this shitstorm, but when I walked into the room and saw her sitting there, the pain in her eyes had been almost tangible. Rippling around her like a forcefield, and it nearly killed me. After Lo left the hotel, I'd almost gone out of my mind. A war had raged inside of me. Did I go after her and risk undoing the last few weeks, or stay out and risk losing her for good? It was my father who made the decision. One stern glance in my direction and the fight left me. Because he knew.

Knew what was at stake and he used it to buy my silence.

So I let her go. Hating myself for the pain in her eyes, knowing I was the one who had put it there. When she finally picked up my call later that night, she sounded fine. Of course, I knew she wasn't. But I was too fucking exhausted to argue. And things had gone from bad to worse. Her silence and weak smiles were almost too much to bear, but I didn't know how to fix things.

How to fix us.

Ever since, the fight in her eyes had slowly started to dull. We still stole moments together, but the reality of the situation hung over us like an angry storm brewing. And eventually it would come to a head.

I don't think either of us wanted to admit the truth. To acknowledge what would happen if Gentry's man couldn't figure things out. But deep down I knew. If there was no way out, no fresh start, I'd lose her. Maybe I'd end up at East Bay or maybe I'd lose my shit and bring down everyone with me, but one thing was for sure, Lo and I wouldn't survive the fallout.

~

"Maverick, my god, you look…" Mom sniffled, dabbing the corners of her eyes as I entered the kitchen. The collar on my shirt was too fucking tight and the tuxedo jacket felt like a straightjacket. I could barely breathe. But it was prom. Even Trey, the laziest most unkempt player on the team, had rented a tux.

"You clean up good, son." Gentry came over and extended his hand. I took it, giving it a firm shake. Silent understanding passing between us.

"I'm so proud of you baby." Mom ducked around Gentry and enveloped me in her arms. "And I'm so sorry, for everything," she whispered, her voice laced with regret and I swallowed over the lump, pulling back to meet her eyes.

"You just wanted to protect us."

I got it. She'd done what she thought was right at the time. It was a mistake she'd have to carry with her forever, and that was punishment enough.

"I should head—"

"Prince? Holy shit, is that you under all that formalwear?" Amusement hung in Kyle's voice as he joined us, a smug grin plastered on his face. "I never thought I'd see the day."

"Stone," I warned, holding his attention with my hardened glare.

His hands shot up. "Hey, man, you look good. You'll be fighting them off with a stick." It was a joke. I knew that. But the second the words were out of his mouth, his easy smile slipped, morphing into something darker.

"I should go. I'm already late."

Gentry slung his arm around Mom's shoulder as I straightened my bow tie. He wanted to say more. But it could wait.

I had a date.

Just not the one I wanted.

"I guess I'll see you tomorrow?"

"Don't do anything I wouldn't," Kyle's voice followed me out of the door and I shook my head. *You have no idea.*

~

I was in hell.

The Coastal had been turned into a James Bond film set. The huge martini glasses filled with colored beads, and the black and white feathers that filled vases positioned either side of the projection of 007 himself, might have been impressive if it wasn't for Caitlin's shrill voice every time she greeted someone as we made our way inside.

"Oh my god, it's amazing, isn't it amazing?" she gushed, smiling up at me as if I actually wanted to be here. With her.

Together.

"I need a drink," I grumbled, my eyes searching out the bar. What I really needed was a beer, or two or three, or a whole six pack, but I'd settle for drowning myself in soda. "I'll be over there."

"Maverick, wait—"

But I was gone. Moving through the gathering crowd. Luke and Trey waved me over and my gaze immediately went to the flash of silver as Trey slid his hand into his jacket. "Please tell me that's what I think it is," I said as I reached them, raising an eyebrow.

He smirked. "As if I'd come unprepared. These things are a fucking drag."

"So, why'd you come?"

School events weren't really our thing. We played basketball, occasionally partied. But organized dances, not so much.

"It's prom. Mom would've had my balls if I didn't give her this one. She made me and Christi pose for like a million photos."

"Speaking of Christi, where she is?"

He shrugged taking a swallow of his spiked drink. "Fuck if I know. She and Jessa got here and went straight to the bathroom."

"And how is the lovely Jessa?" I winked at Luke and he flipped me off.

"You know I only asked her because my mom knows her folks."

I ordered my drink and when the bartender turned his back, held my cup down for Trey to do his thing.

"And how is *that* going?" Luke flicked his head over to where Caitlin was with some of the girls from our class, lapping up the attention of being my date and one of the few juniors here, no doubt.

"Remember that time I got the shit beaten out of me by some hulk at the warehouse and spent three weeks benched? Times that about ten and I'm somewhere around there."

"She looks hot."

Luke slapped Trey upside the head. "Think before you speak, jackass."

"What?" He shrugged. "She does. I mean it's not like Prince didn't already tap th—"

"Go find your date, fucker," I ground out. "Before I do something I regret."

Trey took the hint and disappeared, and Luke said, "He has no filter," as we perched against the bar, watching the scene before us. "But seriously, what is going on there?"

I took a long drink, my mouth flooding with acid at the afterburn of Trey's secret ingredient. "Honestly, it's better you don't know."

"Whatever you say, man. I just hope you know what you're doing."

That was the million-dollar question.

Silence stretched before us. This was it. The end of high school. Soon we'd be collecting our diplomas and then it would be summer vacation and then the rest of our lives.

"You ready for college?" I asked Luke.

"I think so. It'll be different, but I feel ready, you know? And we ended on a high." He raised his cup, and I chinked mine to it. "Too fucking right, we did." I said. "State champions twenty-seventeen."

"I know you don't want to talk about it, but have you really thought East Bay through? I mean…" His words trailed off as Caitlin approached.

"There you are." She flashed me an irritated smile. "Luke." She all but dismissed him.

"Hey, Caitlin." He eyed me sideways and mouthed, "I guess I should go find my date."

"I'll catch you later," I said. "Tell Trey to come find me." I'd need more of whatever he had concealed in his jacket. Soon, if the glint in Caitlin's eyes was anything to go by.

"I want to dance." She trailed perfectly manicured nails up my chest until her palm slid over my shoulder. It was a claim. Caitlin was marking her territory in front of the entire senior class and I wanted to roar at the spectacle. But I played my role, refusing to smile or return her suggestive gaze, but I didn't flinch at her touch either.

My father would have been proud.

"Come on." She took my hand and led me to the dance floor as if she was the one in control.

The room at The Coastal was grand with its high ceilings and a polished parquet floor. A stage was positioned front and center with round tables set up in sweeping arcs looking onto it. Kids parted to let us through. To them we were Wicked Bay High royalty. I hadn't realized how much I resented the pedestal they put me on until recently. Sure, breaking records on the court helped, but they didn't want, envy or crush on me because of my ball skills, it was my name.

I was a Prince, and they wanted in my kingdom.

What they didn't realize was I'd been a prisoner held under duress. Forced to live a lie.

"Maverick," Caitlin snapped, and my eyes fixed on hers.

"What?"

"Could you at least look like you want to be here," she said through her pearly white smile, not wanting everyone to see the cracks. The deep fault lines. Her body pressed against me as she slid my arms around her waist, sighing softly, letting everyone know how much she loved my touch.

As if it was a prize to coveted.

The sooner this ended, the better. Just a little while longer and then it'd be done.

We swayed to the music, some sappy love song, while Caitlin's fingers clung to my shoulders. But it wasn't her I felt. It was Lo's soft curves against my hard lines. Her silky hair brushing my face. Her smell surrounding me.

Jesus, this was fucked up. But it was just a little longer.

The band kicked into something more upbeat and couples broke away, dancing in small groups. I straightened, putting distance between us, and Caitlin raised her eyebrow in annoyance.

"I need a drink," I announced.

A strong one.

"I'll come—"

"Caitlin, come on. Dance with us," some girls yelled over the music. She looked torn. Did she let me out of her sights or miss out on the opportunity to brag to her friends?

"You should go dance." I made the decision for her. Almost sounding like I cared.

I didn't.

I was so far past caring, it was a miracle I was still here.

Chapter Thirty-Two

Lo

My hands trembled as I slipped inside the room. At first, no one noticed me. But then a couple of girls saw me, their eyes widening with recognition, brows pinched with curiosity as they began whispering to one another.

Then another group noticed.

And another.

Until the rumble of whispers crept over the music. But I ignored them, searching the room until my eyes found him. Everything slowed down except for the pitter patter of my heart as our gazes collided. Surprise widened his eyes, and we stood there, drinking one another in, until we were breathless and moving. Slowly at first, and then quicker.

Like attracting magnets.

The entire senior class watched Maverick as he closed the distance between us. He strode with certainty where I walked with hesitation. He commanded people's attention where I drew their judgement. He was the star of this show and people couldn't help but watch him.

I couldn't help but watch him.

But it didn't matter because the second we reached one another there was only him and me.

Me.

And him.

The heated stares and suggestive comments all melted into oblivion.

"What are you…" he stuttered, rubbing his face as if he couldn't believe what he was seeing.

"I came," I said holding his eyes, trying to say everything I should have already said. "For you."

"But Caitlin?"

"Doesn't matter anymore. You're mine, Maverick. As much as I'm yours. I refuse to pretend anymore."

"You're fucking amazing, do you know that?" He smirked, sweeping his arm around me, but it quickly morphed into a broad smile. God, it looked good on him. He always stole my breath, but tonight, in the fitted charcoal tux that hugged his body like a second skin and with his hair styled to perfection, he looked like sin.

"She's going to flip her shit," he whispered as his lips connected with the sensitive skin just beneath my ear and a shiver rolled up my spine spreading out into every nerve ending and setting my body alight.

"She can bring it," I said pushing any thoughts of her out of my mind.

There wasn't time to back out. This was happening.

Consequences be damned.

Maverick took my hand, squeezing gently just as a shrill voice yelled, "What the hell is this?"

He was there in an instant, pushing me behind his body, shielding me from Caitlin. But I wasn't here to hide, I was here for him.

With him.

I placed my hand on his arm and moved to Maverick's

side. "Caitlin," I said. "You look really pretty." A smile curved my lips. It wasn't fake or smug. If anything, it was a little sad because I realised now, things never needed to get to this point. If I'd made this stand from the beginning, if I'd fought for Maverick the way I should have, we wouldn't be here.

Her face paled with fury. "Wh- I don't understand," she choked out, trying to school her panic. But she knew. It was right there in her wide unforgiving gaze.

"It's over, Caitlin. The games, the lies." Maverick's fingers dug into my hip as the words flowed out of me. And before I could stop him, he'd spun me into his arms and was kissing me. Tongues and teeth. Until our chests heaved, and my body sang. I almost missed her gasp.

Almost.

Peeking out from the comfort of his chest, I smiled again, and her whole face transformed, anger radiated from every pore. "You played me? This was all for show, wasn't it?"

He didn't answer. He didn't need to. Actions spoke louder than words and we'd just given her all the proof she needed.

"Wait until my father hears, you won't get away with this." She seethed, hands fisted by her sides. "I'll make sure you both—"

"Cat, enough." JB stepped up beside her and she swung her head around to meet him.

"Are you fucking kidding me, JB? You saw what they did. What he did. Are you just going to stand there and let him get away with it? They made me look like a total—"

"I said, enough."

Caitlin shoulders sagged, realisation and defeat heavy on her face. "Fine. You won't do anything about it? I will!" She stormed toward the door and out of the room, and Maverick slipped his arm around my shoulder, tucking me into his side.

"Some show, Little Stone," JB smirked at me and I shrugged.

"She had it coming."

"Yeah." He ran a hand over his face. "Yeah, she did. We good here, Prince?"

Everyone was still watching, wondering what could possibly be happening that Maverick and JB were in the same room, breathing the same air, and not trying to kill each other. But they didn't know the whole story—they never would. Not even Maverick knew the whole story yet, but he would soon enough.

When he didn't reply, I nudged his ribs, and he choked out, "Yeah, we're good."

None of us moved. JB's hand flinched as if he might try to shake Maverick's. But he didn't. And that was okay. Some fractures were simply too deep to repair.

When I'd gone to him and revealed the truth, as much as I could without compromising Maverick's darkest secrets, he didn't want to believe the story of a man who cared more about business than his own son's future. And despite knowing his sister's reputation for being a grade A bitch, he didn't want to accept Caitlin was a willing participant in Alec's game. But the truth was a powerful motivator, and deep down I think he knew. JB knew something didn't add up. I suspected it's why he warned me about her, he just hadn't fully understood all the players and pieces then. Caitlin wanted Maverick and he knew that put me in the firing line. And maybe, in the beginning, part of him did want to use me to get back at Maverick for hurting her. But somewhere along the line, I was right—JB had a soft spot for me, and despite his strange way of showing it, when it counted, he'd come through. For me.

For us.

"I hope you know what you're doing, Little Stone. My

sister is something else. She won't forget this. I can rein her in while I'm around but come fall, you're on your own."

"I know."

Maverick tensed beside me, but he didn't need to worry, I could handle Caitlin and whatever she threw at me.

JB shook his head, a flash of amusement in his eyes. "I guess I'll see you around." His eyes levelled to mine and for a second I saw regret there but then he was gone. Back to his date and friends.

Show over, the crowd went back to dancing. To drinking and laughing and enjoying their final moments of being high school seniors.

My stomach danced, and my pulse thumped in my chest as I turned to Maverick and said, "What now, Prince?"

"Now." He lowered his mouth over mine. "Now, we give them a real show."

~

"Come on, Rick, you have to come, it's our last official party as seniors." A sloppy grin tugged at the corners of Luke's mouth as he clung onto his date.

Maverick hugged me closer as we walked out of The Coastal. It was only just after midnight, but a lot of kids had already moved onto the various after-parties. We'd stayed until the bitter end, dancing until the lights came up and the cleaners moved in.

I'd never seen Maverick so carefree and happy. It touched somewhere deep inside me, and I knew tonight was the night.

"We can go, if you want," I whispered to Maverick, but it wasn't low enough and our small group cheered while the quiet boy beside me groaned.

"The only place I want to be right now, is in you." His

lips ghosted over my skin and my eyes fluttered with the weight of his words.

"Maverick." I pinched his sides and a deep rumble of laughter built in his chest.

"Too much information, dude," a very glassy-eyed Trey said. He was toasted. So were Luke and Aaron. I'd tasted alcohol on Maverick's lips when we kissed after watching Caitlin flee the dance, but he was sober now. And like a drunk thirsting for their next sip, hunger radiated from him.

"Sorry, I tried." I said to his friends, and they booed as Maverick steered me away from them and back into the hotel.

"Hmm, Maverick, home is that way." I glanced back at the door.

"We're not going home." He tugged me to a row of elevators. One pinged open, and he nudged me inside, stalking behind.

"What did you do?"

"You're not the only who's been keeping secrets," was all he said as he hit the button and we started moving.

We rode to the top floor in silence. A slither of air between our bodies. Our hands and waists. The fine hair on my arms and his jacket. Electricity danced between us, and when the door pinged open again, I sucked in a sharp breath. "What is this?" My eyes scanned the room.

"This is the penthouse suite."

"But... what..."

He wrapped me into his arms, tugging me against his firm chest. "This is ours for the whole night."

"But..."

Warm lips brushed my neck. "Stop. Talking."

I couldn't have said anything if I tried. My words had died. Stolen away by the sheer beauty of this place. It was unlike anything I'd ever seen. A huge glass window looked out over the Bay. The sea glistened under the moon, a blanket of stars twinkling like tiny diamonds.

"It's beautiful."

"You're beautiful." His voice cracked, and I wanted to know what he was thinking. What he felt when he saw me standing there. But questions could wait, this was our time, and I didn't want to ruin a single second.

Maverick's hand slid down over my shoulder and down the sweetheart neckline of my dress. "I've waited all night to do this." His lips chased a warm path over my skin, sending shivers rippling through me.

"I love you," the words tumbled out, and he stilled. One hand poised on my waist the other on my stomach.

"What did you say?"

"I said,"—I turned in his arms, staring up at him—"I love you, Maverick."

"Fuck, you don't know how long I've waited to hear that." Relief flashed in his eyes quickly followed by awe.

But I did know. And a part of me hated myself for not saying it sooner. "I'm sorry I made you wait." It was a whisper.

His eyes darkened capturing me in their intensity. "You were worth the wait, Lo. Worth every damn second." His Adam's apple bobbed. "And what you did tonight... no one has ever... Do you want a drink or anything?"

"A drink?" I raised an eyebrow. And then it hit me, he was nervous.

Maverick Prince was out of his depth.

"Help me," I said, turning and brushing my loose curls off my neck. He wasted no time, his fingers making easy work of the zipper. The dress slid down my body like warm butter until I was standing in nothing but my new lacy underwear. From the sharp intake of breath Maverick took, I made a mental note to thank Laurie for forcing a last-minute shopping trip on me.

When I turned back around, Maverick's hungry gaze swept down my body. Everything had built to this. Five months of secrets and sneaking around. Of heartache and insanity. Of feeling, more than once, like I was drowning.

He closed the distance between us, shedding his tux jacket and dropping it to the floor. My fingers went to his shirt buttons, yanking and popping. Next went his trousers. A blur of clothes and kisses, breaths and touches. Until he lifted me up and carried me to the bed. Nothing between us.

No secrets.

No Caitlin.

Nothing but skin on skin. Love on love.

And it was enough.

More than enough, it was everything.

~

"Can we stay here forever?" I sighed, tracing lazy circles over Maverick's abs. He tightened his arm around me, answering with a kiss. "Hmm, I want to wake up every morning like this."

"Good because I plan to move you into the pool house for the summer," Maverick said as if it was the most natural thing in the world. As if us playing house was no big deal.

And maybe it wasn't. But the tension in my muscles, the little voice in my head, said otherwise.

"Relax," he chuckled. "I'm only joking. We can alternate. But first you have some explaining to do, *Little Stone*."

Rolling onto my stomach, I leaned up on my elbows readying myself for a conversation we should have had last night. But I think we'd been too relieved to want to go there.

"After seeing you with *her* at Valencia, well, it almost broke me. God, I wanted to kill her. But I realised something too."

"Oh yeah? And what did you realize?" He raised an eyebrow.

"I realised I didn't have to just stand by and wait for our fate to be sealed so I went to JB." The quiet boy beside me tensed at the mention of his enemy's name. But I leaned forward, brushing my lips over his. "I love you, Maverick. I've loved you for a long time. I've already lost so much, I won't lose you too. So I did what I needed to do. JB might be a jerk but he isn't a bad guy, not really. He was just looking out for sister. Once he knew the truth—

"So you told him?"

"I told him what he needed to know. I mean it, Maverick. I won't lose you. Even if your dad—"

"He won't."

"What?" I rocked back onto my ankles, my pulse thrumming in my chest.

"Gentry's man came through."

"But how? I don't understand?"

And why the hell was I only just finding out about this?

"Gentry got the call two days ago. I should have told you, but I didn't want *him* hanging over us anymore, Lo. I wanted to look you in the eyes and make promises to you knowing I could keep them. Knowing that nothing and no one will come between us again." He leaned up pressing a tender kiss to my lips. When he pulled away, love and promise shone in his eyes. "It was my plan to bring you here last night, all along. I just needed Caitlin to believe for a little while longer. I arranged this the second Gentry told me. I wanted to celebrate with you. To spend the night with you. With all of this behind us."

There was so much I wanted to say. To ask. What his plans for summer were? Did he plan on moving to Steinbeck before freshman orientation? Did he have to attend summer camp? But I couldn't find the words. Not when I'd just got him back.

All of him.

For the first time, I didn't have to share him with anything. Alec, the team, the pressure of getting into college; it was all gone. I finally had all of him even if it was only for a brief moment.

I didn't want to think about what happened when he left. Not here. Not today. I just wanted to enjoy it. Savour the moment.

He broke the silence first. "You have that look."

"What look?" I gave him a coy smile.

"The one where your mind is working overtime and you want to say something."

"I do not."

"Yes," he said. "You do."

"I love you," I blurted out. Now I'd said it, I couldn't stop. All night, as he loved me, I'd said the words. Over and over. But Maverick didn't seem to mind. In fact, he seemed to enjoy it.

"Fuck, I love it when you say that." He leaned up and captured my lips, sweeping his tongue into my mouth but I fought him off, shrieking, "Gross, morning breath, I need to brush my—"

Maverick slipped his arms around me, pulling me down on top of him and rolling us until he had me pinned to the bed. His legs slid between mine and a soft moan slipped from my mouth as rocked into me.

A smirk tugged at the corner of his mouth as he pulled away. "You were saying?"

"I—"

He slid inside again, and my body ignited. I ran my hands over his shoulders as he brushed his nose across mine moving in and out slowly, setting a delicious pace. And for the rest of the morning Maverick made me forget nothing and promised me everything.

CHAPTER Thirty-Three

Maverick

"Son, wha—" The color drained from his face as Gentry and Mom stepped into the room behind me. They were here, supporting me, but I wanted to be the one to deliver the final blow.

"I thought you should have this." I thrust the letter at him and watched with satisfaction as his eyes pored over the words.

"What is this? I don't understand."

"That, is my ticket to freedom. I'm done. With you and your fucked up mind games. You don't control me anymore."

Surprise was the first emotion I saw flash in his inky depths—the eyes I inherited from him. But it soon melted away replaced with something much darker. Anger. Humiliation.

Betrayal.

He rolled back his shoulders, a cold mask slamming down over his face. "Think carefully about this, Maverick."

Not son.

Maverick.

As if I didn't deserve the title any longer. As if he no longer considered me his son, his heir.

"It doesn't matter anymore, *Dad*," I emphasized his name. The one I would never say again after today.

Because I meant it—I was done.

Free of his games and rules and his toxic expectations and demands.

"Rebecca," he finally addressed the other two people in the room. "For the love of God, talk some sense into him."

"No, Alec," Mom's voice was shaky, and I knew how hard this had to be for her. But it was long overdue. "This has gone on long enough. It ends today."

"Rebecca—" he started, anger rippling from him, but Gentry stepped forward, moving around me until I was shielded behind him. Mom stepped up beside me, reaching for my hand and clasping it in hers.

"My lawyer will be contacting you later, but in the name of common courtesy,"—Gentry handed him the thick manilla envelope—"if you ever come near my wife or my son again, I won't be held responsible for my actions." He turned and stormed out of the room, Mom's cracked sobs echoing off the wall.

"Come on, Maverick," she urged.

But I slipped out of her hold and said, "Go. I'll be right there."

She hurried out of the room after Gentry as if she couldn't stand another second breathing the same air as the man who had abused and manipulated her. Ran after the man who had called me his son. Who had been more of a father to me than I ever realized. It was something I would need time to accept, time to fix, but I'd try.

After this was done, I'd really try. Because Gentry deserved it, unlike the man standing before me.

"Well played, Maverick, well played indeed. It would appear we are more alike than I ever gave you credit for." Alec leaned casually on his desk as if this was just another day's business. But I saw the cracks. The flash of concern in his eyes, the way he'd clutched at his tie as he read my acceptance letter to Steinbeck University.

"I learned from the best," was my reply. "It's over, Alec. I'm going to walk out of that door and never look back."

He raised an eyebrow at the unfamiliar term. But that's who he was to me now.

No one.

And it was more than he deserved.

I turned to leave. To get back to Lo and the rest of our lives. Fuck, that felt good.

Our lives.

Together.

But as I reached the door, his voice stopped me in my tracks. "I'll never forget this, Maverick." Icy cold and emotionless, it sent a chill down my spine. But he no longer held the power.

I looked back at him one last time and said, "Neither will I."

~

"Congratulations, Prince." Kyle clapped me on the back pulling me in for a guy hug. It wasn't my style, but I let him. It was the least I could do after the last few months. If it wasn't for him and Laurie, I doubted Lo would still be here. By my side.

"Thanks, for everything." I said out of earshot of the rest of my family.

"Photos, I need photos," Mom ushered us into a group, and I wrapped my arm around Lo, pulling her close while Kyle, Macey and Summer arranged themselves around us.

"Smile on three. One, two, three." The flash blinded me for a second but then Lo was there grounding me, brushing her lips over mine.

"Seriously, you guys," Macey grumbled. "You can't even wait until we leave?"

"Sorry," Lo chuckled against my mouth finally breaking free when her dad cleared his throat.

"Congratulations, Maverick. We're all very proud of you." He held out his hand and smiled.

"Thanks, Uncle Rob." I shook his hand, keeping one arm firmly around Lo. He still wasn't sold on the idea of us together but after everything—after the truth came out—he'd given us his blessing.

"Thanks for coming, Dad."

"We wouldn't have missed it for the world," Stella said offering Lo a meek smile. While Lo and her dad had found solid ground again, things were still strained with Stella, but my girl was trying. Finally opening her heart up the idea of a new family.

And from the conversations I'd overheard between Gentry and Uncle Rob, that was about to happen sooner rather than later. But I'd be there to pick up the pieces. To hold her up the way she'd held me.

"Prince, get your sorry ass over here," Coach Callahan boomed across the field and everyone laughed. It was a strange feeling. Having them all here, for me. For my graduation.

After everything, it felt right. And, although there was still healing to do, it felt a lot like a fresh start.

"I'll be back," I said to Lo. "See you guys at home later?"

My family nodded eagerly, Mom dabbing at the moisture in her eyes.

"Go, I'll wait." Lo wriggled out of my hold but I leaned down capturing one more kiss before I slipped into the crowd.

As I cut across the field and around the back of the bleachers to the gym, I shed the gown. Graduation was done. I'd got accepted to Steinbeck. Not because of my name or who my father was, or a huge check signed by his hand, but because I'd earned it. And that was something no one could take away from me.

And it felt fucking good.

Better than good; life was finally great. SU campus was only twenty miles away and while I would move into dorms, it was close enough for Lo to come and spend the weekend and I could drive home whenever I needed. And they had been more than accommodating when I'd come clean about my learning disability. Finally, it was my time to shine.

To step out from the shadows and live in the light.

Arriving at Coach's office, I knocked on the door and entered. "Maverick, son, take a seat," he said.

I sat down, raking a hand through my hair and Coach Callahan smiled wide. "I'm proud of you, Prince, real damn proud. I trust it all went well?"

Lips pressed together, I gave him a small nod. He knew the deal, well, most of it.

"Well it's a good day to celebrate, son."

"Thanks, Sir, for everything." My eyes went to the trophy sitting proud on his shelf. We might have won it, but it was Coach who got us there. His belief in the team, in me.

He waved his hand through the air. "It was nothing. You did all the hard work. I have some news, though. It's why I called you in here."

"Okay." I shuffled forward wondering what he could be about to say.

"I ran into Coach Baxter over the weekend. He's excited to have you starting at Steinbeck in the fall. What do you know about Zac Lowell?"

"He captains the Scorpions, right?" I'd done my homework. As soon my acceptance letter came, I'd dug up everything I could on Steinbeck and their basketball team. They had some good players, names I recognized. But from what I could tell they were lacking something. Last year, under his captaincy, they'd missed out on progressing to the elite eight because of—according to press reports—his screw up.

"He's good. But he plays games. Thinks he's bigger than the team. If you ask me, he should've been benched a long time ago. But Lowell has connections." Coach rubbed a hand over his face. "Be careful, Maverick. You're good. One of the best. Not everyone will appreciate that." His narrowed eyes bore into mine and I got the message. Zac Lowell was a problem. But I'd dealt with worse.

"I just want to play ball, Sir."

"I know and like I told Coach Baxter you could go all the way. Keep your head down, work hard, and don't get pulled into any bullshit, you hear me?"

"Yes, sir."

"Good, now get out of here. I've had enough looking at your pretty face to last me a lifetime." He smirked and stood to hold out his hand. I slid my palm against his. "Thank you, Coach, for everything."

"Ahh shit, Maverick, get out of here before you make this old man tear up."

Our laughter filled the room and then I was gone.

To find my girl and start looking forward to my future.

~

"Are you sure you don't want to go out? Kyle is sulking."

I rolled us, caging Lo to the bed, my face hovering millimeters from hers. "This is exactly where I want to be."

"But—"

"No buts. Just let me have this. We can go party later." My lips brushed over hers. Once. Twice. Like a direct line to my blood, heat flashed through my body and I rolled my hips against her soft curves.

Lo's hand slid up my chest twisting into my t-shirt. "I can't believe it's over. You did it, Maverick. I'm so proud of you."

I eased away, staring down at her. "*We* did it. No one's ever believed in me like you, Lo. I love you."

"I love you too, so much sometimes I think my heart's going to explode."

Hearing those three words would never get old. When she'd said them to me the night at The Coastal, I felt like I was the motherfucking king. And I knew I could do anything, be anything. With Lo by my side, everything would work out.

"What's the matter?"

"Nothing, why?" Lo said but her eyes gave her away and I knew she was lying.

"London..."

She let out a soft sigh. "It's just things are going to change again. You're going to leave and I—"

"Hey, hey." I nudged her cheek with my nose, running it along her neck and kissing the soft skin there. "It's a few miles. We'll see each other all the time. I thought this was what you wanted?" Pulling back, I searched her eyes for the truth.

"I do." Lo's lips curved a fraction. "You deserve this, Maverick, you deserve this so much. I just... It doesn't matter. Forget it," she said around a strained smile. "Did I tell you how proud I am of you?"

"You might have mentioned it once or twice." I smirked but when I saw the hesitation in her eyes, I rocked back onto my haunches. Lo pushed up on her elbows with a frown.

"Nothing will come between us again, Lo. I know I'm leaving. I know I won't see you every day, but nothing will change. I promise." But as I said the words, my mind worked overtime. Everything was finally great. We'd come out of this thing with my father, in one piece. The worst was over. Only I wasn't naïve enough to think that was it, that the road ahead would be smooth.

Lo was right, I was leaving, and we would have to find a new routine, adapt to me being in Steinbeck and her being in Wicked Bay. Then there was the stuff with Stella. That would rock Lo's world again and I wouldn't be here to comfort her. But Kyle was ready to step into the hole I left, and after the last few months, he'd earned my trust. And finally, Coach's warning. He hadn't brought up Zac Lowell for nothing. He thought he was going to be a problem. And maybe he would. But distance… Stella… Zac Lowell, we'd survived worse.

Lived worse.

And I meant every word I said—nothing would come between us again.

Nothing.

PLAYlist

Lust for Life – Lana Del Rey ft. The Weeknd
Couple of Kids – Maggie Lindemann
Flux – Bloc Party
Unforgettable – French Montana ft. Swae Lee
Into the Night – Madeline Juno
Another Love – Tom Odell
Mercy – Shawn Mendes
Plot Twist – Sigrid
Thunder – Imagine Dragons
Nothing Else Matters – Metallica
First Time – Kygo, Ellie Goulding
There's Nothing Holdin' Me Back – Shawn Mendes
No Promises – Cheat Codes ft. Demi Lovato
Your Song – Rita Ora
Now Or Never – Halsey
Something Just Like This – The Chainsmokers, Coldplay
Glorious – Macklemore ft. Skylar Grey
Green Light - Lorde

AUTHOR'S note

Writing a sequel is no easy feat. In fact, it's pretty stress-inducing. So many of you enjoyed Wicked Beginnings that, as I was writing Wicked Rules, I couldn't help but keep second guessing myself and the direction of the book. But over the last three years, I have come to accept that if I don't let my characters lead, I am not staying true to myself or their story. So, in the end, despite the back and forth and the 'am I getting this right?', I let them do the talking … and I hope it paid off. I have so much more planned for these characters (even the ones you might still be on the fence about) that I hope you stick around for the ride.

It takes one person to write a book, but a whole village to publish it.

To Andrea, Anna, Ginelle, Jenny, Lucy, and Nikki. Some of you help me to polish my words, some of you are just there to listen, but I appreciate each and every one of you and I'm glad I get to call you my friends.

To my readers group and ARC group. Thank you for

loving my characters as much as I do and for helping share my stories.

To the bloggers who help spread the word; whether it be signing up to review an ARC or share a promotional post, I am so grateful.

To my family for allowing me the time and space to continue writing and following the dream I never knew I had.

And finally, to the readers who continue to buy my stories, thank you. It will never be enough.

Until next time,

Lianne

About The Author

ADDICTIVE ROMANCE

Author of mature young adult and new adult novels, L A is happiest writing the kind of books she loves to read: addictive stories full of teenage angst, tension, twists and turns.

Home is a small town in the middle of England where she currently juggles being a full-time writer with being a mother/referee to two little people. In her spare time (and when she's not camped out in front of the laptop) you'll most likely find L A immersed in a book, escaping the chaos that is life.

L A loves connecting with readers. The best places to find her are

www.lacotton.com

www.facebook.com/authorlacotton
www.instagram.com/authorlacotton

30799159R00166

Printed in Great Britain
by Amazon